VARSITY SERVANT

BWWM Hockey Romance

LAGUNA GROVE VIPERS
BOOK I

JAMILA JASPER

www.jamilajasperromance.com/blog

ISBN: 979-8-3303-3669-2

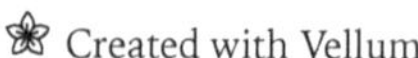

This book was updated in November 2023 with grammatical updates and a new book cover.

The McGraw College Minotaurs

Varsity Possession

Varsity Surrogate

Varsity Stalker

Cole & Kya's Story

This dark and spicy romance story is filled with triggers that will potentially disturb some readers including violence of all kinds, explicit language, and behavior portrayed that is downright criminal and morally depraved.

Cole may disturb your sensibilities at first, so if you are sensitive to this type of content, proceed with caution.

This is a work of fiction and Jamila Jasper does not endorse any illegal or unethical behavior IRL.

In my book universe… all bets are off.

Prepare yourself for triggers and behavior that will horrify most people.

Through the twists, the turns, the mess and the drama, I have a spicy, deliciously dark interracial romance story with wintery hockey themes, lots of heat between the sheets and a NO cheating guaranteed happily ever after ending.

DESCRIPTION

Get on your knees, or I'll tell everyone your secret…
A brute on the ice and a beast in the bedroom,
Cole Seabrook needs a new campus servant and he's found
the perfect woman.
Kya Ambrose. She's African American, curvy, beautiful, and
100% disinterested in chauvinistic hockey players.
Cole has exactly what he needs to blackmail and keep Kya
under his **firm control.**
She **must** obey all his commands… *no matter how depraved.*
The only thing Cole can't force her to do is fall in love.

Our first pre-season meeting with Tuck Murphy has us all shitting ourselves. Tuck's a fucking Laguna Grove legend. If he hadn't broken his wrist, he might've been playing right at home in Boston. He was that good. He is that good, even when he's off the ice. The team leans forward, each of us bending our heads to avoid Tuck Murphy's terrifying gaze while he reams us for another massive puck-related fuck up.

"Laguna Grove has been undefeated in the league for the past five years. I leave this campus and you motherfuckers are not putting that record on the line, understand?"

"Yes, coach."

One year as our coach and then maybe he'll play in the AHL. NHL if he hits a jackpot. But I wouldn't count on a jackpot in this game. You have to fight hard to get to the top and even then, a slipped disk or a fucked up knee could ruin you. Not me. I will always focus on getting exactly what I want.

"Cole," Tuck snarls, his cruel stare fixed on me. If I hadn't skated with Murphy for the past two years, he would have scared the crap out of me. I know he just plays tough in the locker room and everywhere else, but Murphy's a fucking teddy bear. Just look at his girlfriend. She's like an angel with huge tits. No offense, Murphy.

Tuck continues. "Your drives are weak. Every time you're up against Barkov, you fumble it. You need to get it in the corner of the net. Every time. If you can score against Barkov, the other schools in the league don't stand a chance."

"Got it. Better drives."

Tuck nods and moves on to his next victim. "Jayce, your penalty record last season was a goddamn embarrassment. Fight cleaner. Rathbone… what do I even say about you? You could be the best on the team if you weren't such a piece of shit."

"Those were all good hits," Jayce grumbles.

"You broke a kid's femur and laughed yourself out of ice time last year. Pull that shit with me and I'll break your fucking femur."

Snickers travel around the room. You can't fuck with Tuck Murphy. Not even if you're Jayce or Dustin — especially not if you want ice time. At least Dustin's only a frosh. Again. He didn't have the grades to make it to sophomore year with Jayce. I'm a junior, so it's my job to keep those little shits in line, especially if I want to make captain.

"There's one more thing," Tuck says, leaning in. "Sex."

"Yeah, no homo," Jayce throws out quickly, earning a dirty punch from Rathbone and a series of snickers floating around the room.

"You all need to get laid more. The team has a shit reputation because you're all a bunch of assholes. We need people at those games. Lighten up. Get some girls over."

"Technically, we only need one girl," Dustin says. "We can all share her."

A murmur of approval travels around the room until we all notice Tuck's serious glare.

"No sharing girls. That's a great way to get the team off the ice. Don't fuck with the school. Don't fuck with your grades. If any of you want to play hockey after college, you'll take this shit seriously."

We all give him dumb looks, which makes Tuck scowl. "You're all dismissed."

We pound Tuck's fist as we walk out of the room. Except Tuck doesn't pound mine. His hand falls and his stern expression deepens. Fuck, I'm in trouble again…

"I need to talk to you, Seabrook."

"About what?"

"The league. Your career."

My stomach flips. My career is just a dream right now, but Tuck Murphy has connections — connections that a kid like me from Silver Hollow just doesn't have. He puts his hand on my back and rises.

"Let's talk in my office, Seabrook. This shit is game changing."

Tuck shuts the door behind him and rolls up the sleeves on his blue shirt.

"I have to keep it real with you, Seabrook. You're close to getting into the league. If you land a half-decent agent, you'll have one skate on the ice."

I nod. I know I'm good. I put my heart and soul on the ice. Nothing else matters but hockey. No girl. No class. Nothing.

"You need to be outstanding this year," Tuck says. "Our team hasn't taken a big hit in players like this since three years ago. We have too many young green guys on the team and they play rough, but you need to be more than rough to win games."

"I understand."

"The guys need a captain who can lead them. They need someone they can look up to who won't guide them down the wrong path."

"I get it."

"Good," Tuck says, his icy eyes suddenly glazing with a flicker of frustration.

"When you're off the ice, I need you to socialize, get the campus excited for the team again. Talk to women. Don't terrify them. Talk to them."

"With all due respect, Coach Murphy, none of us have problems with women."

Tuck raises an eyebrow. "That's not what Anijah says."

The coach's lady is in my year at Laguna Grove — a junior — and she's everything to Tuck, which is exactly why he never brings her around a sick pack of hyenas like the boys of the Laguna Grove Vipers hockey team. We're bigger assholes than this preppy college has ever seen and I. Fucking. Love. It.

"We have a reputation for being tough. That's not a problem."

"Maybe not," Tuck says, suppressing the flicker of irritation I caused. "But stay out of trouble, Cole. Don't let girl trouble screw you out of your dream."

"Is that what happened to you?" I reply, a cocky smirk on my face that I know will piss Tuck off even more than he's already pissed. Hey, that's what he gets for suggesting that I would ever stop taking hockey seriously. If Tuck thinks that, he has the wrong guy…

Tuck's gaze steels further.

"No," he snaps. "Anijah's a gift. She always has been. But she's one in a million. Don't let some chick distract you from the NHL. I know you, Cole. I remember when you came here as a freshman and you have had recruiters' attention for a long time. You're nearly 21 years old. This is your shot. Your one shot."

I nod, because no one understands this better than me.

"I'll give you ice time. I'll give you a chance to prove yourself, but then you have to prove yourself. Work harder than Clutterbuck, get nastier than Rathbone, and you'll find yourself with a $10 million contract and all your troubles will melt away."

"I would be living the dream."

It's hard not to let visions of fame and fortune dance in front of my head. I don't want to get too distracted. If you stop thinking about the game and only think about the money, that's when you fuck up.

Tuck's stern voice brings me down to earth. "Stay out of trouble, Cole. I mean it."

"Yes, coach."

Trouble? Where the hell would a guy like me find trouble on a small college campus like this? I appreciate Tuck's concern, but... Laguna Grove is too boring for trouble. Lucky for me, all I need is smooth ice and a fast puck to make me happy.

RAPE CULTURE

COLE SEABROOK

"Excuse me!" Kya shrieks, raising her hand so high it nearly comes out of the socket. This frosh needs to chill. It's a fucking Gender Studies class and it's eight in the morning. How is she even awake right now, much less waving her hand like a maniac and nearly knocking over my damn coffee?

I had practice until midnight and I can't keep my eyes open in this stupid class, especially not with the chick sitting next to me getting all nerdy over... what the hell are we reading again? It has to be something about rape. These campus feminists sure love talking about rape. I don't even know why. I think we can all agree that rape is gross. Duh.

"Kya, you already answered a question. What about... Cole?"

Kya snickers. She mutters under her breath. "Right. Like a stupid hockey boy understands rape culture."

"Uh… what was the question again?" I mumble, necking back more black coffee from the campus cafe.

Professor Cooper repeats the question.

"Uh… Well. Like. If a dude in high school bangs a teacher, that's just different because like… he has the dick, you know? He can just… go soft."

I can feel 15 pairs of eyes on me and I know I've done it again. My cheeks turn red and Kya Ambrose, instead of shutting the fuck up and knowing her place, clears her throat.

"Professor Cooper? I just think that it's disgusting that Cole would advocate for a child molester to have free and open access to victims in an educational environment."

"Miss Ambrose…"

"Attack ideas, not people," Kya says with her stupid, stuck up voice. "Right."

Kya throws me another glare, which Professor Cooper misses. Kya leans over to write in her best friend's notebook, her stupid gold pendant bouncing over her cleavage. I could actually appreciate her tits for once if she could just chill out. I lean over to see what she's writing.

He is so fucking dumb. Omg.

Dumb?!? I seriously can't stand this chick. I'm sitting right on the other side of her and despite what she thinks… I can read. Just because I got into Laguna Grove on a hockey schol-arship doesn't mean I'm fuckin' illiterate. But bitchy former high school valedictorians like Kya don't get it. She oozes money, just like the other assholes at this school. Whatever. I don't care about that shit. I only care about the game. The ice. And winning.

"That's not what I meant," I blurt out. I can't keep letting bitchy Kya Ambrose win.

"What did you mean, Cole?" Professor Cooper inquires impatiently.

"It's nothing. Just something stupid."

"Can we move on?" Kya snaps. "I just think it's funny how we have one guy in the class, yet he monopolizes the speaking time."

I am going to kill Tuck Murphy for making me sign up for this stupid fucking class and subjecting me to Kya Ambrose and her big mouth. He promised me I could get an A, but all I'm getting is A pain in the ass.

Seriously, if I had things my way, she'd be on her knees in the hockey house, putting those crazy lips to good use. All she does is make my life a living hell and shed black curly hair all over the fucking table.

Whatever... she'd probably call me a chauvinistic bastard for even thinking something like that.

I'm thinking about what it would be like to shut Kya up with my dick in her mouth when Professor Cooper calls my name again. Kya gives me a worried look and I wonder if I missed something.

"Stay after class. Both of you."

Shit.

I hate that this chick can get under my skin. She's one of these new 'woke' people at Laguna Grove and I don't have time for chicks who don't understand that college is for getting totally fucked up and having the craziest four years of your fucking life. And hockey. Can't forget hockey.

I wish hockey could be my girlfriend, honestly. Obviously, I can't have a girlfriend. No time for anything but hitting it and quitting it. Plenty of girls hang around the hockey house hoping to get laid. I just need to choose one. I don't even need to ask their name. I'm Cole Seabrook. Life will just keep getting better once I'm in the league. I won't have to worry about what annoying chicks like Kya think of me.

Kya glares at me, like it's my fault for being so "dumb". Whatever. Maybe it's her fault for giving a shit. Why bother? She's wasting a lot of time that she could spend getting laid. You know what? I should say that. I should raise my hand and explain that's the problem with women's rights. A lack of sex.

First of all, a chick like Kya probably never met a guy who could give her an orgasm. These wimpy little poetry guys who sniff around feminist pussy can't possibly fuck worth a damn.

Whatever. Here I am getting distracted again thinking about her pussy. I bet she never had a guy eat it. She's a frosh. These girls are totally innocent. Totally. I don't even think it's hot. It just makes them uptight, which is totally lame.

After class, we're the only ones left and standing side by side in front of Professor Cooper. Kya's really short next to me. I'd love to spot her at our next hockey party... settle our arguments outside the classroom. I bet she'd come dressed like the rest of the girls at this school, showing too much skin and crying over the same assholes she pretends to hate in class. Whatever. I like when girls dress like that. Kya has a nice chest. She'd look good in one of those girl tops with all the skin showing from the bottom. It's like wow. I'm hard just thinking about her tits...

Kya's voice snaps me out of the moment. Fuck, how did I zone out for so long? This coffee must be mostly water.

"Hi Professor Cooper, I am so sorry. I guess I just get emotional…" she stops and whimpers and then a single tear falls from her right eye. Give me a break.

Kya continues, "As a black woman on this campus, you don't know how hard it is being around people who trigger you on a daily basis. Cole knows what he's doing. This is what they do. The guys on his team are bullies. I don't even know how they infiltrated this safe space."

"How did I trigger you?" I ask, folding my arms and raising an eyebrow. "And infiltrate? I signed up online like everyone else. I attend Laguna Grove."

"You know how to use the internet for something besides porn?" Kya snaps.

I throw her the fiercest warning look I can. Kya glares right back. Professor Cooper sighs.

"Listen, Kya… Take a deep breath. Okay? And Cole? Don't say a word. You two come from… totally different walks of life. Cole, you're a privileged white male from an upper class family just outside of Boston, right? And Kya, you fought for your scholarship here straight out of the hood…"

"Actually, I'm from Hollywood Hills. My dad's Dwayne Ambrose, the basketball player," Kya says, not even concerned about the fact that she's bragging. Dwayne Ambrose? Damn. I wonder if he knows his daughter is an enormous pain in the ass.

"Right…" Professor Cooper says, turning pink.

"I'm from…" my ears turn red. Really red. This chick is from Hollywood Hills? And wow. What the fuck is she wearing because her ass looks amazing? Wait, Cole… she is your worst nightmare, so stop looking at her ass. I wonder if she ever put a finger up there. Damn it, Cole, focus.

Professor Cooper interrupts me anyway.

"You two need to learn to speak each other's language. Life isn't a Twitter feed. Cole, you can't be a cruel troll and Kya, you can't attack back ten times harder. You both need to learn and grow, and communicate like adults. Look at each other. Talk to each other. I'm assigning you both an extra assignment. Together."

Kya looks at me and then makes a not-so-subtle gagging noise. I just smile. This is punishment for her, not me. I don't mind spending every day making her life a living hell.

"This is… oppression?" Kya whispers, horror crossing her face.

"Kya, you are in college to learn, right?"

"Of course! Sorry, Professor Cooper. I'm just… I'm shocked. I mean… will this affect my grade? I think Cole and I have different grades in the class."

"What you mean is you think I have bad grades?"

"Um… yes. That's exactly what I think," she says.

The rest of the class is silent. The gay kid whips out his phone and blatantly starts recording us. Something Satterfield, I think his name is. Another Laguna Grove dumb fuck probably looked to go viral and prove I'm just another racist white male.

"I read all my assignments. What's a matter? Think I can't read too?" I snap.

The class snickers. My cheeks grow hot. Like I give a shit what a bunch of virgin nerds think about me. When I'm in the NHL, they'll all brag that they knew me and I'll have the last laugh.

"Um. Yes. I am 100% sure you can't read," Kya says, earning a feminist fist bump from the super dark-skinned chick sitting near her. I think they're friends.

"That's enough!" Professor Cooper interjects.

"I can't write an extra essay. I've got hockey."

More snickers from the class. Seriously? I can't believe Tuck told me to take a class with a bunch of losers like this. He acts like he's had one too many pucks to the head.

"See? He's already dragging me down. Please, Professor Cooper… do not subject me to this… patriarch."

"How can I be a patriarch when I'm not even a dad and I have zero control over you?"

"Professor Cooper!" Kya whines. "Please… don't drag another black woman down."

"My decision is final. I want an email report on your first meeting in 24 hours. You're both dismissed."

Kya turns to me and hisses, "You are the worst."

"Don't worry, babe. We got this."

Kya glares at me. She would be pretty scary if she wasn't short as fuck.

"Babe?" she hisses. "You are disgusting."

God, I love winding her up. It's so freaking easy. And it's perfect revenge for getting the whole fucking class to laugh at me.

"All chicks are babes, sluts, or nothing. Take your pick."

"Yet another one of your demeaning ideas surfaces from the deep. We'll meet tonight after your stupid hockey practice in the library... if you even know where that is."

"Can't we meet in the hockey house?"

"I'm not going to your rape den to work on our assignment."

"Practice ends at 9. Meet me at the rink. We can work on it wherever you want after that, babe."

She glares at me, which makes her look sort of hot. You know, if you're into nerdy black chicks with big hair that they shed all over your notebook.

"Where is the hockey rink?" She asks.

I can hear my ears ring. She's just a frosh, so maybe that's her excuse.

"Figure it out, babe. If you're late, I'll report back to Miss Cooper that you're neglecting your studies."

Kya straightens her back and smiles triumphantly. "Right. It'll probably be way harder for you to find the library."

Before I can shoot back, Kya turns on her heel and disappears, her fluffy black hair bouncing with each step.

❦ 2 ❦

ARROGANT WHITE A**HOLE

KYA AMBROSE

My heart races as I storm away from Cole Seabrook.

I don't know what his problem is, but I know I hate Cole Seabrook with all my heart. He sits next to me in my Gender Studies class and he's just like every other arrogant white asshole at this school.

Actually, I take that back. Cole's worse than the average dick head at Laguna Grove because he's on the hockey team.

He looks at my notes all the time, probably copying everything I write, and he takes the hair I shed and makes little piles to put back on my notebook at the end of class.

Hello, we're in college. A black woman can have her natural hair however she likes without some annoying white guy pointing out how much her curls shed. I don't even know why he keeps sitting next to me when there are nine other women in our class who would kill for the so-called honor. Ew.

Ugh. Cole is the worst. I don't even feel bad about calling him dumb. He's like… pet rock levels of intelligence. That's not my fault. He should try picking up a book instead of spending half his free time getting hit in the head.

People at Laguna Grove worship hockey guys. They're seriously treated like gods on this campus. I don't even know why. He probably expects me to get weak at the knees just because he talks to me.

I assume that's why he puts on that stupid, fake-smoldering expression whenever I talk to him, even if it's obvious we hate each other. Just because he has super blue eyes, like a Midwestern sky, doesn't mean everyone's going to fall to his knees.

Three minutes after my horrible interaction with Cole, who's not just a white demon but the bane of my existence, Makeba bursts out of her physics class. I can't wait to see her. Thank God I have someone who can help me work through this.

I glance over my shoulder nervously, just in case Cole followed me. He has the creepiest criminal stare, and he's always gawking at me like he wants to eat me or commit a hate crime — I can't tell which.

Probably the hate crime thing. Hockey boys don't like black people. Period. Everyone knows that. I heard they don't allow black people on campus to come to their parties, but I don't go to any parties, so I can't exactly confirm that.

"Hey, queen," Makeba says, pushing her notebook into her backpack. "You good?"

She whips her braids out of her face, nearly whacking the girl exiting class behind her in the face. Makeba is one of those people who is charmingly clumsy.

"No. I have some stupid extra assignment to work on with Cole," I grumble.

I forgot we agreed not to say his name until Makeba follows with, "The white devil?"

She knows all about my various verbal altercations with the annoying white guy in my class. I'm never going to let him get the upper hand. I nod and Makeba grins, expecting I'll have some tea to spill.

"Let's get lunch with Raven. We'll dish," Makeba says. She is such a sweetheart. My black girl crew is the only part of Laguna Grove I actually like.

It's not like I can go back to California. I am so over the west coast. It's too much being Dwayne Ambrose's daughter over there. I want to get an education, not spend all day fielding questions about my famous dad. No one on the east coast gives a crap. I can be myself here. I can have normal friends — normal black friends.

It's so different from trying to fit in around Los Angeles.

Makeba brushes crumbs off her ankle-length denim skirt. She probably snacked all the way through her physics class. She loves pretzels. And snacking.

We walk to lunch together where Raven already has a table, which she's guarding with a stack of romance novels spread out so no one steals our seats. She goes through these books like toilet paper. I've never met someone who finds so much time to read during college.

Raven paints a broad smile on her face and waves us over, taking off her gold-rimmed reading glasses. Who needs to worry about assholes like Cole when you have friends like Makeba and Raven? Makeba and I plop down at Raven's secured lunch table and heave our bags on chairs next to us.

"Hey, ladies!" Raven says excitedly. "What's popping?"

She has some pizza and an apple on her plate, plus a bit of apple juice. I'm starving, but waiting for the salad bar to clear out before I make myself something light. I glance over at the salad bar, giving Makeba the opportunity to answer Raven first.

"Kya had another incident with the white devil," Makeba blurts out.

Raven wriggles her eyebrows.

"Oooo, did you finally tell him off?"

"Yes. A little. Professor Cooper got mad at me though."

"Girl, they can't stand a strong black woman," Raven says, defending me before she hears the entire story. Seriously, what did I do to deserve friends this loyal?

I've never had friends like this before — friends who didn't just like me because my dad plays professional basketball.

"I know. I thought Cooper would be on our side, but you know..." I trail off because I don't really know what the hell Professor Cooper was thinking. Isn't she supposed to be a feminist? Ugh.

"Teachers love hockey boys," Makeba reminds me. "Even if they're all assholes. There's one in my physics class and seriously, he's dumb as dirt."

I nod. How relatable. Cole's dumb too. Raven doesn't seem to care how stupid the hockey boys are.

"I hear they're having a big party this weekend," Raven says salaciously.

"Who cares?" Makeba says sadly. "We don't go to parties. We aren't cool. Let's be real. We're going to spend all weekend in our dorm rooms studying and watching Joseph Gordon-Levitt movies."

"Ugh, he's so hot," I breathe. He's been my celebrity crush forever.

"We aren't uncool," Raven mutters, although we are definitely uncool.

Everyone in our dorm gets invited to parties except us. I try to tell myself that it's not related to the fact that we're at a predominantly white institution and the only three black girls in our hall…

Even the black people here don't seem to like us, like we aren't part of their clique. I guess we're the wrong type of black girl. At least that's what it feels like.

"We're definitely uncool," I mutter bitterly.

Raven's tired of our defeatist attitude toward socializing at Laguna Grove. She sits up with renewed vigor, like she's getting ready to lead us into battle. Given the social situation at Laguna Grove, she probably is.

"We should just go," Raven says. "We don't need an invitation to go to a party."

"Do you really want to go to a seedy white people party and watch them awkwardly bump against each other and call it grinding?"

"It could be fun," Raven says. "Come on, Kya. Be positive!"

"I am positive that I don't want to go to some creepy hockey boy's rape den. It's bad enough we have to write an extra essay together."

"Hold up, you have to write an essay with the white devil?" Makeba asks.

I nod solemnly.

"Can he write?" Makeba whispers.

I shrug. I don't even know if Cole Seabrook can actually read or if he just manipulates some poor girl into doing his homework. Ninety percent of the white girls on this campus would kill to be near Cole Seabrook and at least sixty percent would kill to do his homework.

Seriously. Most of the people in our gender studies class stare at Cole the entire time and barely take notes. I mean, seriously? He's not even that cute except for his hair, jawline, nose and eyes. But what about his personality? He's trash. Like most guys. Trust me, my dad plays pro-sports. I know trash guys and I can spot them a mile away.

No offense to my dad, but... he did cheat on my mom. Four times. Or maybe it was seven? And they're still married. She loves him that much. Or at least she loves his salary.

"You'll probably have to do the whole essay," Raven says. "But I'm serious. We sneak into a party this weekend. A white people party."

"What about a black people party? Anijah's coming back to campus and her friends are throwing her a kickback."

"I don't want to go to a kickback," Raven says, her voice burning with passion. "I want to rage."

I raise a skeptical eyebrow. I think Raven reads too many fluffy stories. She has her head in the clouds half the time. Her college fantasies are all too good to be true. So far, college has been homework, homework and more freaking homework.

"Have you ever raged?" I mutter to Raven.

"No."

"Do you even drink?"

"No. But we're in college. I don't want to be boring. I spent all of high school living like a total nerd. We should have fun," Raven says.

It's scary that she's the fun one in our group since she falls asleep at 9 p.m. every night and spends most of her free time curled up alone reading romance novels. Since when does she care about the fact that none of us have a real social life?

"Studying is fun," Makeba says unconvincingly. "I mean, what do you think will happen? We'll head to some dumb party, totally hate it, and go home."

"Or…" Raven interjects, "We'll each meet a cute guy and fall in love."

"Ew," I grumble. "A cute hockey player? Do I need to remind you they're all assholes? Cute bodies, maybe. But they're demons. Racist demons."

Raven sighs with disappointment. I hate killing her vibe, but… I'm right.

"I'll text Anijah," I say, trying to revive the dead vibe. "But she's totally changed since she started dating Tuck Murphy. It's like… she wants to be part of that world, you know?"

"I don't even get it," Makeba says. "I like our world. Our boring black girl world."

"Is that our clique, then?" I sigh with disappointment. "The boring black girls?"

"Hear, hear," Raven answers, rearranging her stack of romance novels to bring the kinky historical one to the top.

Our little chat sours my mood. I don't want to be known for being boring. I mean, I don't want to be known at all, but if I have to be known, I want it to be for my quick wit or something, not how boring I am. Maybe my friends are right about us. Maybe we need to shake things up.

Cole walks into the dining hall, and I lose my train of thought. His grey sweatpants are slung low on his hips and he's wearing a Laguna Grove Vipers jersey over his hoodie. The green on the jersey makes his eyes stand out a lot, and his hair glows like a golden halo as he walks through the door. I glance away as quickly as I can. He's hanging with his hockey buddies — a pair of tall brunette guys who look beastly — and I pray he doesn't see me. Of course, I noticed him, but only because it's my instinct to avoid him. I can't avoid him if I don't know where he's lurking.

I'm lucky. He doesn't notice me at all. He and his friends too busy staring at a table of blond sorority sisters and whispering to each other. Thank goodness.

What was I thinking, anyway? Cole Seabrook would never notice me or any of my friends in a crowd. We're boring black girls. That's just who we are. We aren't the type to go out with hockey players and not the type to go to parties. Not the type to catch Cole Seabrook's attention unless I'm sitting right next to him.

"I'll get a head start on that dumb essay after lunch," I tell my friends. "Anyone down for a library trip?"

Raven and Makeba nod eagerly.

3

A RIDE ON THE SEABROOK TRAIN

COLE SEABROOK

This assignment is the perfect chance for revenge. I get my gear on and skate onto the ice. I'm early with Jayce to practice shooting. He spits his mouth guard out and says, "You look pissed, brah."

"Yeah, man."

Pissed is an understatement. I don't want to hang out with Kya when I could stop by the house and find a willing puck slut to take upstairs. I'm backed up, and this chick is totally killing my vibe.

Thwack.

Jayce laughs as I miss the corner shot. By a lot.

"Fuck. You must be really pissed."

"I don't want to talk about it."

"It's the Gender Studies chick," Jayce says, teasing me, as fucking usual.

"Shut up."

"It's always her."

Thwack. Thwack. Thwack.

He hits three pucks in rapid succession, each one hitting exactly where Jayce wants. Fuck, he's good. Murphy's right that I'll need to step up my game if I want a recruiter to give a shit about me. Laguna Grove is good, but it's no Harvard hockey team. To make it out of here, I need to stand out. And get Jayce to back the fuck off.

"It's not always her."

"Every single time. Can you believe what Kya said? Just bang it out, brah. Take her back to the house and get some."

"Great idea. That way, I can get charged with rape and never make it to the NHL."

"Oh, you'd still make it," Jayce says calmly. But you know what? Jayce Clutterbuck is a pretty smart dude, and he's pretty good with girls. Maybe there's a good idea in there somewhere.

"I need to teach her a lesson."

"Sex. Sex solves everything," Jayce says.

Thwack. I finally make a good fuckin' shot and then it comes to me. I already had a good idea. Get Kya on her knees. I'll make her suck my cock, I'll film it, and then I'll make sure everyone knows the truth about her. I'll turn her into a total slut and make her beg for it and then… I'll humiliate her.

How's that for a dumb guy?

I may be dumb, but I've never had a problem getting a girl to suck my cock. It won't be any different with Kya Ambrose. Imagine how quiet it will be with something in that loud mouth…

Jayce laughs. "You had an idea, didn't you?"

"Fuck yeah."

"You gonna bang her?"

"Something like that."

"Cool, brah. Invite her to the party. She's a frosh, right? There's not a frosh alive who wouldn't show a sliver of pussy to get an invitation to the Pesthouse for herself and her bimbo friends."

"I don't think she's that kind of girl."

Jayce's face twinkles. "Every girl's like that, brah. Every girl."

Tuck starts off practice by making us sprint our asses off. Sorry, I mean Coach Murphy. We really have to pretend like Tuck Murphy isn't the craziest motherfucker to grace the ice at Laguna Grove. His last semester was epic. He got married to his frosh girlfriend, knocked her up, and Laguna Grove won the championship against Wisconsin. Fucking Wisconsin.

Tuck's a damn legend, but he wants us to work harder than I've worked in my life. My body hurts constantly, and it hurts even more when Tuck blows his fucking whistle and calls my name.

"SEABROOK. YOU FUCKED THAT ONE UP. DO IT AGAIN."

Fuck. There are no shortcuts when you're dealing with Murphy. The only reason he's not in the NHL is the crazy injury he's still healing from. Something involving a fire and a frat house. I was totally out of it that semester. Now, he's breathing down my neck over one foot of ice. I skate faster. Harder. I skate until I'm dripping in sweat and my pads smell like the thousands of practices I've had in them.

I take my helmet off after our drill, shaking the sweat out of my hair. Tuck gets on the ice and skates over to us, holding a timer aloft.

"You all skate like a pack of fat pandas."

"Thanks."

"Look at this," Tuck says, shaking the timer furiously. "You think these sprints will get you to the championships? Because they won't."

"He's doing his best, brah," Clutterbuck says, throwing a wad of spit onto the ice. Tuck glares.

"When I ask your opinion, Jayce, you'll know. Now Seabrook… what the fuck is wrong with you?"

"Nothing," I mutter. I can't fuck this up. I can't piss Tuck off. I'll skate harder and faster if I have to. I'll do anything for my shot at the NHL. Anything.

By the end of practice, I'm dripping in sweat and the last one to leave the ice. I take my helmet off, my head of blond hair dripping in sweat. My beard is getting way too long and my hockey hair is the shortest it's ever been at the start of a season. I feel like a beast with a chest desperate for oxygen and a body desperate for rest. I totally forget that she's meeting me here until I open the door and step off the ice with my skates.

I stayed behind for a few after practice to shoot on the empty net, totally forgetting about this dumb meeting. Isn't she early, anyway? Of course she's fucking early. Nerd. My body hurts like hell.

Thunk.

I hear her gasp and then remember. Kya. I glance up and my eyes meet hers. Naturally, her face crinkles with immediate revulsion.

"It's 8:45," I tell her.

"I know. I've never been down here. I gave myself extra time in case I got lost."

I try to hide my smirk. She's such a nerd.

"Whatever. I need to shower first. Can you wait?"

"Um… how long are you going to take in the shower?" She asks calmly.

I expect her to sound more annoyed, but she just keeps giving me this weird look. What the fuck is she looking at? I swear, I don't get that chick at all.

"Five minutes. I'm the last guy here."

"Right."

"How long were you here?"

"Hurry and take your shower," she snaps. "I'll wait on the bench."

"You can sit outside the locker room. Come on."

She's skeptical, but I eventually get her to grab that purse thing and follow me. I take my skates off, but she's still tiny next to me. Kya follows me down the hall and it's blissfully silent. It's almost like the girl next to me isn't Kya Ambrose.

"So," she says awkwardly. "Our essay. Have you thought about it?"

"Nope."

"Great," she mutters. "This has to be the worst punishment ever."

"I couldn't agree more," I grumble.

Then there's ice between us. We're standing outside the locker and in our first conversation, all we've done is acknowledge that we fucking hate each other. It isn't exactly inspiring.

"I'll go in and take a shower. You can wait out there."

"Cool. Hurry."

"Yeah."

I walk into the locker. My cheeks feel more flushed than usual. There was something so weird about her out there. Whatever. I get naked and step underneath the hot water. Fuck, it feels good. I soak my head and soap up. As my hand darts around my cock, the picture of Kya's face flashes in front of my head. Her lips especially. I try to focus on keeping clean, but I can't help it. As I wash myself, I'm thinking about her and I'm getting really hard.

She's right out there. I could drag her in here and fuck her in the shower. She'd probably like it. I could say all the sweet bullshit she probably wants to hear. I try to stop myself from being such a sick fuck, but I can't help it. At least I cum quick and there's no one else around. I get dressed in grey sweatpants and a t-shirt. I forgot my stupid boxers. Fuck.

"So. Where do you want to work?"

She stands up, abruptly shoving her phone into her pocket.

"Not your rape den," she snaps.

"For the record, I've never raped anyone in my den."

"Athletes commit 87% of campus rape," she says. "Sorry, I'm not taking my chances."

"Citation please?"

"I don't need you to mansplain to me, Cole," she huffs. "Let's go do this dumb essay at Dory's."

Dory's is the on-campus cafe named after an illegally kept Macaw on campus that was passed down from frat house to frat house for her entire 100 year life span.

"Fine. I'll get you a Macaw-fee," I tell her.

Once we leave the rink, the brisk air makes Kya shudder. She's wearing a thin pink sweater and once the cold Mass air hits her, goosebumps break out over her skin. I have a hoodie slung over my shoulder, so I take it and put it over hers. She stops shivering. Much better.

"I'm not a damsel in distress. I can handle the cold," Kya snaps.

"Is it suddenly feminist to get hypothermia?"

Reluctantly, she puts the sweater on and instantly stops chattering like a nervous beaver. We're only a few more minutes away from Dory's.

"I won't do all the work for this essay. Just so you know."

"I know. I do homework, you know."

"Right," she snorts.

"I can hear your skepticism."

"Can you spell skepticism?" She snaps.

"Is there a reason you're such a bitch?"

I know this is going to piss her off which makes this a dick move, but I don't care. First, I had to jack myself off while this chick sat on her phone and now she's sassing me while wearing my damn hoodie.

"I'm a bitch, as you so eloquently put it, because you're the type of guy who calls women a bitch. That is a misogynistic slur and you know it."

"That doesn't answer the question."

"Yes. It does."

"Got a boyfriend?"

"How dare you!" She yells — as usual — stopping dead in her tracks. "Are you implying that I hate you because I don't get laid enough?"

"Maybe."

"You are a pig, Cole Seabrook. Once this essay is over, I never want to hear your name or see your dumb face again."

"The feeling's mutual. But until then… we go to the same school. We work on the same projects. Maybe we even go to the same parties."

"We do not go to the same parties," she grumbles.

She looks livid. This is the perfect time to ask her…

"Want to come to Pesthouse Friday night?"

"What?"

"We're having a party. Invitation only. You can bring three of your frosh friends for company. Girls only."

"I have plans."

"What plans?"

There's no way some frosh has better plans than showing up at Pesthouse.

"Important plans."

"More important than socially establishing yourself at this cutthroat fucking school as a freshman?"

She folds her arms, clearly considering my point, while pretending not to. "How do I know you won't just invite me and then embarrass us by kicking us out at the front door?"

"You have my word."

"Wow, that means so much to me," she mutters sarcastically.

"Fine. I'll text you an invitation. You can show it to the guys on the team. They'll let you in."

"You don't have my number," Kya huffs.

"We have to work on this stupid project, so... give it to me."

At least we're walking again instead of freezing our asses off. She gives me her number in the doorway to Dory's. I feel something weird about getting her number, even if she's just an annoying frosh and of course she gave me her number...

"I'm not going because I care about that stuff. It's just... my friend Makeba is having a really hard time here. It would mean a lot to her."

"Cool. Wear something hot."

"I'm not dressing to please you," Kya snaps, thrusting the door to Dory's open and storming to the counter. I walk behind her, trying not to look at her bubble-you-know-what. She's so high maintenance it's ridiculous.

"I'd like a 16 oz vanilla latte with half soy and half almond milk, a half pump of sugar free caramel, a half pump of chocolate with sugar, and half ice please with two extra shots of espresso on the side and a spoonful of matcha mixed with almond milk in another cup."

I lean over and whisper into her ear, "What the fuck did you just order?"

"I like what I like. And I'm vegan."

"Of course you're vegan."

"What's that supposed to mean?"

"Sir?" the kid behind the counter asks.

"Decaf. Thanks."

"Decaf?" she says, totally unimpressed. "That's your fuel for a hard night of studying?"

"It's my pregame for going home to pound back some beer."

"Ugh."

"That'll be $11."

"Oh, we need separate checks," Kya says.

Before the asshole kid behind the counter can say anything, I slam the exact amount on the counter. Seriously? She wants to 'split the check' on coffee? It's like her major is annoying studies.

"I got it," I interject.

"I don't need you to buy me coffee."

"It's $11 Kya. If you really want to pay me back, I have some ideas. Didn't think you'd charge as little as $11 though…"

She glares at me and exchanges sympathetic glances with the asshole kid behind the counter.

"Thanks for the coffee," she mutters to me.

We get a table in the back and Kya pulls out her laptop and opens a document with some insane color coded outline.

"I drafted this in a few minutes while you were playing. You can make edits."

I look over at the document.

"This is intense."

"Yeah. It's called getting As."

"You are such a bitch."

"Only because you keep calling me a bitch."

She slurps on her irritating coffee, sprinkling some of that green mixture on top.

"I need to go pee. Watch my stuff," Kya commands. And then she struts off. I adjust my grey sweatpants. She's hot. That makes it all so much worse. It's always so much better when the feminists are ugly. It turns out that was a bullshit lie. Every feminist is drop dead sexy. Even Kya with her big dick sucking lips makes me reconsider women's rights and wrongs…

While she's gone to take a piss in this cafe restroom, I can't watch her ass anymore. Sigh. I move my hand over the pad on her laptop and then a document pops up. A document with a really weird title.

Bound & Gagged By The Fraternity Brother

Holy shit. What is this? I'm immediately intrigued. I can't look away, actually. I have to whisper the words out loud to believe what the fuck I'm seeing.

This shit is perverted as fuck. I click on it without hesitation. It's a long document. A very long document and when I click around, there's a folder with several more like it. And boy, is it detailed. Kya's a feminist. She's not supposed to write the dirtiest shit I've ever read in my life.

I don't know what the fuck I just found on Kya's laptop, but this isn't what I expected. There are dozens of these documents, each with similar filthy titles. Believe it or not, even Cole Seabrook has his fucking limits. She writes stories about dudes with power. Most of them are about domination, rough sex and worse... holy fuck. This is the mother lode.

I mess around for a bit and see that she posts them on some website for nerds who use words to cum. She has a fan following on there of about 4,000 sick fuckers who probably don't realize a college feminist is the one crafting their twisted fantasies.

It's erotica... She is such a fucking nerd that she literally needs literature to cum. But this isn't Jane Fucking Eyre. This is dirty girl porn about the worst things a woman can fantasize about. Holy shit.

My heart races with excitement. I finally have something on her. Finally. It's a fucking gift from the heavens. I think about her stupid, smug mouth calling me names in class and this shit just hits different. My decaf suddenly tastes very caffeinated.

Kya might just be expressing herself, but I wonder what her little women's club friends would think if they knew she was a bad girl who fantasized about this.

This is the perfect blackmail, even better than my video idea, and Kya just dropped it into my fucking lap. I email the documents to myself and get rid of the evidence all before Kya gets back. Man, it's hard not to look at her different. It's hard not to plot her downfall with each bitchy little step she takes.

"Thanks for watching my stuff," she says, with an expression of mild disgust and no trace of appreciation on her face. Don't worry, babe, I'll give you a reason to get really pissed off soon.

"No problem."

"We'd better write this then?"

"Uh huh."

"I'm not a bitch," she says. "By the way."

"Right. But you're a total slut, huh?"

"Excuse me?" Kya snaps.

"Nothing."

"I thought so. Crazy ass cracker…"

I pretend I don't hear that last part, because I'm generous. And I'm about to ruin Kya fucking Ambrose's weekend. That's worth the wait. Maybe after I'm done ruining her, I'll bang her too. I bet she'd moan my name while I did it. I bet I could get her to beg. One thing is crystal fucking clear.

Nobody knows the real Kya Ambrose now and once they do, she'll have to change her fucking attitude.

Working with Kya is worse than taking a puck to the head. She controls everything and my only saving grace is my fantasy about getting her on her knees this weekend and putting my dick into her mouth. What? Trust me, it's nothing worse than what she's fantasized about.

I read her stories on the way back to the hockey house. This shit is almost too good to share. I want to keep this secret to myself and then keep Kya under my control. That would be perfect.

I want her so badly that it's driving me crazy. I don't want to force her or anything… but I want her to want me. That would humiliate her. Unfortunately, if Kya has ever fantasized about taking a ride on the Seabrook train, I can't find it in her collection of dirty stories.

But God, I can't wait until the fucking weekend.

❧ 4 ❧

THE BLACK GIRL SQUAD

KYA AMBROSE

"*Cool. Wear something hot.*"

Can you believe what that asshole said to me? I keep thinking about it for the rest of the week. I hate that I'm thinking about Cole at all. That's the problem with assholes. They always do dumb asshole things that you have to think about in all your free time.

Dumb assholes with their dumb asshole blue eyes and dumb asshole cocky smiles. I hate them.

Makeba's searching for a dress in the pile of clothes on my floor. I hate her little pile of outfits, but she's sort of crashing in my room until she can sort out the drama with her white roommate. That hoe is crazy with a capital 'C'. She spat on Makeba's toothbrush. I mean, that's disgusting... who does something that?

Raven's my roommate and we normally agree to keep our room spotless. We exchange a nervous glance as Makeba mixes her dirty socks in with her clean ones accidentally during her search.

Sigh, it's the right thing to do to let her crash here, even if she's way too messy.

"What the hell are we supposed to wear to go to a hockey party, Kya?! This is way too last minute. I'm freaking out," Makeba practically screeches. Her braids fly into her face and she scrambles to push them out of the way so she can continue her search. Raven has a much more level-headed reaction than I expect.

"Who cares," Raven says. "I'm wearing sweatpants and I'm still going to kiss a guy. I have powerful vibes on my side."

"You've never kissed a guy," Makeba says, fussing with her hair in the mirror. "What makes you think it's going to happen tonight?"

"I bought a spell from a hoodoo witch I follow on Instagram," Raven explains, as if this is the most normal thing in the world.

"You mean you got scammed," Makeba grumbles.

"It's not a scam. I've been rubbing jojoba oil beneath my feet for the past two days."

"Your witch told you that moisturizing your feet is how you're going to get a man?" Makeba snaps, ready to get into it with Raven and her mysterious internet spells. The first week of school, she tried to curse Makeba's roommate and that might have led to the whole spit on toothbrush thing.

"Can you two stop arguing?" I grumble, holding up two halter tops. "Which one looks better."

"Your boobs will hang out," Makeba says. "Unless that's the look you're going for."

No. If I wear a top with my boobs hanging out, he'll think I'm trying to dress up for him. That's the last thing I want Cole Seabrook to think. I throw the halter tops as far away as I can and wrinkle my nose with regret when they land on Makeba's metastasizing sock pile.

"What about the black velvet dress?" Raven asks.

She goes through my clothes all the time borrowing stuff and practically has everything cataloged. I get it. My dad gets a lot of designer stuff for me for free, so people get really excited to borrow stuff from my wardrobe. That velvet dress was a gift from Prada for a cologne commercial he did a few years ago. It's pretty cute. And tight. It shows my boobs too, but not too much.

"She's right," Makeba chimes in. "That one is cute, but not too slutty."

"Makeba, you need to wear something short," Raven says. "Attract a white boy with a fat ass."

"Why would I want a white boy with a fat ass?" Makeba replies.

"I don't know. To put stuff in there," Raven says. "I read it in this self-help book for women seeking interracial relationships that white guys like ass play."

"Ew!" Makeba screeches. "I've barely even kissed a guy. I'm not jumping straight into butt stuff."

"You're seeking an interracial relationship?" I grumble to Raven. "Since when?"

My dad would kill me if I dated a white guy. Actually, he'd probably just kill the white guy. It's not like he has to worry about me dating anyone at Laguna Grove. I'm basically invisible here, which has its perks, but it makes for a sad love life. Raven ignores my question.

"Whatever happens, happens," Raven answers in a sing-song voice that sounds very New York. Raven's from Harlem, Makeba's from Jamaica, Queens. They don't know how cool that makes them to me. I love New York City. The best months of my life were when a couple of New York teams were courting my dad, trying to convince him to move out East. Instead, we got stuck in stupid dusty Los Angeles with its shitty traffic and lungfuls of toxic smog. Don't even get me started on the fires.

"Hell no. I'm wearing jeans and a sweatshirt. I'm not trying to impress anyone," Makeba responds to Raven's butt stuff suggestion.

"Why not?" Raven complains. "You have nice boobs. Push them together. Go for it."

"You just said you were wearing sweatpants," Makeba accuses.

"Well now, I don't want to be a lame, so I'm dressing up. Kya's dressing up. I don't want to look like her frumpy sidekick."

They turn their attention away from fighting for once while I'm jumping to get my butt into the velvet dress. I feel like the freshman fifteen hit me like a bus. Thankfully, it's all gone to my butt. Unfortunately, since I'm from LA, everyone thinks I've had surgery. Ugh.

"Oooo," Makeba teases. "Are you dressing up for Cole?"

I look in the mirror and want to die. This definitely counts as dressing hot. But this dress is also perfect. I look even better in the dress with the freshman fifteen. I look more full-figured. Especially my boobs. I scowl as I observe how noticeable they are in the dress.

"That is so not funny. He's an asshole. I'm only going to this party to humiliate him, not impress him."

"You have a plan for that?" Raven says.

"Yes. Maybe not the greatest plan, but… it's a plan."

Honestly, I don't have a plan. My plan is to wing it. My plan is to find some way to make Cole feel like an idiot. That shouldn't be too difficult, considering he is actually an idiot.

"Cool. Should I wear this hoodie or that one?" Makeba asks about two identical black hoodies.

Luckily, Raven and I choose the same hoodie for her, so we don't have to argue about it longer. Raven borrows a tan wrap dress from me and a pair of heels from Makeba. We do our hair, but I'm the only one who does my makeup. Some habits from LA die hard, although I'm happy to live somewhere more chill about appearances than Los Angeles.

Everyone in our dorm hall is talking about partying and which parties they're going to and for once, we aren't planning to lie in bed all weekend watching 10 Things I Hate About You for the five-hundredth time. It's almost exciting. Then I think about running into Cole, which is way less exciting.

Raven really wants to go out and be a part of things here at Laguna Grove. I get it. I was left out all the time as a kid. We moved around a lot when my dad changed teams and Los Angeles never felt like home. It sucks feeling left out, even if you can pretend not to care sometimes. Maybe one day I'll find somewhere that really feels like home. College is fun and I'm learning a lot, but Laguna Grove doesn't feel like home either. At least I have a black girl squad.

We're all dressed up and we look so different. Raven pulls her braids back with a tortoiseshell hair-clip which looks incredible. Makeba twists her braids into a high bun that makes her look like a West African queen. I let my hair go all natural and wild. I like it better like this — in a big fluffy afro — even if my dad hates it. He forces me (and my mom) to get our hair straightened for media appearances still.

"I got vodka," Raven says. "I'll pour us shots."

"Wait, I've never done a shot," Makeba says nervously as Raven pours her suspicious vodka into tiny plastic shot glasses she bought from the pharmacy.

"Neither have I," Raven replies. "Hold on, I'll Google that shit."

She glances down at her phone when I hear soft tapping at the door.

"It's me, BJ."

BJ is more Raven's friend than ours and he's definitely not a part of the black girl squad but Raven insists that he's lonely and needs friends so I guess she invited him to the party tonight. I think Makeba likes him, but I don't really get why. He's not my type. At all.

"You invited BJ?" I whisper before walking to the door.

Raven shrugs. "Maybe he'll be your first kiss."

The thought rankles me.

"I've kissed a boy before," I grumble. Unlike Raven and Makeba, I'm not a virgin. Well, not exactly a virgin.

I throw the door open and greet BJ with a smile.

"BJ! Welcome. We just got dressed. We're doing shots if you want some."

"Cool," he says, glancing up at me with hooded green eyes.

He reeks of pot, which is probably why Raven befriended him. She's not a complete stoner or anything, but she's super high strung and vapes once in a while to calm down.

BJ might be cute if he were taller. I don't know. I guess he's just not my type. Makeba assumes he's gay. Raven doesn't care, she's just made his social life her personal pet project to distract from the fact that our social life here at some small ass liberal arts college sucks.

"You're wearing that?" Raven asks him. "Sweatpants and a hoodie? How are you going to find your poetry white girl?"

BJ shrugs. "Yeah. I'm not trying to hook up or anything."

He shoves his hands in his pockets. I roll my eyes. Only a guy would think that the only reason to dress up is for sex. You would think at a fancy college like this, where everyone is supposed to be super smart, people would be way less shallow. You would be dead wrong.

"Can we drink or what?" Makeba says. "I want a shot."

"You should probably chase that with some Gatorade," I warn her.

Makeba sucks her teeth. "My dad's from the Caribbean. We can handle our rum."

"That's vodka," Raven says.

Makeba shrugs and takes a deep inhalation. Her face wrinkles and contorts in horror.

"Why does it smell like poison?"

"Because it is poison," Raven says. "Now drink it. I want to see if you die first before I try mine."

Makeba holds her nose and downs the shot. She immediately starts gagging and then coughing. She dramatically flops onto her pile of clothes and groans.

"That is nasty. Oh, God. That shit is nasty. Kya... help me..."

"Are you going to throw up?"

"Maybe..."

"Okay, well, don't throw up on your clothes."

"Wait," Makeba says. "Hold on. I'm fine. I think."

"Is she dead?" Raven whispers, tiptoeing around BJ, who pounds back his shot without flinching.

"She'll be fine."

"BJ, help me up," Makeba groans. He helps her up, and she leans against the wall.

"I'll take one. I'll certainly need it to face that asshole," I grumble, forgetting that BJ's standing right there.

"Which asshole?" BJ asks me.

See? This is why we don't let boys into our little group. Now, I have to explain 'the asshole' to BJ, and he's probably going to think I'm making a big deal out of nothing. It's not like I can tell BJ that Cole's a white devil. That wouldn't be politically correct.

"There's this guy on the hockey team in Kya's class," Raven says. "He's an asshole, and he called her a slut."

"Damn. That sucks," BJ says.

"Yeah. Don't worry. I'm getting revenge."

"You have a plan?" BJ asks. What the hell is it with everyone and this stupid plan. Do I need a plan?

"Not yet."

"Here," BJ offers, "You need more liquor."

Maybe he's not so bad.

He pours me another shot. What choice do I have? I take the shot. I'll probably need it to get through a night of confronting Cole Seabrook.

❄ *5* ❄

DOPE ASS HOCKEY PARTY

COLE SEABROOK

There are three ingredients to a dope ass hockey party: ice, puck bunnies and vodka. Laguna Grove's new head coach gave us one directive before the next game. Get laid. My plan for getting laid is going to walk through my front door in about... thirty-five fucking minutes. Kya Ambrose walks around like she has a stick up her ass, so she'll probably show up pretty early.

Then I get to mess with her head.

I can't fucking wait. She totally deserves it for calling me an idiot. She deserves it for looking down on me. Clutterbuck and Barkov man the DJ station and play the nastiest fucking rap we can get our hands on. That shit is great and beer gets me going. I feel alive. And with enough beer in me, I can't feel how fucking sore my muscles are.

When the party officially starts, I walk downstairs in a tank top and shorts to find seven puck bunnies gathered around the keg, shrieking loudly and asking Dustin Rathbone about cocaine. He's more than happy to provide if it means all eyes in the room are on him. Plus, he enjoys making women do sadistic shit for coke. He'll make his tarantulas crawl over their bare boobs or make 'em stick their hands in his snake's tank. All pretty funny shit — even funnier if you're on coke, apparently.

I don't do drugs. I can't if I want to make it to the league. But that doesn't stop the other guys on the team or the girls at the party from wanting them. The music pounds harder from the other room and I hate that I'm searching for Kya in the crowd. I'm wrapped up in my revenge. That has to be it. I grab a beer and say hi to a few of the girls. Bethany, a chick whose name I just learned, follows me when I walk away from the crowd.

"Cole! Cole, we need to talk."

We do?

I turn and sip my beer.

"What's up?"

"I want… can we go upstairs to talk?"

Great. That takes care of getting laid. I'll send Bethany upstairs, find Kya, threaten her, and have sex with this chick who I just met.

"Yeah. Can you wait for me? I'm in room four on the third floor."

"Oh. Cool."

"Be naked when I get there, okay? I don't want this to last a long time."

"Oh. I was wondering if like… we could talk for a bit before…"

"Get upstairs, babe," I tell her, kissing her cheek and patting her on the ass so she gets out of my hair and I can focus on ruining Kya Ambrose's night. We're an hour into the party and I'm shocked she hasn't arrived with a gaggle of freshmen. Bethany's still waiting for me upstairs and somehow, she got my number. Seventeen texts in an hour. Geez, this chick is desperate. At least I know she'll wait for me.

Clutterbuck's at the door checking phones for invites.

"Yo, have you seen a black frosh come in?"

Clutterbuck smirks. "Is that what you're doing tonight? A black chick?"

"No way, dude. Not really my type," I laugh.

"You play hockey, bro. I think you can snag a blonde," Jayce teases.

I already have a blonde waiting for me upstairs. It's boring. Predictable. What's totally fresh will be seeing the look on Kya's face as I announce that I'm about to ruin her life. Fragile masculinity, my ass.

If I can't find Kya, the least I can do is work on getting properly sloshed. Hammered. Totally fucked up. Which means I'll need more damn beer. Dustin's already on the table, shirtless, forcing Barkov to down a Smirnoff Ice when I guzzle back PBR.

Drugs are a no-no, but alcohol just gets pissed out, making it the perfect thing to get totally numb on the weekends and just forget about the NHL. Forget about everything but getting my hands on a hot piece of ass tonight.

Then I finally see her. My hot piece of ass crawling into the party with her nerdy frosh best friends. I'm a junior, so way too old for freshman chicks, but damn…

Kya's the tallest of her friends and that big mane of curly hair that sheds all over my notebook, she's finally tucked back in some tight bun that lets me see her cheekbones better. And her lips. I don't think she sees me.

Her friend tugs her arm and I can read her lips from across the room saying something like, "This place is crazy. It's too wild."

Too wild? Oh, babe. The party hasn't even started. She'll see.

Kya's friends link arms with her — for protection, I assume — and they wander over to the little bar we set up where we serve the alcohol. Typical fucking freshmen, out at night with ridiculous eagerness to drink underage. Even innocents like Kya and her friends.

If I don't act now, I might lose my chance to ruin her night and finally to wipe the smug look off that annoying frosh's face. I slide past two guys who have a redhead chick pinned to the wall and both of them have a hand up her skirt.

I think I recognize the chick from biology class. I didn't expect her to be a slut. And I didn't expect my prey to walk willingly into my trap.

"Excuse me!" Kya says, thrusting her hand over the bar. She can't see that I'm there yet, pretending to work the bar so I can get an excuse to talk to her. I lean over and smirk.

"Sorry, frosh. I don't serve alcohol to underage people here."

Her friend tugs on her sleeve and whispers, "See, Kya? We're not welcome here. Do you see any other black women?"

"Relax, kid," I tease the other chick. "You can both have a drink. I was just messing with Kya."

"Do you know that guy?" Her friend asks, wrinkling her nose as if knowing a hockey player would be the worst thing in the world.

"No! He's just some guy in my class."

I hand them the drinks. Kya gives me a weird look. Unbelievable. She's totally not cool, but she's looking at me like I'm the freak.

"Kya, can we talk?"

"Sounds like he's not just some guy..." her friend mutters.

"Raven, can you chill?" Kya hisses.

"Let's hit the dance floor," the other friend says. Kya rolls her eyes.

"I'm coming. I just need to talk to him first."

"Okay," her friend, apparently named Raven, says, giving me a disapproving glare, which I've totally done nothing to deserve.

"Come on, Makeba," Raven says to the other friend and they disappear with their drinks toward the dance floor, leaving me utterly alone with my delicious prey.

"What do you want, Cole?" Kya says, in that prissy, uptight tone I hate so fucking much. She's a snob and soon I'll get back at her exactly the way she deserves.

I can't help the smile on my face. Especially not because I'm six or seven beers deep.

"I want you to come upstairs with me."

"What do you mean, come upstairs?" She asks in a violently sassy tone.

"I mean, come upstairs to my bedroom. Get on your knees and then suck my cock."

Her mouth goes round — the perfect shape for the act I just described — but she's not scared yet. Just disgusted. Don't worry. That's all about to change…

"You are revolting! I'm not doing that. I'm never doing that. Is that why you invited me here tonight? Because let's get one thing straight, Cole… I am never and I mean never —

As much as I love her hot little rants, I clamp my hand over her mouth and shut her up. She glares at me, her well-mani-cured eyebrows furrowing over her innocent black doe-eyes. She's so hot. But so fucking annoying.

"Listen, frosh. I have evidence of just how fucking dirty you are and I will tell your friends, your teachers and everyone you know that you spend your free time writing the dirtiest sex stories that I've ever read."

I drop my hand from her mouth because I know for once, I will have made Kya Ambrose speechless. And man, I love the silence.

Eventually, the frosh comes to her senses. Her pretty lips form an 'O' as she gapes at me.

"I don't know what you're talking about."

I recite one of my favorite sentences from her dirty story from memory.

"My older neighbor wraps his hands around my neck, pressing me against the wall as he slides my skirt over my thighs. He puts his gigantic cock inside my—

"Cole, stop!" She screams. There it is. Kya's misery. And fuck, it brings a smile to my face.

"This isn't funny," she stammers. I can practically see her nervous freshman heartbeat.

"I agree," I answer with a smirk. "It's pretty fucking sick. What do you think Professor Cooper would say?"

"You wouldn't dare show it to her. This is such a freaking violation of my privacy. This is why I—

"Watch the way you're talking to me, princess. I hold your fate in my hands, remember? I own you."

"You fucking asshole," she hisses, dropping the good girl act just like that.

"Good," I whisper. "Get angry. Now come upstairs with me, or you'll regret it."

Suddenly, her face gets all scared. Terrified. Like she thinks I'm going to do something unthinkable to her once we get up those stairs. I run my tongue over my lower lip slowly and watch her struggle to hide the signs of terror from her face.

I definitely own her now.

"I'm not going upstairs with you. Never leave with a perpetrator to a second location."

"A perpetrator?"

She scowls and I can just tell she's going to run. Not so fast, Ambrose. My hands close around her wrist and I pull her body against mine. She presses her free wrist against my chest and attempts to push me away, but... it won't work.

"Your friends are still around," I whisper, taking my free

hand and pushing a curl out of her face. "I bet you wouldn't want them to see you out here kissing me. And loving it."

Kya keeps struggling. I like that she has so much fight in her. It's a turn on. Her fighting spirit only makes me want to chase her down harder and make the conquest that much sweeter.

"I'm not going to kiss you. Not out here. Not upstairs," she hisses, practically quaking with outrage.

"Come upstairs, Kya. Seriously. You're pissing me off."

I sense the fight draining out of her at my harsh tone, and her voice falls to an uncharacteristic whimper.

"Promise you won't hurt me."

"I can't promise that."

"Fine," she says. "Promise you won't… rape me."

Her eyes flutter to mine and I can tell from the look in her eye that she's fucking serious. Honestly? Kya Ambrose has got me twisted up in knots. She thinks she gets me, but she fucking doesn't.

"Seriously?"

"Promise."

"You realize, if I were a rapist, I'd just lie."

"Thanks, Cole. That's comforting."

Good thing I wasn't trying to comfort her.

"Fine," I whisper. "I promise. Now, come. We have unfinished business."

My promise gets the job done, and she follows me upstairs to my bedroom. Her arms shake where I'm holding onto her. I don't give a shit if Kya's scared. That's exactly what I want. To punish her.

✨ *6* ✨

THE HOT BULLY'S BEDROOM

KYA AMBROSE

Cole's bedroom smells horrible — like a disgusting man cave. I hold my nose.

"Did you kill someone in here?"

"Hockey pads," Cole grunts, as if that justifies being putrid.

He shuts the door behind us and my heart stops. What the hell am I doing? Yes, Cole knows something horrible about me. Something I don't want to get out. But how the hell is following this cretin to his bedroom going to help?

There's a loud yelp, and a figure moves beneath Cole's sheets. I scream too. He already has another fucking victim up here?! The girl worms her way out of the sheets and stumbles out of Cole's bed — completely naked and totally plastered.

"COLE! I came, and you didn't come. You didn't want to cum inside me..."

Wow. She's really drunk. She's not just naked, but super thin — the typical type Laguna Grove guys go for. My stomach tightens and I try to avert my gaze out of respect. I couldn't be that skinny if I tried. She stumbles forward and I fight my instincts to throw a blanket over her and carry her out of there, mostly because I don't know what's going on and I doubt Cole would make it so easy for me to escape.

Is she Cole's girlfriend? I didn't know he had a girlfriend.

"Sorry, cupcake," Cole tells her. "But… I need you to get the fuck out of here."

Okay, so I guess she's not his girlfriend, either that or he's even more of an asshole than I thought. The blonde girl stumbles forward, barely able to keep her balance as she jerks toward the door to Cole's bedroom. She's leaving, and she's my ticket out of here.

She's unencumbered by both clothing and shame. I tell myself that she'll save me if I beg, even if her death stare tells me she'd rather cover me in Old Bay and spit roast me.

"Wait!" I plead with the blond girl as she glowers at me. "Take me with you. I don't want to be here."

She pushes my hand off her and delivers a wad of frothy spit on Cole's bedroom floor. "Slut," she sneers. At me.

"I'm not a slut," I protest, even if this chick definitely doesn't care.

She glares at me as if I want to be in this stupid bedroom with Cole Seabrook. Any decent woman would have tried to save me, but she's jealous. Freaking jealous!

And did this trick really just call me a slut? She gives me a little shove as she pushes past the door, and Cole shuts the door behind her. I definitely had too much to drink earlier. I'm in control, but not in control enough. I should have just fought him and run instead of listening to that jack hammering anxiety in my chest.

Cole turns his key in the lock and then shoves it into his pocket. Damn. I should have run.

But there are four of Cole's teammates waiting in the hallway and they're loudly sexually harassing every girl who walks past — including the unfortunate Becky that Cole just kicked out of his bed.

I don't even think he knows her name.

"I totally forgot about her," he says, grinning at me like that revelation should flatter me or something.

I need to think carefully about how the heck I'm going to get out of this. That shouldn't be a problem, right? I'm much smarter than Cole.

Once the door closes, he looks me up and down with a blatantly animalistic stare. I feel small. Trapped. My throat tightens, and that reaction apparently impresses him.

"You dressed hot. Just like I asked. Sorry about that girl. Don't even know her name."

"I didn't dress for you," I snap. "And that's not something to brag about."

"Sure you didn't," Cole continues. "Just like you totally didn't wear that short magenta denim skirt in tenth grade to get your math teacher's attention. Or was that part of your kinky sex story fiction?"

"It's all fiction," I snap, although that part wasn't fiction at all, "And you had no right to hack me and view my private information."

I want to act like this doesn't affect me, but Cole knows I wouldn't be up here unless he had something that could ruin my life. I guess I've showed my cards. I need to be smart, even if I can already feel my world crashing around as I imagine my dad hearing about my stories. My private stories that Cole had no right to lay his filthy hockey player hands on.

"I didn't hack you, princess," he says, stepping closer to me and practically pushing me up against his door. Without touching me, of course. The only thing I'm grateful for is that I can smell something besides his disgusting hockey pads for a change.

Him. Cole Seabrook. The smell hits my nostrils like a gust of wind. A perfect gust of wind that smells like vanilla and something spicy. Maybe nutmeg? He pulls away from me and it's back to the gross smell of Cole's nasty ass hockey pads.

"What do you want, then?"

"I think you know," he murmurs. His minty breath has a hint of a hoppy smell to it. If I've had too much to drink, Cole definitely has. And now he's trying to use this dick head act to lure me into his bed. I knew it. These sick hockey creeps always try it.

"I'm not sleeping with you."

He laughs. "Is that the first place your mind went? Can't say I'm surprised, considering the nasty shit you wrote."

My cheeks are burning. There's even sweat on the back of my neck and I know it's going to mess up my curl pattern. Even my palms are sweaty and I feel small and awkward. How the hell did I lose Makeba and Raven so quickly?

I hate that he's threatening me and that he has something on me that could really ruin my life. I'm such an idiot. I don't know how, but I let my worst enemy get his hands on my biggest secret. My voice drops.

"N-no. I mean… Can you just stop? This isn't funny. I get it. We hate each other, but this is too far."

"No," he whispers. His eyes are ice. I've never even seen eyes that blue, and it's unfair that God gave those perfect blue eyes to a freaking monster like Cole Seabrook.

"Tell me what you want," I snarl.

I have to show him I'm not afraid of him, even if it's a total lie that I barely believe myself.

"You."

He's still smiling like a cocky idiot.

"I'm not sleeping with you."

He's clearly suffered one too many head injuries on the ice, considering how often I need to repeat myself.

"That's not what I'm asking for, princess. I want you. As my personal slave."

"Your slave!?"

My hand clenches into a fist and without thinking, I swing on a crazy ass white boy almost a foot taller than me. He grabs my fist and stops me. Duh.

"Hey," he says calmly. "Slaves don't hit their masters."

"That's not funny," I snap, pulling my fist away and shaking it off, because I hit Cole's stupid gigantic palm pretty hard.

"You're right," he says. "It's just… it's the only way you can stop me from publishing this stuff to the internet, sending it to your dean, maybe even seeing if TMZ wants some real dirt on Dwayne Ambrose's slutty daughter."

"I am not a slut," I hiss at him. Suddenly, I want to hit him again. Cole gives me a warning expression, like he can read my mind and he wants me to know that this is a totally bad idea.

"Really? If you aren't a slut, why did you write this…"

Cole clears his throat. "He bent me over in the shower and slid a well-lubricated finger into my anus."

Did he memorize every freaking word I wrote?!

"Stop…"

He doesn't stop. Obviously. He continues criticizing me like he's a freaking erotica expert or something.

"Into your anus? I mean, come on, Kya. Word choice…"

"Stop," I whisper again. Because I finally feel like he's broken me. This is too humiliating for words. And it's not like Cole doesn't know who my father is. Everyone does. Cole could for real ruin my life. If daddy even knew about this. "Please…"

Cole's completely unsympathetic, but his cold blue eyes eventually crinkle around the corners as he laughs at my pain.

"I love watching you beg."

"This isn't funny!"

"I know," he says. "It's satisfying. You are so fucking stuck up, Kya, and I hate the way you look at me like I'm nothing."

"You're less than nothing," I snarl at him, hoping it hurts him more.

"Maybe," he says. "That doesn't change the fact that I own you."

"You don't."

"Don't test me, Kya. You don't want to see how badly I want to fuck your life up."

"Why do you even care?"

"I don't. But you're a bitch and I need to teach you a lesson."

"Don't call me a bitch!"

"Fine, servant. I won't call you a bitch."

It's so lame that I think to myself, at least he isn't calling me a freaking slave anymore. The bar is in the basement of this stupid house.

"I want to go back to my dorm. I need to talk to my friends," I tell him, hoping he'll get over his stupid revenge plot and let me go. I don't want to play games with Cole Seabrook.

"Give me your phone," Cole commands with a potent bass in his voice. Just because he uses a silky jazz voice doesn't mean I have to listen to a word he says.

I fold my arms over my chest. He'll never figure out that I tucked my phone into my bra. Cole gives me an infuriated look once I refuse to budge. Then he realizes where my phone is. A cocky expression crosses his face and before I can react, Cole freaking sticks his hand down my shirt.

"COLE!"

I shriek as he moves his hand around my bra. His hand is super cold, and he's touching me. Holy fuck, he's touching me. My body tenses as Cole's wandering palm cops a purposeful feel of my breast. I gasp and the tip of his crude index finger grazes my nipple before he touches it.

"Gotcha," he whispers, grazing my nipple again and withdrawing the cellphone from my bra. My body reels from the contact and I nearly fall backward against the door.

Bile rises in my throat. Cole Seabrook just touched my breasts. I can't believe he just did that. Without asking for consent, he stuck his stupid hand in my bra and then he had the audacity to touch my nipples in this really weird way that sent this horrible feeling through me. I can't handle it. My heart's ready to jump out of my throat and take off down the hall.

"YOU FONDLED ME!"

"I'm helping you," he snaps. "Now unlock this."

He holds it up to my face and apparently there's no setting for "don't unlock me if I'm making a terrified face". He glances through my text messages and leaves a voice note in my group chat.

"Hey Raven, Hey Makeba. Kya's totally occupied for the night with a complete gentleman who will only show her the utmost respect. All she asks for now is that you leave the party without her. She's totally taken care of."

He sends the message and lifts my phone over his head until we hear the little sound the phone makes when a message has been passed through the ether and has officially become a part of the irretrievable record of embarrassing shit you've done. Crap…

"Give me that!"

I finally come to my senses and lunge for the phone, but it's too late. Cole sticks my phone into his boxers, wriggling his hand down there so it's tucked away really deep. I gag at the thought of the phone I put up to my face nestled against his dumb wrinkly ball sack.

"EW!" I screech.

Cole smirks and walks over to his bed, moving his hips a little to settle my phone disturbingly close to his asshole, and sitting on the edge. He's considering me, but I still can't read what his intentions are. I'm definitely too terrified to look the junior hockey player in the eye. Unlike our gender studies class, this isn't a safe space and I know I can't get away with my harsh quips when I'm utterly at Cole's mercy. I still haven't moved away from the door. It doesn't feel safe.

"Come over here and get your phone," he says, using the voice again. I glare at him.

"No. Fucking. Way."

"Why not?"

"Because. Your dick is in there."

"Fine. I'll keep your phone," he says. "Your choice. So… let's get to work."

"What?"

I swear he's so dumb that communicating with him is fucking impossible. Get to work?

"You're my servant. This place is a mess," he explains.

At least he's right about his bedroom being a mess. He makes Makeba look like a neat freak. There are piles of clothes everywhere, books strewn about, empty beer cans, too many pairs of Air Force 1 sneakers and hockey pads. The worst part is the stink — which I can definitely blame on the pungent hockey pads.

"I'm not cleaning anything. There's still a party downstairs. I came here to party and go home."

Maybe if I can trick the dumb caveman into partying, I can get him even more drunk and escape out the back door. He doesn't take the bait.

"Right. You want to service some of my friends first, then?"

How dare he threaten me with that.

"Cole! No!"

"Fine," he grunts. "You're stuck here for the night and I'm super drunk, so I'm going to go to bed."

"Let me out! Please, Cole. I promise I won't make fun of you again."

"You would say anything to get out of here. Too bad. You're mine."

"How long is this stupid arrangement going to last?" I snap. "Because I don't want to be your servant. Ever."

"It lasts until I get what I want."

"Which is…?"

"I need peace of mind while I train for hockey, princess. You stumbled into my lap at just the right time. Now go to bed."

"Where exactly do you want me to sleep? On the pile of your disgusting hockey pads?"

"Get into bed, princess. I don't have a problem sharing."

Cole has officially lost his cracker ass mind.

"I am not sleeping in your bed, you pervert."

Cole's still sitting up in his bed, snickering at me like I'm a freaking joke. But I'm serious. If I crawl into Cole's bed, he could attack me. He's looking at me like he wants to.

But his annoying loud laughter makes me think I need to attack him first.

Through his laughter, he grunts out a sentence or two. "Pervert? I'm the pervert? You have over 100,000 words on your hard drive about all the ways you like to take it up the—

"It's fiction!" I screech.

"I. Don't. Care. You're mine, princess. Now get to bed because you have a long day ahead of you tomorrow. You know… being my personal servant. Or slave. If you change your mind."

"You don't have to do this, Cole."

"Believe me, I do. Don't make me repeat myself." There's the voice again. This time, I can tell he'll punish me for fucking with him.

I slowly approach the monster's bed. If I want to get my phone and call for help, I'll need to put my hand down Cole's pants, which is the last thing I want to do. Unlike Cole, I have boundaries. My cheeks grow hot again with the recent memory of him sticking his hand into my bra. And brushing up against my nipples.

"I don't want you groping me, either."

He definitely did that on purpose. I don't care about the fake-shocked look on his stupid ass face.

"I didn't grope you," Cole balks. I don't want to bring up my nipples. That would only encourage him.

"I hate you so much," I breathe as I sit on the edge of his bed next to him.

"Get close to the wall, princess. I wouldn't want you tumbling out of bed in the middle of the night in a drunken stupor."

"You mean you wouldn't want me escaping?"

"The keys are in my boxers too. Sorry, princess. You're stuck with me for the night."

I kick my shoes off and feel suddenly self-conscious that they're going to smell terrible. I comfort myself with the reminder that Cole's bedroom smells far worse than my feet ever could.

"You live in a pigsty," I snap.

Sassy comments are the only thing I have now. He's completely broken me down.

"You'll fix that tomorrow," Cole grumbles. "Now lie down."

"I can't lie down without fixing my hair," I snap.

Seriously? This man is so ignorant, so utterly consumed with himself, that he doesn't realize that my hair actually takes work. I can't just leave my hair wild and free like a freaking blonde ass mop. He gives me an even dumber expression than normal, which truly worries me.

"What? Is that when you take the curls out?"

Cole is honestly the most annoying person on the planet. I am sure of it.

"Take the curls out? Are you an idiot? My hair grows like this."

"I'm not an idiot. And watch your mouth, servant."

He is such a demeaning misogynist. If this asshole wants to make me his servant, I won't make it easy on him.

"Whatever," I snap. "I need to tie my hair down."

"With one of those kinky whips and chains from your books?"

"No. With a satin scarf."

"What about an old t-shirt?"

"Is it clean?"

"No."

"UGH!"

Whatever. I don't even know why I care about my stupid hair anymore. I hope it suffocates Cole in his sleep. That's my best hope for getting away from this asshole anyway — killing him with my hair. I huffily climb into his bed, hating the relief that floods me when his sheets are actually soft and clean, considering the rest of his bedroom is a trash heap.

I curl up against the wall and face away from Cole Seabrook. I hate him so freaking much.

7

MY FIRST BLACK GIRL

COLE SEABROOK

Cool. I'm drunk and Kya's in my bed. She's finally my prisoner. My mind turns around my plans of defeat excitedly. My servant. What a brilliant idea. I can think of a hundred tasks I can make Kya do to annoy her… humiliate her… ruin her.

It's enough to make a man crazy, you know? Just the idea that I could ruin the stuck up chick who makes my life a living hell… Yes.

Seabrook always wins. Tonight, Miss Ambrose is going to learn a tough lesson.

I grunt and slide myself onto the bed next to her. I know I ought to face away from her, but it will piss her off a lot more if I spoon her. I curl my body around hers and wrap my arm around her.

"What the fuck are you doing?" She snaps, but as she wriggles, I only hold on to her tighter.

"We're cuddling," I tease. "Aren't you having fun?"

"You smell like beer."

See? She's having plenty of fun. Beer's great, right? I push my face into her cloud of suffocating hair and consider shaving her head. That would stop the annoying freaking curls falling all over my notebook, but... it smells incredible. I rake my fingers through it instinctively.

"Cole, stop," Kya snaps, her little feet thrusting aggressively against my shin.

"I'm getting comfortable."

"You're getting comfortable turning my hair into a freaking nest. I'm your prisoner, not your friend. Stop cuddling and go to fucking sleep."

"Mmm," I murmur. "I like when you talk dirty to me, baby."

Kya kicks me in the shin again. Hard. She's so small, it's not like she can hurt me or anything, but it's definitely annoying.

"Kick me again, servant, and I'm going to sleep naked."

"If you slept naked, you'd have to take my cellphone out of your sweatpants and then I'd run away."

"Actually," I whisper, getting real close to her ear, "I'd put your phone between my butt cheeks."

"COLE!"

She elbows me in the stomach. Hard. I groan, and she makes a frustrated harrumph.

"Why is your stomach so hard?" She grumbles, as if I ought to have made it easier for her to beat the fuck out of me by turning into dough.

"Abs, princess. Want to feel 'em?"

Most chicks want to feel my abs.

"No."

"Can I feel yours?" I tease her.

"I don't have abs, Cole. Now leave me alone."

By my definition, she's my servant. I don't want to leave her alone. I want her total humiliation and I'll do whatever it takes to get it.

"Fine," I whisper. "Stay here. With me. Cuddling. In total silence. If that makes you happy."

It definitely makes me happy to have her body pressed against mine. Don't get me wrong, I still think Kya can be such a b-word. But she's soft, and she smells great and that annoying fucking hair of hers is pretty sexy up close.

"You smell like coconut," I whisper.

"COLE!"

She turns around to face me and I'm grinning from ear to ear, mostly because I know it will piss her off and she'll probably hit me or grab my shoulders or maybe even bite me if I'm super lucky. Uh… I mean, unlucky.

"What?"

I know I'm goading her, but it's pretty easy to piss Kya off.

"Stop smelling my hair. Stop being a creep."

"A creep? I'm too hot to be a creep, servant."

I sniff her hair again, and she shoves me. Again.

"Why do you hate me? Why are you even blackmailing me?"

"According to you, I'm a misogynist. Maybe I hate all women."

"I don't believe that," Kya says. "Well, I believe you're a misogynist, but you have a mom. You don't hate her."

"Leave my mom out of this, servant."

I want to pull her closer. I mean, I want to do all kinds of crazy things to Kya. Pulling her closer is just one of many ways I want to touch her.

"I am not your servant," she responds slowly, her tongue darting over her lips after. Those lips are so hot. I adjust beneath the covers. I can't focus on torturing her when I'm looking at those lips.

"Yeah," I whisper. "You're a pain in my fucking ass."

"If I'm such a pain in your ass, why are you enslaving me?"

The argumentative parakeet lying next to me makes a good point. If I want to stop her chirping, I'll have to give her a pretty good answer. But lying in bed next to Kya, there's only one answer coming to mind, and it's pretty fucking stupid.

"Because," I whisper. "I want to."

"That's not a good reason."

"It's a good reason to do this."

I lean forward and I kiss her. I know it surprises her, because her lips purse together instinctively at first. I keep my lips pressed to hers, because there's no way in hell I'm pulling away until Kya kisses me back. I feel the moment her resistance melts away, and I feel like I've almost won something totally impossible.

It gets me hot. Excited. Her lips part and I press my tongue into her mouth. I hold her face and keep kissing her until I don't want to anymore. When I pull away, Kya's lips fall apart and her hand connects with my face in an incredibly hard slap.

"Ow!"

"You fucking bastard," she breathes and then Kya climbs on top of me and kisses me back. I feel her thighs parting as she straddles me and her soft butt rests against my thighs as she positions herself on me. I'm reeling from her slap. My cheek stings. But I have to soak up every moment of her body touching mine, even through clothes.

She bends forward and grabs my cheeks to kiss me, running her fingers through the gentle sprinkling of stubble across my cheeks. She parts her lips again, allowing my tongue to explore her mouth and tease hers. Then she nearly collapses on me, more of her weight pressing into me as she kisses and kisses me.

When she pulls away from me, her thick black hair cloaks us in a fallen curtain of coconut-scented curls. Our faces feel even closer with the shroud of hair encircling us and I can see how wide Kya's eyes are in my dark room with only a bit of light from the hall peeking under the door.

"I never did that," she whispers. "Because it was really stupid and I really hate you."

I need her to stop talking. Stop thinking. I nod and gesture toward her lips. She knows what I want and now, I know she wants it too. Maybe we're both just too stupid drunk to lie in bed together and expect nothing to happen because this definitely isn't attraction. Kya hates me.

Her hips move forward as she inadvertently presses them into me to kiss me better. I haven't made out with a girl like this in... a long time. Hook-ups move fast. You don't take your time. Half the time, I'm thinking about something hotter than some Laguna Grove frosh — like scoring a hat trick at my next game. Stuff like that.

With her, it's just fucking wild. Her lips are bigger than any girl I've been with and they're about ten times softer. Everywhere on her body is soft and when I kiss her and tease those lips, I realize I kinda like big lips. Really big lips like hers. They taste better. They feel better.

My desire gets the better of me and I roll her onto her back to kiss her more.

"Cole..." Kya whispers as her head hits my pillow, and she's practically buried beneath my navy blue sheets. The less I allow her to talk, the better.

I kiss her again and I touch her hips this time. Now that I'm on top and now that we've been kissing for a while, it's definitely okay to touch her. I move my hand under her dress, but I don't go straight for her tits. I just touch her hips and her stomach, feeling her breath moving in her body as we kiss and her hips wriggling when I do something with my tongue that she enjoys.

I pull away from her for a second because I'm definitely about to go for her top, but I want to make sure she doesn't plan on kneeing me in the balls once I do it. I can feel her phone sloshing around my boxers, making my freshly sported hard-on impossible to handle.

"Princess," I whisper. "That was pretty hot."

"Stop. Calling. Me. Princess."

"Okay," I whisper. Then I kiss her neck, and she makes this almost strangled moan. I've never had a chick react that way to me kissing her neck before, so I chuckle.

"What was that all about?" I whisper, running my tongue over the spot. I kissed. She whimpers again and every part of me stiffens. That sound is heavenly.

"It's nothing," she answers.

"You're moaning and I've barely touched you."

"I'm just… If you're going to make fun of me…"

"I'm not," I interrupt, before my little parakeet squawks the moment away. "It's hot. You're hot."

I kiss her neck again and she makes that stupidly sexy moaning noise. I could give her a nice big hickey right there. She'd probably kill me, so I resist the urge and pull away for a moment. I'll have plenty of time to enjoy Kya's crazy hot body tonight and until I've had enough of revenge.

"Have you always moaned like that?"

"Can you please stop talking?" Kya whispers.

"I'll stop talking if you let me take your dress off."

She gives me a worried look, like this might go too far and she doesn't know how to stop it. I wait because I'm pushing my luck and I don't want her to freak. This is a game to me, but it's just a game. I want revenge, but I don't want her to get all traumatized or anything. I just want to play.

"Fine," she whispers. It's like she's scared to speak up around me for once. Her sharp-tongue ended up not so sharp after all. I kiss her on the lips again, settling her and I feel her stomach until her breathing relaxes, and she's just letting me make out with her hard.

I reach up to her breasts and touch the curve for the first time through her bra.

"Is there a zip on the back?"

She nods. I flip her over, and she makes a little grunt. I roll to the side and wow. Her butt. As she lies on her stomach, I can't focus on anything but her ass. It's fucking hot. Beyond hot. I reach for the zipper and slide it all the way to her lower back.

She's wearing a black bra underneath, and she has a tiny tattoo on the right side of her lower back. It's an outline of Africa, I think. I want to kiss that spot. I want to kiss every spot on her back. I start at the base of her neck, positioning myself on top of her again and pushing her hair out of my way.

There are wisps of thinner hairs on the base of her neck and they tickle my lips as I kiss her. She gasps and her hips tilt toward me, which means her ass presses into my crotch and holy fuck. I have never been harder in my life. I want to pretend its anyone but Kya underneath me, but she smells incredible and there's no way I could touch that hair and think of anyone but her.

Once I get her neck, I move down to her bare shoulder blades and roll the sleeves of her dress down as far as I can until I get to her bra. I unhook it with my thumb and forefinger and gently run my fingers through the indentation in her skin where her bra cinched too tightly around her torso.

I kiss the middle of her back and then keep working my way down to her lower back and that freaking tattoo. I run my finger over the slightly raised ink and then kiss it. Then I roll her dress off, over that perfect ass. It's pretty cold, so she's wearing tights beneath the dress. I can't wait to rip them off. But first… her butt.

I kiss her butt through the tights, and Kya makes a desperate little grunting sound. I pull the tights over her bottom, exposing the mounds of soft dark brown flesh. Fuck.

My heart pounds like crazy. It seems so stupid now that I have her here, but I feel like I'm doing something forbidden and wrong. I've never been this close to a black girl's ass before. Guys on the team joke about how they have better butts, hot butts. But it's just a joke.

You don't take black girls upstairs at hockey parties. You don't find out for yourself if the rumors are true. I don't know if they're true about every black chick at Laguna Grove, but they're definitely true about Kya.

I've gone too long without kissing her and she unconsciously gives her ass a frustrated wriggle and the way it moves gets me too hard to think. I kiss her butt. A lot. I can't stop massaging the soft flesh and moving it around and kissing her as she makes soft whimpering noises and slowly spreads her thighs.

I lose control when she spreads those thighs because I can finally smell her and it drives me wild. Every part of her smells incredible, but down there smells like heaven. I want her. I need her.

I graze my teeth along the back of her thighs and she whimpers again. Oh, I'm not done with you yet, princess. Don't worry.

My tongue follows my teeth on the backs of her thighs and then I spread her cheeks apart and press my face between her legs. She's still wearing a skimpy black thong — my favorite. It's totally soaked and difficult to pry from her curves, but I manage the task before I press my tongue between Kya Ambrose's legs.

8

RUMORS ABOUT WHITE GUYS

KYA AMBROSE

I've heard rumors about white guys. I heard they like going down on women. A lot. I don't believe in racial stereotypes or anything, but holy shit. Cole really just went for it. It's like he just expects it to be the first thing a guy does. It freaks me out. (I won't bother lying about that.)

I've never met a guy who just goes straight for it. I hate that the guy going straight for it is Cole, but I'm sober enough to know what's happening and tipsy enough to allow myself to want Cole Seabrook's tongue between my legs.

I moan as he runs his tongue between my lower lips and then presses it right against my butt hole. I squeal and he grabs my ass, pulling me against his face and pinning me there. He's strong. I couldn't wriggle away from his tongue if I tried. Not like I'm trying very hard because even if the tongue belongs to a monster, I'm still a heterosexual human female and his tongue against my pussy feels like heaven. I just need to forget that tongue is attached to an asshole.

He slides his tongue over my back door and then attempts to jut it in. When I moan, he pushes it out and rubs his tongue over my clit again, focusing his attention on massaging the tiny nub with his soft tongue. Oh shit.

His lips are even softer than his tongue and as his tongue moves against his clit, he kisses my labia with the softest lips I've ever felt. I've never had more than a reluctant 30 seconds of head before and this is...

"Oh my God..." I gush as a surprising climax erupts and I feel warmth spreading between my legs.

Cole pulls his face away from my pussy momentarily and I feel his tongue all over my thighs as he licks up whatever liquid just erupted between my legs. Once he cleans my thighs, he doesn't stop or anything. The fact that I just had an orgasm doesn't deter him from flattening his tongue and using his fingers to spread my lower lips before he presses his tongue against my exposed pink flesh.

He's doing this because he enjoys it. For himself. I moan again, and Cole moves his tongue faster. I didn't even need to explain to him what I liked. It's as if the moment he figured out how to make me cum, he just figured it out. His tongue and fingers hit all the right spots and even if I'm soaked from one orgasm, I easily yield to another. Easily.

Cole doesn't stop. I'm sweating when he finally does, and I lost track of how much I came. My hair is a puffy cloud/nest around my head, and Cole uses his fingers to push my juices inside me. I moan again because... Cole Seabrook's finger is inside me.

His tongue is one thing, but any part of Cole's body penetrating mine feels so wrong, but... so good. I've never been with a white guy before. I never thought it would be different... but it is so different. Holy shit.

I moan again as he moves his finger around in there. He's quiet, except for heavy breathing. Thank God. Hearing his voice would only snap me back to reality. I'm hooking up with Cole Seabrook.

We all have different definitions, sure, but his finger is so deep. I wriggle my hips back again and he takes his thumb to rub my clit while his finger's inside me. I cum again and Cole removes his hand. I glance over my shoulder to watch him sucking my juices off his fingers, and then he licks me off his palm.

Oh God. I face away from him again, because I don't think I could look him in the eye after this. I feel his body hovering over mine, still clothed, and his crotch pressing into my ass. He pushes my hair out of the way and his lips are so close to my ears that I can smell myself on him. I can hear him licking his lips and I feel a shiver travel straight to my crotch.

"You taste good, princess."

"Th-thank you."

I hate that I sound like a whimpering mess — like one of those desperate girls always hanging around the hockey house hoping Cole or one of his sociopathic jock teammates pays them any attention. He chuckles and I hate that I'm enjoying the sound.

"You make a great servant so far," he whispers, reminding me that he's an asshole. "But I'm pretty fucking tired, so you can blow me tomorrow."

He kisses my cheek and then rolls off me. My throat feels tight and even if I had enough orgasms to lose track, I feel a strange pang in my chest. Disappointment? No. There's no way I'm disappointed that Cole didn't drag me up to his rape den and have sex with me. I told him I didn't want sex. And I didn't.

But… I mean… I didn't expect him to use his tongue on me. I didn't expect him to be good at doing that stuff. When he lies on his back, I suddenly want to cuddle with him. But I force myself to turn around and face the wall.

Cole literally wants to enslave me. It's 2021. We know better than to let white boys who want to make us slaves get in our head, right?

I don't remember falling asleep, but the smell of Cole's hockey pads wakes me up in the morning. I roll over and my chest tightens as I realize I'm in bed with a man. I'm freaking out, ready to beat this strange guy to death, and then I remember. A shock of messy blond hair pokes out from beneath the blanket and there's absolutely no space for me to move in this Twin XL standard issue bed with Cole's gigantic ass next to mine.

I can't even climb over him or rifle through his boxers to find implements that might aid my escape. I roll over to face him — and because I'm considering smothering him as my next way out — and then he opens a single blue eye.

"Good morning, servant," he mumbles groggily as his eye roves over me.

I guess he's done with the princess crap, but servant isn't exactly an upgrade.

"It's not a good morning," I hiss, pushing against his bicep, trying to chase him out of his own bed.

I feel a little like a bitch for my response, but I'm sober now and it's daylight and I'm in Cole Seabrook's bed, so I'm rapidly coming to my senses. I let Cole go down on me last night. Why the fuck would I do something so insane? He's black-mailing me currently and if I thought allowing him between my legs would encourage him to liberate me, I was wrong.

I can tell from the cocky smirk on his face that he's far from finished and he definitely doesn't have any plans to let me go.

"I wondered if you'd try to escape," he murmured. "Glad you stayed. It would have been such a shame to email your dad about your slutty secret."

"Well, I didn't escape," I snap, ignoring his cruel threat. "But I'm hungry."

Rule #1 of being a captive, never make it easy on your captor.

"Perfect," he mumbles sleepily. "Clean my room, suck my cock, and then I'll get you breakfast."

"Are you fucking kidding me?"

His smirk falls away. He can be terrifying when it suits him.

"No," he says. "Get out of my bed and start working."

There's that stupid disappointed pang in my chest again. What did I think? Did I really think I could hook up with Cole Seabrook for like an hour and he'd totally change his attitude toward me? He's definitely the type of guy that pumps them and dumps them. At least I didn't allow him to humiliate me completely by giving in to my tipsy desire to sleep with him. What the hell was I thinking? You can't just sleep with asshole guys because they're hot.

I still have my pride as long as I don't sleep with him.

"I'll clean your stupid room," I snap. "But I'm not sucking your dick."

"We'll see."

He doesn't make it easy for me to climb over him and leave his bed, and he makes sure to get a good grope of my butt as I'm doing it while I glare at him.

"You have a nice ass, Kya."

"I can't believe you actually know my name."

"Yup. I also know what your pussy tastes like," he answers with a cocky grin smeared across his face. I swear I want to kick the crap out of him.

"Can you shut up? That was a total accident. I was coerced."

"Isn't that what all your sick stories are about? You're welcome."

I glare at him, but he doesn't seem to give a crap.

"Hurry," Cole urges. "I really need my cock sucked."

He is the most entitled, misogynistic, stupid, and annoying bastard on the planet. I regret not hitting him over the head with his dumb hockey equipment and escaping without succumbing to his stupid wishes.

"Why don't you call that desperate blonde who warmed your bed up last night?"

"I don't know her name. And I don't want her lips. I want yours."

I roll my eyes.

"How long are you going to keep blackmailing me?"

"It's been less than 24 hours, so it definitely hasn't stopped being fun yet."

"This is fun to you?"

"Kya," he says sternly. "You aren't cleaning up. It's a pigsty in here. Come on. Get a move on."

I pick up a few sweaty shirts and nearly gag.

"Have you ever heard of a fucking laundry hamper?" I snap, although I really want to "hamper" Cole's breathing by shoving his disgusting shirts in his face. My rage doesn't affect him. At all.

"Yeah. It's in my closet."

He closes his eyes and I see my perfect chance to strike. The only problem with killing Cole is that then I'll have to get rid of the body...

"Your phone's vibrating like crazy," he says. "It's getting me hard."

"That's disgusting."

"It's right between my nut sack and butt," Cole murmurs. "Pretty gross."

"I fucking hate you," I hiss at him.

"Keep cleaning, Kya. Keep cleaning."

I put all his dirty clothes in the hamper, which cuts back on the smell slightly. But only slightly. There are still disgusting hockey pads in here, not to mention beer cans, homework assignments, jars of protein powder and all kinds of weird jock stuff.

I can't believe how many girls at this school worship guys like Cole.

"You're like a messy little boy," I chide him.

"Oh yeah? You're like a super annoying mom."

I make an irritated noise which has absolutely no effect on Cole, whose hand has moved under the covers and suspiciously close to his crotch. I'm working on collecting the beer cans. Most of them are half-full, making the task inherently risky if I don't want to spill gross beer everywhere.

"Your phone's vibrating again."

I ignore him this time. I'm just his servant, right? I don't need to talk to his annoying ass, I just need to serve him. His hand is moving around his crotch like he's adjusting himself or maybe reaching for my phone to carry out some nefarious deed, and I hate that I'm even looking in Cole's stupid direction.

I stop paying attention for one freaking second when I move Cole's helmet and shriek when I see what's hidden beneath it. I hate boys. I hate men. I hate the entire race of men and I don't care if it makes me sexist. Because no girl would ever live like this. Ever!!

"WHAT THE FUCK IS THAT!?"

❧ 9 ❧

OVIE

COLE SEABROOK

"Can you stop being dramatic?" I grumble at her.

Sheesh. Kya loves making a big deal out of stuff, but this is definitely not a big deal at all.

"THERE'S A SNAKE. THERE IS A LIVING WILD AND DANGEROUS REPTILE IN YOUR BEDROOM."

"Dustin's boa got out again. Big deal. Keep cleaning," I say to her, falsely expecting my sensible explanation to calm her down. She's going to freak him out if she keeps screaming like this. He doesn't like noise.

"Big deal?! It's a six-foot snake coiled up in the corner of your fucking bedroom!" She shrieks. Then she makes another dramatic wailing sound and calls me a bunch of names.

She's totally going to make me get out of bed for this, isn't she? Kya doesn't realize the last thing she wants is Dustin coming up here.

"Relax. He doesn't bite. Often."

She shrieks again and jumps back.

"It opened its fucking eyes! Cole! I quit. I quit."

She screams again, like the fucking snake's going to give a shit.

"You can't quit," I remind her impatiently. "You're my servant. And will you relax? You'll wake the guys. And they're a lot worse than I am when they're horny."

She shoots me a glare which I definitely don't deserve and continues having her snake-induced meltdown.

"It's moving! Cole, it's going to EAT US!"

She stumbles backward and throws my desk chair between her and the snake.

"Maybe it's just going to eat you."

"This isn't funny!"

She scrambles across the room again and onto the bed, which means she has to scramble over me, which is very hot. Trust me. Her body's fucking crazy, which makes sense because Kya's definitely nuts in that hot way girls have.

I still want revenge, don't get me wrong, but I can get revenge on a hot girl, too. Equal rights, baby.

I finally sit up and glance at Rathbone's creature.

"Ovie," I mutter. "You are such an asshole."

"The snake's named Ovie?"

"After Alex Ovechkin. One of the greatest hockey players of all time."

"Ugh, who cares about stupid hockey? Get this freaking disgusting snake out of here!"

I lazily text Dustin about his snake. Kya's done a great job with the room so far, but I need this place in much better shape before morning skate.

"Get to work, Kya. I'm tired of your bitching."

I smack her ass. Hard. She looks at my pillow like she wants to smother me with it, and just in case I stick it behind my head.

"I. Hate. You," she snarls. Then she climbs over me again, giving me a great view of her sexy ass and she glares at Ovie, as if glaring would make a difference. I can hear Rathbone's animalistic stomping down the hall. Ovie gets out all the time. I swear I searched for him yesterday and didn't find him. Ah, well.

Kya picks up a few more beer cans before Rathbone opens the door. He doesn't even look at me — or at Ovie.

"Hey, hot stuff," Dustin says, his eyes roving over Kya and then lingering on her ass. He turns to me and grins. "You sharing?"

"Nah, bro. She's helping me out."

Dustin chuckles. "Right. Sure she is. Great tits, babe."

Kya ignores him.

"Babe," he yells. "I said great tits."

Kya's messing with the wrong dude by ignoring Rathbone. Or maybe I have the situation all wrong.

"I heard you," Kya snaps. "I don't care what you think about my boobs."

Dustin steps into the room, towering over Kya, who glares at him like her eyes can bore holes through him. I prop my head up on the pillow, watching it all crumble around me. Kya draws herself up to her full height, glowering at Dustin Rathbone like he's peanuts, even if one swat from his giant hand could knock her across the room.

"Come on, babe. If you'll be a slut for Seabrook when he talks so much shit about you, you'll be a slut for anyone. Call me when you're done riding his cock."

Before Kya can react, he leans over and kisses her cheek. Kya pushes him hard, but Dustin gets checked daily by men twice Kya's size. He doesn't budge.

"Seabrook, what on earth are you doing with this one?" Dustin responds — to me — bemused.

"She's cleaning up after me. And after that, who knows…"

Dustin knows exactly what I mean by "who knows". He knows exactly what he'd do with a pretty girl like Kya. Hell, he'd probably mess with her worse than I did.

"Wow," Dustin says. "That's pretty hot. Mind if I touch her?"

"Go ahead," I answer, because it's definitely going to piss Kya off. I think he's going to touch her face or something but Dustin Rathbone takes a firm hand and gives Kya's hot ass a big squeeze. She shrieks in surprise and stumbles backward, losing hold of the giant pile of semi-filled beer cans cradled in her arms.

The beer spills… everywhere. Dustin can't stop laughing as she picks her way through the pile of cans. Kya's soaked and now my room smells more like beer than ever before. It's hilarious.

"Chill out, chica," Dustin says. "You've got a great ass."

Dustin steps over her and grins once he sees Ovie.

"Ovie! Come with me, buddy."

He sticks his hand out, and Ovie knows exactly what to do. Kya stares horrified as Ovie flicks his tongue and then moves his head forward to slither over Dustin's hand. Dustin wears the snake over his shoulders and without saying goodbye, he peaces the fuck out with his giant snake.

Kya rises to her feet, eventually peeling herself free from the piles, and tosses an empty beer can at me, which I catch and set on the windowsill.

"Chill out, Kya. You just made a huge mess. Better clean that up."

Her face is all scrunched up with rage. She's kinda hot when she's angry…

"I hate you! I hate your gross sticky beer. I hate your filthy, smelly room. Your friend just sexually assaulted me!"

"He grabbed your ass, Kya. Come on. Are you traumatized?"

"YES!"

She flings another beer can in my direction. Fuck.

"Can you stop that?" I grumble as I catch the beer can.

"You're an asshole."

"Yeah, and you're still mine," I snarl. "So get this shit cleaned up, Kya. Now. Or I swear, I will ruin you before breakfast."

She glowers at me, but she's not willing to risk me spreading her shameful sex stories to TMZ or whoever. I wouldn't know where to start or anything, but Kya doesn't need to know that. She just needs to make sure my room is fucking spotless. This is way too easy.

But watching her clean with that furious scowl on her face is just... making it super fucking hard to think about how I'm going to torture her next. Yeah. Super. Fucking. Hard.

Kya interrupts my daydream about all the things I want to do to her mouth.

"Seriously?!"

"What?"

"You have.... Oh my God... this is so gross..." she says, basically hyperventilating as she shrieks. "Cole... you have an... erection. Oh my God! Cole! Cover it up."

Fuck. My blanket's doing a pretty terrible job of giving me privacy. Ah, well. What's the point. I throw the blankets off and Kya shrieks as if she's seeing two ghosts doing it doggy-style and not just... me.

"It's HUGE," she screams. "I mean... COLE! Put that away! This is harassment!"

"Come on, babe. Just ignore him."

"Ignore him? Ignore him?"

She does this thing when she's mad where she just repeats stuff. It's pretty funny, but I think she's going to toss a beer can at my head again.

"You're almost done," I tell her. "Keep working."

She throws the last of her beer cans in the trash and then glares at my hockey pads again. She casts a furtive glance over her shoulder at my dick. She tries to hide it but... I've lived with this dick my entire life. I know how women react to it. She might be a super annoying feminist chick, but Kya's still a flesh and blood woman. A delicious woman. Tasting her was one of the best ideas in a while, even if it's totally messing with my head. Fuck.

There's no way in hell I'm getting rid of this boner without help.

"Want a break from cleaning?" I offer, softening my expression as she uses a Clorox wipe on my desk. I haven't seen the surface of that desk in weeks.

Kya tosses the wipe and flops down on my gaming chair.

"Yes... thank you."

"Good. Come over here and suck me off."

There's that angry scowl again. What the hell did I do wrong? I offered her a break.

"You are disgusting."

"What? You don't like a big dick?"

"Only an asshole calls their own dick a big dick."

She mocks my voice to make me sound super dumb and I remember that prissy little Kya is the last person on earth I should sympathize with.

"Come on, Kya. This is the biggest you've ever seen. Don't lie."

"You are so arrogant. And that's not even the point. You are disgusting because you want to blackmail me into giving you head."

"Can you imagine another scenario where I get head from you?"

"I guess that makes it totally fine to blackmail people if you get a blowjob out of it."

"See? Even a dumb guy can have some pretty good ideas."

"I'm not sucking your dick."

"Right. And you're going to explain your story, Locker Room Sex With My High School Bully, to your daddy on Dr. Phil."

"I hate you," she screeches. And she fucking means it. Her eyes well with tears and holy shit. Is she really going to cry? I think she's faking it for a second, but there are some things you can't fake — even if you're a spoiled L.A. princess.

"Come on. Don't cry. That'll spoil the experience for me."

Her glare lingers. I like when she looks at me, even when she's pissed off. It's almost as fun as chasing down a puck.

"I hate you, Cole. You don't understand. This is humiliating."

"Why? You really think you're that much better than me?"

"I don't hook up," she snaps. "I don't give my body to random guys. I'm not like you athletes or whatever. I don't go out every weekend and get naked with strangers. Those stories I write are just fantasies and you're treating me like I'm this… like I'm just a slut. I don't do that stuff."

She cries harder, which totally kills my boner. I slide my pants back on and groan as I get out of bed and walk over to where she's sitting. I guess I'll have to take matters into my own hands.

"Get up."

She turns her teary gaze up at me with a pleading look on my face, like she thinks I walked over there to stuff my dick in her mouth. But she stands while she fidgets nervously. Her heart must be beating like a hummingbird because her chest is all fluttery.

"I think you seriously overestimate how many people I sleep with," I tell her.

"Oh yeah? How many girls have you slept with?"

"We're playing this game?" I tease. "That's usually a conversation you have with someone you're dating."

"Well, we're at absolutely zero risk of dating, so you shouldn't have a problem telling me," she snaps.

Then she looks all scared again because she thinks I'll punish her for that sassy quip. I just raise an eyebrow. No need to traumatize her. Yet.

"4."

She snorts. "You are such a liar."

"I'm not."

"There was a half-naked girl in your bed before I got there."

"And I kicked her out. Listen, babe. I'm totally focused on my game. I'm going to the NHL. I don't have time to screw around."

"Okay. I'll try to believe that."

"What about you? How many guys have been inside you?"

"It's complicated."

"Complicated?"

"Well, I've never told anyone."

"You're my servant. You have to do everything I say. Including tell me."

She scowls. "I'll tell you if you promise not to sexually assault me."

"I already promised that."

"Promise again."

"Fine."

I think she gives up too easily for her tough girl act. She could have argued for way more out of me. I don't know. I just got kinda curious about what makes this annoying feminist tick. I guess that will just make it easier to get what I want from her. Or something.

She sighs all dramatically before telling her story because Kya is very dramatic 100% of the time.

"I technically had sex with three guys but... I have terrible luck with guys and all my boyfriends ended up having..."

"Having what? A secret pussy?"

She glowers at me with that "I think you're a fucking idiot" look she has plastered on her face whenever she looks at me.

"No," she snaps. "A micro-penis. I lost my virginity to a micro-penis."

"What the fuck is a micro-penis?"

"Seriously?" she says, her haughty know-it-all voice returning. "You don't know? It's a serious medical condition that affects 0.6% of men."

She has that annoying know-it-all tone which makes it impossible to hold back my laughter as she reveals her secret talent at attracting micro-penises.

"And you found three of them in a row?"

"They're drawn to me," she says somberly. "I can't help it."

I know this is her super secret dramatic story, but it's kinda fucking funny. I stifle a laugh and she pushes my arm.

"Can you stop?"

Sigh. I'll give her a tiny break since she's crying and everything. It's not that much fun watching her cry anymore.

"Yeah. I'll stop. Listen, babe. Are you hungry?"

"Yeah."

"Let's get some grub. Then you can do your homework at the rink while you watch me skate."

"Are you serious?"

"Yeah, babe. It's the weekend. I'm not letting you out of my sight."

"My friends are going to get suspicious. I need my phone."

"No problem. It smells like my ass, though."

She wrinkles her nose, but she's too desperate to get her phone back to complain about the butt-phone.

I continue my severe warning. "You know what will happen if you try any bullshit. I think my all-time favorite was Hooking Up With My Chiseled Youth Pastor. That was fucking filthy. The candle wax? The orange peels? And what was that oil called? Jojoba? Kya… Come on."

She scowls and looks away from me, remembering that she hates my guts. I kiss her forehead and unlock my bedroom door. Breakfast time.

10

I'M HIS SLAVE

KYA AMBROSE

Raven folds Makeba's clothes, taking one item off the floor at a time and conducting a thorough sniff test before folding each article. Makeba lies back on my roommate's bed, taking no interest in Raven's attempts to clean up after her. My friends have been here for an hour already, but I just got out of a meeting with Cole and Professor Cooper. He sent me here to pack my things. I guess I'm moving into the hockey house — unofficially.

My hot pink Longchamp weekender bag sits on my bed as I stare at my clothes and try to figure out what to bring to Cole's so he doesn't think I'm flirting with him. I'm his freaking slave. Sorry, his servant. Like that makes a difference to him. I choose a couple pairs of leggings. They're comfortable, making them a good choice. Then I find an old sweatshirt from high school that only has two holes in it.

"So... are you going to tell us who that guy was?" Makeba asks.

"Yeah, Kya. We haven't heard from you in like... two days," Raven adds. "The only white guy we know that you talk to is the white devil. That wasn't him, was it? Because you went upstairs with him."

I don't know how the hell I can explain my weekend to my best friends. Nothing more happened between me and Cole, but after our breakfast together, he worked me like he was serious about the servant thing. He even sent me to get his stupid skates sharpened. How the freaking hell can I explain how degrading this is to my best friends without exposing my secret?

"I know. I know," I grumble under my breath. "I've been cagey as hell. I'm sorry."

Stupid Cole. His very existence makes my life a complicated hell. Like I didn't feel guilty enough for ditching my friends at a party, he'd sent them some dumb message and made my life fifty thousand times more complicated. He was so annoying.

"He's just some guy I met," I offer after my friends punctuate my silence by staring at me with large, guilt-inducing brown eyes.

"Some guy you met at Pesthouse?" Makeba asks. "But you knew him... before? Are you sure he's not the white devil?"

I feel like she's attacking me, even if this is 100% normal girl talk. If they find out that Cole and I kissed or did any of that stuff... they're going to judge me. They're going to hate me.

"Didn't you two meet a guy? It's not like my phone has been blowing up with texts from you guys or anything."

Raven gives Makeba a shifty glance, and then her nose wrinkles as one sock she picked up from Makeba's pile emanates a disturbing stench.

"What was that look about?" I grumble, referring to the shifty glance rather than the stinky sock.

"Some guy asked for my number," Raven says, grinning. "He was hot too."

"At the hockey house?" I answer, wrinkling my nose. Although a part of me has to admit that I'm impressed that Raven's oily foot rub spell actually worked.

But my crinkly facial expression makes me seem too judgmental, even if I have no right to judge her, considering where Cole Seabrook put his white boy tongue less than two days ago.

"How hot is hot?" Makeba asks, even if she's clearly already heard the story.

"HOT!" Raven says. "I didn't even know what to say. I almost gave him Kya's number."

"Thanks..." I mutter.

The last thing I need is more annoying hockey guys in my life.

"Is he on the team?" Makeba asks.

"I don't know," Raven says. "He was hot, though."

"Do you know his name?" I ask her. I've unfortunately spent enough time in Pesthouse that I know a couple of their names. Cole made me serve nachos and beer to him and his best friends, Jayce and Dustin, while they played video games. They humiliated me.

"Dustin," Raven replies. "I didn't hear his last name. Something like Crafthole."

"Ew," Makeba says. "What kind of name is Crafthole? It sounds perverted."

"You mean Rathbone?" I correct her.

"Oh..." Raven says nodding. "It might have been that."

"Ditch his number," I say. "Seriously. He's a total asshole."

I shudder just thinking about that gross snake. What type of freak keeps a reptile as a pet? White boys. White boys are the freaks.

Makeba pipes up, "Since when are you an expert on hockey guys?"

This is my moment of truth. I can either lie to my friends and save my skin or I can tell someone about what's happening to me. Cole would definitely retaliate if I told the dean, but he never said that I couldn't talk to my friends about this. He'd probably love hearing about my inevitable fall from grace. I throw a sad white t-shirt into my bag and sigh.

"I have a confession to make about where I've been all weekend."

"Banging a hockey player?" Makeba says.

"No! Definitely not. Ew. I'm still the same old Kya. Trust me. I would never."

Except for letting Cole's tongue touch the darkest corners of my thigh creases. In my defense, that doesn't exactly change who I am as a person.

"Cole Seabrook has enslaved me," I announce seriously. This

only confuses my friends, unfortunately, and I won't get out of the situation without giving them answers.

"Huh?" Raven asks, giving a thankful glance to the heavens that the thong she just pressed to her nose was clean. Makeba's still on her phone, blissfully unaware of how much work Raven's putting in to clean up after her. I would help, but I'm not exactly thrilled by the idea of cleaning up after anyone else after the weekend I've had serving all the stupid hockey boys.

"I am Cole Seabrook's slave," I repeat. "He has made me his slave."

"Girl, slavery's over," Makeba whispers, looking over at me like I've hit my head or something.

Raven stops folding clothing and rushes over to me, tiptoeing to put her hand on my head.

"Do you have one of those bird flu diseases? That affects the brain?"

I don't think Raven has a clue what she's talking about. I shake my head.

"No," I say. "I'm not sick. I'm not an actual slave... but Cole's blackmailing me. And he has something big."

"Go to the dean," Makeba says.

"I can't," I say. "The second he found out, he'd ruin my life and trust me. This would ruin me. Not just that, it could screw with my dad's career. It's terrible guys..."

My friends are sweet and innocent. I never want to do anything to break their hearts or to drag them into my mess. They just don't deserve it. Raven's hand drops from my forehead and she takes my hand.

"Don't freak out," she says. "Cole's an asshole. He's just trying to scare you."

"I spent all weekend in his bedroom. He's serious."

"Did he hurt you?" Makeba asks. "Blackmail or not, he has no right to touch you. You could go to the police."

I shake my head.

"He hasn't hurt me. He just… he's making me do a bunch of stupid stuff for him, like clean his room and serve him and his friends. It's so dumb."

I explain as much as I can, detailing my weekend from the moment Cole brought me upstairs. I skip the part where we kiss and have a weird sort of hookup. I rant about the stupid snake Ovie for more time than necessary because the stupid snake snuck into bed with me while Cole was at practice one night. My friends are dismayed. It's good to have a consensus that Cole is a freaking asshole.

"There's only one way to deal with bullies," Raven says. "At least according to romance novels."

"Should we really make life decisions based on romance novels?" Makeba mutters.

Raven throws her a sharp glare as if she finds Makeba's suggestion genuinely offensive.

"We need to get back at him," Raven continues, convinced that her idea is worthwhile despite Makeba's protests.

"How?!" I tell her. "Remember, he has all the power over me."

He has hundreds of my stories. Hundreds. And apparently, he's not too stupid to remember the plots, characters, sex scenes and the exact quotes of my filthiest stories. I'm so grateful my friends don't push me to confess. I don't want them to think I'm a desperate skank or mentally unstable or something.

"He doesn't have all the power," Raven replies with a smirk. Her confidence catches my attention.

"Can you get to the point?" Makeba huffs. "I want to know how we're going to take him down."

At least it's easy to get them on board with hating Cole.

"Sabotage," Raven announces. Could that one simple word solve my problems?

That's it?

"How!?"

"Do everything wrong. Everything. He'll get so annoyed that he'll probably set you free."

I don't know if I share Raven's optimism.

"Either that or he'll kick my ass."

"If he was going to hurt you, he would have probably done it when he trapped you in his bedroom, utterly at his mercy."

"I guess..."

"Listen, that idiot friend of his? I'm blocking his number. And we're going to find all the ways you can fuck with Cole Seabrook."

"Hell yeah," Makeba says.

"Don't let her get away scot-free," Raven says, glancing over at Makeba, who rolls over to check her texts. "She had a really weird weekend."

"It wasn't really weird," Makeba says.

"What happened?" I ask. I would listen to a manatee mating call playlist if it meant not thinking about Cole Seabrook's torture.

"I'm dating BJ now," Makeba announces.

"Gay BJ?"

"He's not gay. I mean, he's not my type either, but…"

"Then why are you dating him?"

Raven answers that question for her. "She wants to get laid. Guys here are like impossible to pin down."

Makeba nods and smiles. "And BJ's easy. He's right there. I mean… isn't that the best guy to sleep with? The guy who's right there?"

"That doesn't sound romantic…" I grumble.

"Making out in the basement of Pesthouse isn't romantic either," Makeba insists. "I just need to convince him to like… do me."

"You're dating. That should be pretty easy," I tell her.

Makeba's parents basically kept her locked in a study throughout her teen years, so I don't blame her for being a little naïve about guys. But BJ? I just don't see it.

"I don't think she should date BJ," Raven chimes in, looking to me for an ally. "But that's my opinion."

"So you want to support Kya, but you won't support me?"

"I'm not dating Cole," I protest. "I'm his prisoner."

"Fine," Makeba says. "But at least he's a guy and you get to sleep in his bed. I just want somebody. I'm tired of being single."

"What about waiting for the right guy to come along?" Raven asks.

"The black men on this campus hate us," Makeba reminds her. "We're the boring black girls. Not the sorority black girls. Not the dance black girls. Not the cool black girls. Actually, they don't even like any black girls."

Makeba had a point there.

"I'm divesting. I'm bagging a white guy. Even if it's BJ. I mean, how bad can he be? He writes poetry. Slam poetry."

Raven rolls her eyes, even if Makeba's right about the black guys on campus. A lot of them try to get close to me because of my dad's connections, but they prefer chasing after the white girls like the one I found in Cole's bed. My stomach tightens uneasily.

Makeba shoots back at Raven about her 'right guy' comment. "You thought you found the right guy. But Kya just told you to delete his number because he was a secret asshole. There aren't any right guys. Just wrong guys. I want my wrong guy to be a white boy now."

"That is so cynical," Raven protests. I sense a fight about to break out, and I really don't want us all to fight.

"Hey, don't fight," I chime in. "If you're happy with BJ, then you're happy."

"Thank you, Kya."

Raven rolls her eyes. "I know BJ. He's not as innocent as he seems, Makeba. He has a dark side."

"So?" Makeba says.

"Are you attracted to him? Even a little?" Raven pushes.

"You don't need to be attracted to lose your virginity. Can you just support me?"

"Fine," I say. "I support you. When is your first date?"

"Soon. I think," Makeba says. "He said he'd plan it."

"Great..." Raven grumbles. "He's already dropping the ball."

I change the subject.

"Should I bring my white sneakers or my flats over to Pesthouse?"

Raven and Makeba offer me a sympathetic look.

"Bring this," Makeba says, finally getting out of Raven's bed and handing me something. It's a whistle with a blue logo on it that says THREE STREAMS COMMUNITY CHURCH.

"Um... what is this?" I ask her.

"It's a rape whistle. For Pesthouse."

"Thanks... but... only hockey guys live there. I don't know if this would help."

"You never know," Raven says, agreeing with Makeba. I accept the whistle just because I want them on the same side. I prefer them on the same side at least. Raven finishes folding Makeba's clothing and Makeba thanks her by ordering Chinese food for dinner so we don't have to use our meal points. Score.

I want to stay with my friends, hang out, and eat Chinese food, but my phone buzzes. I look down and my friends immediately know it's Cole, from the horrified expression on my face.

"What does that asshole want?" Raven snaps.

COLE: Hey babe. Get back to the house. I let you have plenty of freedom. Hope you didn't fuck your life up. You have fifteen minutes to get back here or I'll come find you. Trust me, you don't want that.

Even if I'm cutting into my fifteen minutes, I show my friends the text message. They give me sympathetic hugs and Raven promises to cast a painful 'dark magic' spell on Cole. I tell her not to worry, but I notice her supply of jojoba oil has dwindled significantly and I don't think she'll spare Cole's spirit her harshest curse.

"You'll teach him a lesson," Makeba says. "I know you will. Stay strong, Kya."

"Our ancestors survived worse," Raven adds solemnly.

My friends walk me to the door of our dorm room, but I'm going back to Cole's place. Alone.

11

MY OBSESSION

COLE SEABROOK

Kya, Kya, Kya. I spend all day thinking of ways to torture her. Classes are boring anyway, and it helps to have something distract me from the pain while I'm skating or while some idiot on the team slams me into the boards.

It's been torture sleeping next to her without touching her. She sleeps on her stomach because her butt is so big and soft that lying on her back arches it too much and she can't sleep. After what happened, I think she's too scared to sleep on her side next to me.

This is better for both of us. I don't know what I'd do if I pressed my dick against her thick butt cheeks again. Probably something super fucked up.

At least we won our game on Sunday, thanks to Kya's excellent work getting my skates sharpened and uniform clean. I'm as superstitious as any hockey player, so I want the same routine for Wednesday's game. Unfortunately, since Monday evening, something has gotten into Kya Ambrose. She's fucking up. And I think she's fucking up on purpose.

She dyed my lucky white boxers green by accident. I found Ovie's skin at the foot of my bed, and she spilled beer all over my textbooks. One more mistake and I swear to God… I'm going to blow the lid on her little scheme to get out of trouble.

If she thinks fucking up will get the job done, Kya Ambrose is 100% wrong. On Wednesday morning, she's the picture of innocence. Maybe she knows I'm onto her or something. Today's task is simple — once she has my laundry, cleaning my bedroom and getting me breakfast out of the way. All she has to do is show up at the rink and film my game on her phone with a tripod.

Coach Murphy says I need a better corner shot and I couldn't agree more. It's better if you have someone take your game footage for you for the closeups and everything. My personal servant is perfect for the task. She promises to get to the rink on time and we only argue with each other for twenty minutes that morning instead of the usual forty-five.

This only makes me more suspicious. What the hell is she planning? If she has secrets, I bet they're hiding in that enormous mass of curls. I've been collecting every strand she sheds on my pillow, and I swear she's like a freaking poodle. Whatever. As long as she gets the game recorded, I don't care what gets into her.

She's crazy, so that probably explains everything. I knew that when I started blackmailing her.

Thankfully, Kya's not crazy enough to miss the skate before the game. She's there with the tripod right on time, but she looks unenthusiastic. It's easy to forget that the only thing Kya hates more than me is hockey. She constantly tells me how contact sports are stupid and the reason I'm a "brain damaged idiot".

When I point out that I can't be that much of an idiot since she's my personal servant, which must make me pretty smart, she gets all mad at me. A hockey player has to handle his business in this feminist college world. That's all I'm saying.

The least she could do is smile. That might motivate me to skate faster or something. Once the game starts, she won't be able to ignore me and half-heartedly stare at the screen. There's a reason Murphy thinks I'm ready for the league. I'm fucking awesome to watch and Kya's got to notice.

We scout the Bayshore University Boars on the ice. The guys are smaller than we are and I can tell they aren't as fast. They have a legendary defensive player, impossible to get past, but the rest of the team looks weak. Looks can be deceiving, but I hope like hell that I'm right.

I have to believe that kicking their asses will be easy. There's no such thing as a sure win in hockey. Anything can happen on the ice.

In our crucial last minutes of preparation, we skate in circles, practicing passes and shooting. Clutterbuck passes me the puck and I flick it to Rathbone, who throws it backward to our first line center, Adam Foote. Foote passes to Dale Miller, who cracks a joke in a sharp South Boston accent as he whips it around to Benji, who finally stopped daydreaming about that brunette he's been chasing. We keep skating in circles and passing before shooting on Vitaly Barkov, the gnarly Ukrainian we have in goal.

Corner shot… I need to work on my corner shot. Barkov saves two of mine, but I get one in past him. If I can get a shot past the toughest of the Vipers, maybe I can sneak one in against the Boars.

Tuck made it a point to remind me that there will be recruiters at this game. Many of them are here for Jason Scuttle, a hulking defenseman for the Boars. If I make a good impression on the ice, maybe they'll be looking at me too.

Rathbone makes all his shots on Barkov — good luck for our game. He's pissed off because "some chick" turned him down. He doesn't want to tell any of us who she is. Dustin just wants revenge and tonight he's taking out his anger on the puck, the way they trained us to since we were kids. I could skate before I could run, according to my mom.

The stands fill up as we skate and soon, it's hard to pick out Kya's premium seat against the ice, normally reserved for family members. Murphy gave me permission to let Kya take one of my seats.

My mom's coming to this game. She'd probably love Kya and imagine a bunch of different hairstyles for her or whatever. Chick stuff. I make sure they aren't sitting next to each other, but I don't use all ten of my tickets and my mom can be chatty… I can only hope she doesn't try making conversation and totally blow my cover.

I can't worry about Kya or chick stuff for long because the crowd goes wild and we play our walk out song. Everyone in the bleachers wears some festive combination of Laguna Grove colors — green, silver and white. Because we're the vipers, everyone has rattles in the audience, even if rattlesnakes aren't vipers, no one gives a shit. Hockey is a place to get drunk, wreck shit, and cheer for the home team until your lungs give out.

At least all of our decked out fans make it easy to see Kya, who chose not to give a shit and refused to even wear my jersey. She's wearing all black.

"I'm mourning the days when I didn't have to watch a bunch of dumb jocks hit each other in the head over a stupid rubber disk," she snapped before we came down here.

Jeez. At least she's doing her freaking job, and I don't have to hear her chatter on the ice. It's game time.

We line up on the ice, and it gets quiet. At least in my head, there's pure silence. I need my mind clear so I can skate, shoot, pass, and move all on instinct. The crowd is probably still going crazy out there, heckling the Boars, who look nervous in their white and navy away uniforms. Out here on the ice, my mind is clear. Quiet. I'm ready to win this shit.

Foote wins the face off and we have the puck. He passes to Rathbone, who races to the Boars' side of the ice. Clutterbuck weaves behind me as I fend off #45 and wait for Rathbone to shoot the puck.

As Rathbone shoots, #45 skates on my right and slams me into the boards hard. I nearly fall over from the impact, but he has the puck and I race down to our side of the ice to catch him.

Clutterbuck saw that hit, and he's pissed. I can tell he's itching for the type of fight that will land him in the penalty box. I can see that fierce look in his eye, like he has some shit to work out on the ice. He thrusts his stick out and snatches the puck from #45 who attempts to get it back and finds himself slammed against the boards with Clutterbuck's fist coming straight at his face.

Fuck. That colossal idiot can't afford to get a penalty this early in the game, but it takes the refs, me and Foote to get Jayce off #45 whose nose looks broken. #45's chest heaves with rage and his face is red, but Jayce already got all the good hits in.

The crowd's going crazy, booing the referee, but this is all Jayce's fault. He knows Tuck is going to kick his ass for this and the giant idiot doesn't even care. He'd better not fuck up again.

2 minute penalty, Laguna Grove Vipers, Bayside University Boars on the power play.

Fuckin' Clutterbuck… We make it through the power play without letting a goal in, but I can hardly breathe by the time Clutterbuck's back on the ice. Murphy calls me off and I heave over the boards as Benji Coyle takes my position. He's only a sophomore, but he's pretty fast and he'll become a good forward with a little more ice time. I can't stop watching the puck. The adrenaline coursing through me refuses to let go.

Tuck rushes over to me, glaring. Coaches are pretty much always pissed.

"What the fuck happened out there with Jayce?"

"I dunno."

"You shouldn't have let that guy hit you, Cole. Keep your eye on the puck, but never let the other guy out of your sight. Got it?"

I nod, but my ears are ringing and I can barely focus on anything but catching my breath. My eyes find Kya in the crowd, even if she's totally a fucking distraction, and she looks more miserable than ever. I can't blame her. We're five minutes into the first period and no one has scored.

I have to get back out there. I need to change that.

"Coach. Let me back out. Coyle needs rest."

Murphy nods and signals, then I'm back out on the ice. No one scores during the first period and by the end, I'm red in the face and almost as pissed off as our coach. If I want to get any recruiters' attention, I have to score. I have five of our ten shots on goal, but not one goes in. Fuck.

Our break will mostly involve getting our asses reamed by Tuck Murphy. The Boars don't exactly have the best record this season and we should have them down 2-0 by now.

"Don't get down," Tuck snarls at us. "Get out there, skate your asses off, and destroy them. Use whatever you have to. Get angry. And Jayce… one more fucking penalty and you'll be doing a thousand pushups after practice tomorrow. Keep it together, guys. We can win this."

Tuck gets us riled up and energized. A break helps a ton and when we're back on the ice, I know what I need to do. Foote wins the face off again. He's pretty fucking good at that. He slides it up to Rathbone and I skate into the Boars' ice as fast as I can. Rathbone passes and I take a crazy shot.

It hits the corner of the goal. It's in…

The crowd goes fucking crazy. I pump my fists and skate over to Rathbone, who locks me in a hug. I fist bump the team behind the boards and feel giddy. This is what hockey games are all about.

First goal of the game to Cole Seabrook, #59 for the Laguna Grove Vipers. GOOOOAAAALLLL!

The crowd goes crazy and I can't help but find Kya. Even Kya fucking Ambrose isn't immune to the magical energy of scoring the first goal at a home game. She's clapping. She's smiling. Fuck yes. Good thing I have more where that came from.

Halfway into the second period, #23 for the Boars slams Jayce into the ice. Jayce Clutterbuck knows what Murphy told him is key. He needs to let that shit slide. But he doesn't, and he slams his fist into #23's face. The crowd goes wild, but so does the ref and for his second offense, he's five minutes off the ice and the Boars are back on the power play.

Tuck's livid. They score twice, making my goal feel fuckin' worthless. We can't let this shit happen. I'm off the ice again, catching my breath, too tired to get another goal in. But I need to do this. I beg Murphy to send me back out there.

"You have two minutes, Seabrook. If you don't tip the puck in, you're finished until the third period."

"Got it."

I skate out there, racing for the puck, too close to the center line. I grab it and whip it around the crease with a stunned Boars defenseman struggling to keep up. Rathbone checks the guy hard and Foote distracts the goalie as I pass the puck to him.

He passes back to me and I weave it around, tipping it past the line.

Another goal for the Vipers to Cole Seabrook #59, with Adam Foote #18 on the assist.

I've tied the game up, but I'm not finished. The Boars win the next face-off, but I'm ready to prove myself. I whip around to the right side of the ice and grab the puck. I take everyone by surprise, weaving around #23 and #67 on the Boars' team.

Cole Seabrook on the breakaway!

I can hear them cheering. I can feel the crowd wanting me to shoot. To make it in. I slam the puck towards the goal. And fuck… it goes in.

Holy shit, he's done it! Another goal for the Laguna Grove Vipers from #59 Cole Seabrook on the breakaway. He's scored a hat trick! First hat trick in the college league this season.

The crowd goes wild as I pump my fists and we end the second period with the score 3-2 in our favor. Murphy can't stop grinning as we walk off the ice. We have the best locker room talk we've had in ages and Murphy hypes us up.

You can win this, guys. You will win this. Huddle. Vipers on three… 1… 2… 3….

"VIPERS!"

The Boars are tough as nails at the start of the third period. They're tired and angry. They want to win this. It would be huge for them, screwing over Laguna Grove, and the score is close enough that we can't get complacent.

We have to win this. Boars win the face-off, which puts us at an instant disadvantage. Our defenseman, Marc Kane, swings the puck up to Logan Hargreaves, our second string center. Hargreaves is a freshman, nasty skater, but not the best at shooting.

He passes to Rathbone as they ease their way deep into Boars' ice. Rathbone shoots it to me, but #67 on the Boars is sticking to me. I don't have a choice. I have to take a chance on the frosh and I pass to Logan. He gives it a big slap with his stick and none of us know if it's in for a second and then it's clear.

He fucking made it. The frosh fucking scored.

GOAAALLLLLLL for the Laguna Grove Vipers, first goal of his college hockey career for number #20 Logan Hargreaves, a Canadian international student and monster on the ice.

Laguna Grove can't control themselves and the Boars are losing steam against us. We're up 4-2. We can win this. We can destroy them.

Rathbone scores the next goal with an assist from Foote. When the buzzer blares, it's hard to believe it's over. Laguna Grove wins, 5-2. I glance over at the crowd and Kya's shrieking with ecstasy, jumping up and down and cheering. So much for hating this dumb sport. I smirk until I see someone I recognize standing next to her.

My mom. *Shit.*

❄ 12 ❄

THE WHITE DEVIL

KYA AMBROSE

I can't believe we won. I didn't know Laguna Grove actually won hockey games. I'm so excited that I hug the equally excited white lady next to me. She's really pretty with great blonde hair and I guess she must really like hockey because she wraps me in her arms and squeals.

"Who are you here for?" I ask her, trying to be polite as I turn off my recording and start folding up the tripod. I just hugged a stranger, so now it's a little awkward. I just got caught up in the moment.

"My boy scored the hat trick," she says. "Do you know Cole Seabrook?"

My heart stops. I appreciate my friends for their advice about sabotaging Cole. I think he notices, but he hasn't said anything about it, which makes my attempts to get under his skin a total work in progress.

But this... this is an opportunity.

125

"Yes," I tell his mom with a brilliant smile. "I know Cole."

She brightens up instantly. I am so ready to ruin Cole's stupid ass life. He thinks he's smart, huh?

"Really? I brought him up on my own, you know. He loves this game, bless his heart. After his dad left, his hockey coach became like a second dad to him. He spent all his time on the ice."

"Wow," I gush. "He's an incredible player."

Thank God Cole didn't hear *that*. But I need to get his mom to like me so when I finally expose that her son is an evil piece of...

"Wow, you really think so, babe?"

Shit... My cheeks turn red and I turn around. Cole's standing behind me in his uniform, his long blond hockey flow sticking to his neck, and his blue eyes fixed on me.

"Cole!" His mom gushes, weaving around me to wrap her tall, sweaty son in a big hug. "You were incredible."

His stern face cracks and I stop, breathless, because I've never seen Cole smile like that. When his mom wraps her arms around him, he looks less like a monster and more like an overgrown boy. It's a bit... cute. He turns red when he notices me watching him and stifling a laugh.

"Thanks, mom."

"I was just talking to Kya! How do you two know each other?" his mom asks.

Cole's eyes meet mine and I smirk. This is the perfect opportunity to humiliate him. I know he loves his mom and when she learns that her son isn't this perfect little angel, maybe she can convince him to back off.

Cole gives me a warning look when he sees the mischief in my eyes, but that white boy can't stop me!

"Cole's my—

"She's my girlfriend, mom," Cole interrupts, smirking at me. "Yup. Kya's my new girlfriend."

WTF? Why would Cole say something like that. Now I'm the one thrown off balance and the desire to punch him in the face is only getting stronger…

He puts his big sweaty arm around me and I don't think his mom notices when I elbow him in the stomach. Hard.

"Your girlfriend!? Oh my goodness, honey… why didn't you say so?!"

Cole glowers at me and I'm too stunned to come up with a response as his mom wraps her arms around me and hugs me like she's already adopted me into her family. No!

I seriously want to kill Cole Seabrook. Maybe one day, I'll get a chance. That would be a freaking dream come true.

Cole looks like he has second thoughts about his dumb lie when his mom says, "Oh honey, we always have dinner after my boy's games. Do you want to come with us?"

"Uh, mom. That's unnecessary," Cole stammers, suddenly getting all awkward and turning pink. Ha. It's funny to see some reminder that he was once an awkward little boy and not an annoying blond pillar of muscle.

"I'd love to have dinner with you," I say, noticing how uncomfortable he is and enjoying every freaking second of it.

It's finally time for Cole Seabrook to sweat. Maybe I have a chance to win this after all…

"I made reservations for two, but it's nothing to add an extra one. Honey, why didn't you tell me you had a girlfriend?"

Cole's cheeks turn bright red as his mom picks up the phone to call the restaurant. Cole's scowl at me after she turns away is the sweetest revenge. Serves him right for keeping me as his servant and then lying to his mom. I hope his entire world comes falling apart after this dinner. It will be great to have the upper hand for once. She seems smitten with her son and ready to spill all his embarrassing stories. After this dinner, we'll see who ends up blackmailing who…

She hangs up after a few seconds and turns to her son.

"Honey, you get dressed and drive her over and oh, I'm so sorry. Bless my heart, I just can't believe Cole introduced me to one of his girlfriends! What's your name, sweetheart?"

"Kya. Kya Ambrose."

"You can call me Tina. And honey, you have such lovely hair."

"Mom!" Cole interjects sharply. "I need to change. Go on."

Tina Seabrook ambles away, excitedly texting someone. I smirk at Cole, enjoying the discomfort on his face with smug satisfaction.

"Serves you right for telling her I'm your girlfriend," I hiss once his mom's out of earshot. I don't want to blow my cover yet. Naturally, Cole ignores what I say and just plunders forth with his own agenda.

"Did you get the footage?" Cole snaps.

"Yes. It's on my phone."

"Perfect. Follow me to the locker room. I need to change."

"I can't imagine a worse place for a woman to find herself than a locker room with a bunch of date rapists," I say to him, hoping that eventually one of my good points sinks into his dumb hockey player skull.

"Not all athletes are date rapists," Cole snaps. "And I'm the last one here. Everyone's outside talking to the press. A recruiter stopped me after the game because of the hat trick. Not like you care."

Well, at least I learned something new today. Everyone in the crowd was talking about Cole's hat trick. Maybe it's because my dad is an athlete, but I've always avoided sports that weren't basketball. A hat trick is apparently scoring 3 goals in a row, what Cole did in today's game, essentially winning it for Laguna Grove.

He's a freaking hero on this campus and even I have to admit, he looked great out there. I mean, I won't admit it to his face. But I can admit it to myself.

"You're right. I don't care."

"Come on," He says. "I need to give you instructions on how not to screw up dinner. Servant."

"I don't see why you're punishing me when you're the one who lied to your mom."

Cole grunts and I struggle to keep up with him, lumbering through the halls in his skates. We get to the men's locker room and I lean against the wall outside.

"I'm not going in there."

"Yes, you are. I don't need you bolting and confessing everything to my mother. I saw that look in your eye and I'm keeping your ass close."

"Oooo, is the widdle baby Cole afraid of his mommy?" I tease.

Cole's intense blue gaze hardens.

"No," He says. "But she's my mom and I protect her from everything. I always have."

"Since your dad left?" I snap, although it's kind of a low blow for me to bring that up in such a sassy tone.

Cole doesn't bark at me over the tone, however.

"Yes," He says. "Since my dad left, I'm all she's got. I want her to think I'm a good guy and I want her to know that I'll take care of her. So yeah, servant. I need to make sure you don't fuck that up with your big mouth."

"I don't have a big mou— COLE!"

He pulls me into the locker room and wow. It's eerily quiet and eerily clean in here. This school seems to have blown its entire budget on a luxurious locker room for the men's hockey team.

Cole strides over to his locker and just starts… undressing.

"What are you doing?"

"I'm changing. Just sit on the bench."

"I don't want to watch you change!"

Cole turns to me, shirtless, with an irritating cocky smirk on his face.

"Really? You don't?"

"What is there to see?" I say, each word dropping out of my mouth painfully slowly as my dumb body has a biological reaction to Cole's exposed chest. He has an eight-pack. I feel how firm he is each night we share a bed, but seeing it in the fluorescent locker room lighting makes his shredded body even crazier.

"I dunno," He says. "Nothing. I guess."

He steps out of his skates, takes his pads off and drops everything. And I mean everything.

"Cole!"

I dramatically cover my eyes, but it's too late and we both know it. My hands fall away and Cole puts his hands on his hips. Grinning.

"See. I knew you couldn't look away. You're too obedient."

"I am not—

"Shhhhh," he interrupts. "Bask in the glory of my perfect body and my big cock."

"You are so disgusting," I snap, but my eyes are glued between Cole's legs because big doesn't even begin to describe it.

I guess this explains why he's such a dick. It has to be at least 20% of his body weight. Okay, maybe that's an exaggeration, but it's thick. Thicker than a Pepsi can. I wet my lips and try to think straight as Cole's bare member steals every drop of my attention.

"Hey," he teases. "Eyes up here, princess."

I'm more than happy to meet his eye. And glare at him.

"I am simply documenting this blatant sexual harassment in my memory palace. Nothing more."

"Document away," He says, toweling the sweat off his body and sliding into a pair of navy boxer briefs that hug his thick hockey butt. He is so muscular it's insane.

"Whatever. You're not all that just because you have a good body."

"Thanks."

"For what?"

"For saying I have a good body."

He crosses the room in just his boxers and in an infuriating move, he grabs my cheek and kisses my forehead. I glower at him from my seat on the bench.

"Hurry up," I snap. "I don't want to keep your mom waiting."

"Mom knows I run late a lot. We have time."

He's standing right in front of me, his hips at the level of my face.

"Plus, if you don't want us to be late, you can just work faster."

"Work faster at what?"

He juts his hips forward.

"No way. I am not blowing you in the hockey locker room."

"Why not?"

"Because it's disgusting and—

"Shut up, Kya. I don't care. I want your lips down there. Now."

"What about—

He clamps his hand over my mouth.

"Remember, I can still ruin you. So if you know what's good for you… do it."

I hate that I don't have any choice but to obey Cole Seabrook. What he wants from me is wrong. Everything about Cole is wrong.

"Why? Why do you even want this from me?"

My hands move to his hips and Cole steps forward. Even his hips are muscular and lean. I run my hands over the outside of his boxers, where his large dick struggles to stay hidden. I was too drunk the first time I saw him. I didn't realize how big he was.

"I can't even fit my mouth around that thing," I whisper.

"With those lips? Sure you can, princess."

"What do you mean about my lips?" I snap, sensing something offensive coming (and sensing correctly.)

"They're big."

I frown and pull my hands away from Cole's hips. He is so annoying.

"That feels racist."

"Listen, princess. You've got great lips. I want them on my cock. And you're going to listen to me or we're going to be late for dinner. Or worse… Rathbone could walk in on us and then you'll have to do him too."

"That's disgusting," I whisper.

But he's right that it will be better for me to get this out of the way quickly. And Cole gave me head, so I guess this was coming, eventually. I pull his boxers over his ass and he groans.

"I earned this, you know," he whispers, sliding his hands through my curls as I wrap my hand around the base of his growing member. "I scored a hat trick. It's only fair I get head."

Cole wouldn't understand fairness if it crawled up his ass and wormed its way to his brain from there.

"This is blackmail."

"Um… yeah. I mean, you can say no if you want to, but… I think you owe me."

"I don't owe you."

"I ate your pussy. You came in my mouth. Now open up."

I glare at him.

"Come on. What's the big deal? You've never been shy about opening your mouth before."

"It's just not romantic," I whisper.

"I don't need it to be romantic. With those lips… you can't screw up."

"Cole…"

"Just do it, princess."

Princess. I hate how that word makes me feel. I hate pretty much every effect he has on me. I shouldn't let some dumb guy make me feel so many insanely conflicting things at once.

I shouldn't let some dumb guy put his dick in my mouth in a freaking locker room. He just wants me to submit to him. He yearns for that feeling of power and there's something so manly about him standing over me, wanting me to yield to him. It's messed up, but it's like Cole activates my horny lizard brain and every sensible thought in my head just gives in to pure lust. It's unlike anything I've ever felt before. It's exhilarating.

His cock jumps to attention, almost hitting me in the face. The large thick meat stick juts forward, practically begging to enter my mouth. If I don't hurry, I'm sure Cole will take matters into his own hands and shove it in there.

"Don't worry," he whispers. "I won't get cum in your hair."

Um!? That was the least of my concerns. I open my mouth to complain and the tip of Cole's dick prods my lips. I move my head forward and tighten my lips' grasp on the head of his cock. Cole groans, his fingers sliding deep into my curls, definitely tangling them up and messing up my curl pattern. Ugh. Cole doesn't care about my curl pattern, or my hair. He wants to control me. He wants to use my mouth for his own sick purposes and I'm going to let him.

He smells too good for me to say no. At least that's the dumb excuse my horny lizard brain comes up with. His dick pushes forward more against my lips and I instinctively spread them apart and move my teeth away from his large but sensitive shaft. I don't think I can breathe with that thing in my mouth, but Cole makes this low groan in the back of his throat and then I don't care anymore. I just want his big dick deeper.

"Do you like my big white cock in your mouth?" He whispers.

I want to react, but he grabs my hair tightly, holding me steady so his dick is buried too deep in my mouth for me to answer.

"It's okay, princess. We don't have to be politically correct in here. I know you like it."

He pushes into me another inch. I can feel him going deeper than I've ever taken a man before, and I brace myself against his thighs. He releases his grasp on my head slowly and allows me to control the pace for a moment. I run my tongue along the length of his shaft and move forward again, taking him deeper than before. Cole groans. He smells like sweat. Logically, I know that. But in this deeply intimate act, I'm convinced that sweat is the most delicious manly scent I've ever inhaled and I don't just want to press my nose to his crotch, I want to suck every inch of his flesh. My grasp around his cock tightens and I take him so deep that I feel the tip of his dick graze the back of my throat. When I start to choke, he slowly removes my head from his shaft until I can breathe again.

I look up and him, and he's just staring at me with those intense blue eyes. I've never seen him look at anyone like that before. I feel like I belong to him properly now and that he considers this, claiming me above everything else. He doesn't have to say anything to get me to do what he wants. I stroke his thighs and attempt to take him deep again.

"It's true," he murmurs, his icy blue eyes fixed on me. "Black girls give way better head."

Again, he pushes into me deeper when I try to say something. Fine. If he wants to keep my mouth around his dick, I'm going to do everything in my power to tease him. Whenever he gets close, I ease my pressure and slow down. He doesn't care about being late, then he can prove it. I can tell he's getting more sexually frustrated. He desperately wants to cum, and I'm teasing him like my life depends on it.

"Fuck, babe. You're perfect," he whispers. "Please... let me cum."

There's something so fucking satisfying about having Cole beg me for something. His fingers tangle deeper in my hair.

"I love your lips," he whispers. "Let me cum in your mouth."

I hate that his encouragement makes my chest surge and my desire to please the hockey beast grows. I take more of him and grab his ass to pull him in deeper. He groans.

"Fuck... that's hot..."

I want to keep teasing him, but I can't keep this up for long. I tell myself that I have to make him cum. I ignore the fact that I want him to cum. I move faster over Cole's shaft, responding to his appreciative grunts.

"I'm close," he whispers. "Oh, fuck... I'm gonna cum."

I tell myself if I pull my mouth off, he'll finish somewhere cruel, like in my hair or on my face. I ignore the weird desire I have to taste him, to share something so intimate and unusual with a man like Cole, who is attractive in every way aside from his entire personality. When I feel his cock finally building to an orgasm, I wrap my lips around him even tighter.

Cole's dick spasms in my mouth as he groans and I feel the hot pumps of cum bursting from his cock head and coating the back of my throat. It's sticky and he cums so much that my mouth feels too full and I gag again. His hands relax in my hair and he groans with pleasure. He's utterly docile for a moment, just breathing slowly with deep satisfaction as he strokes my hair. Good girl, his hands seem to say to me.

Cole slowly withdraws his cock and I swallow the giant load he placed in the back of my throat. Salty. All of him tastes salty now. But then I have this intimate warmth sliding in my chest and I'm soaking wet between my thighs. I feel a pang of guilt over it, but very grateful that Cole has no way of knowing that giving him head drove me to the brink of arousal. To the brink of flinging myself at him.

When I look up at him, my eyes water, a look which only brings him greater pleasure than before.

"I hope you have room for dinner, princess," he whispers, taking my hand and pulling me to my feet. "Come on."

It's not romantic, but I don't care. I still feel the surge of excitement in my chest from having tasted him. Touched him.

Before we leave the locker room, he kisses me on the lips. That makes my conflicting emotions go to war. It's a big, confusing kiss. He even puts his tongue in my mouth, unperturbed that he just deposited a load of his semen in there. He pulls away, red-faced, and repeats himself.

"Come on," He whispers. "I can't control myself around you."

I don't think I can control myself around him, either. I'd never done that with a guy like that before. I'd never enjoyed it. But now, I can't help but feel a sick thought cross through my mind. Maybe he'll expect this often. I can't bring it up, of course. I don't want him to think I enjoyed it. Because I didn't. This was just blackmail. Totally. 100%.

13

MAYBE I DON'T HATE YOU

COLE SEABROOK

Kya's quiet throughout dinner. I knew a dick in the mouth would keep her quiet, but I didn't honestly expect to miss my little parakeet's constant quips. Every time I look over at her, I can't help but picture my cock in her mouth. I know it's pretty fucked up, but holy shit… she was beautiful. It was like her mouth was making love to me.

I never looked down at a chick doing that and felt like… a fucking emotion? That was crazy. She was soft. Arousing. I don't even think she realizes how good it was. I'd never had a girl play with my cock like that or enjoy it so much. What a pleasant surprise…

I feel obsessed with trying again. I'm sure I can convince her to blow me every night. No. Whatever the fuck she does with her mouth is way better than a blowjob. I want a Kyajob. Kya isn't a sick fuck like me, so she's making pleasant conversation instead of fantasizing about head.

She makes it a point to focus on my mom during dinner, keeping me off balance because I have to listen to every damn thing that comes out of her mouth. Pretty hard since thinking about her mouth automatically gets me hard and super distracted. Kya says I have ADHD, but honestly, she says a lot of shit. I can't listen to all of it.

I'm expecting her to fuck up big time at dinner and give me something I can use against her ass later. But she's honestly… perfect. My mom loves her. The second my mom asks Kya about her hair routine, I can't get a word in. They talk about creams and curlers and all types of chick words that I don't understand. My mom never compliments hair. The opposite, frankly. She notices split ends, brittleness, excessive dyeing and bad perms. Mom used to make me help at the salon until I turned thirteen and started taking hockey more seriously.

Apparently, Kya has some of the healthiest hair my mom has ever seen. Whatever.

After dinner, Kya's all glum again. Mom drives back to Silver Hollow, giving me a totally embarrassing goodbye like I'm still a little kid. Kya avoids taking cheap shots at me, and sticks her hands in her coat pockets, looking at her toes. I feel a little bad for making her do that in the locker room. I guess she's more upset about it than I expected. I thought it was amazing but… I know she wants to be like in love with a guy she does that stuff with. And I definitely don't make the cut in her perfect fucking world. Whatever. I don't really want her to feel like shit, so I try to be a gentleman for a change.

"Hey," I tell her. "You were great at dinner."

"Your mom is a sweetheart. I guess the asshole genes must come from your dad."

There's another cheap shot about my dad. I wonder if her dad's perfect. He probably is since he's rich and famous. Kya seems like a daddy's girl.

"Yeah. I guess so."

"Sorry. That was too far," Kya mumbles.

"Listen, I know you don't want to go back to the hockey house tonight. Let's sleep in your room."

"Um… you're not sleeping in my room," she argues.

Great. I should have known she'd find her fire again.

"Are you forgetting the part of our arrangement where you do what I say or I expose your deepest, darkest—

"Fine!" she says. "But I'm only agreeing to this because Raven and Makeba are away for the night at a Summer Walker concert."

"Who?"

"Never mind," she grumbles.

"If you want, I can make you strip tease for the guys back at the house instead. We won the game. I think we've earned it."

"That's disgusting, Cole."

"Babe, you've got a great body. Nothing to be ashamed of."

She glares at me, which is her main form of communication with me, anyway. I take her hand.

"Come on, show me the way to whatever gross frosh dorm you live in."

"I don't need to hear this from a guy whose room smells like sweat 24/7."

Whatever, Kya.

It's nice to hear those quips again. I guess she feels better about the locker room. It's kinda sick that I want her to like it. That I wish some deep messed up part of her would actually enjoy giving the guy blackmailing her head. I don't know. She's probably just naturally skilled at that. I don't know if it's a race thing. I just say that stuff to mess with her, anyway. Messing with her is how I got her attention in the first place. It's fucked up, but it worked.

She's really quiet on the walk to her dorm room, so I get to miss her quips again. She's like, really quiet. I don't mind, I guess. I get to look at her when she's not talking and when I'm not thinking really dirty things... I think regular dirty things like I want to put my hand on her ass or pull her shirt down. I put my hands in my pockets and try to keep up with her angry little power walk.

What the fuck am I doing? I don't know why I'm taking pity on her and giving her one night in her own bed. I could take her back to my place and have her sharpen my skates or make me a pizza from scratch. I could make her feed Ovie his live mouse, which would definitely entertain Dustin and Jayce. I could turn back and change things up on her. I don't owe her anything. But I guess a part of me is genuinely curious about how the annoying frosh actually lives. I want to know Kya's deep, dark secrets.

She unlocks her bedroom door and I am in... a pink explosion. There's nothing dark about her fluorescent pink room at all. At least all the pink appears to be contained to Kya's side of the room. Freshmen have to share rooms at Laguna Grove.

She has a black and white poster of some black woman with an afro holding up a black power fist hanging over her bed. That shouldn't surprise me. Her books are organized and color-coded on her desk, illuminated by a tiny pink desk lamp. She has photos with her friends on the walls and a picture of her sitting on her dad's shoulders as a kid when his team won the championships.

It smells incredible in her bedroom, like vanilla and pineapple. Like her hair. She turns to face me.

"Well? Go ahead, make fun of my chick bedroom."

She's always mocking me in a voice that's supposed to sound dumb. I roll my eyes.

"I don't make fun of everything."

"Yes. You do."

"Your room is super clean. I guess that's why you do such a good job with mine."

"My roommate's a neat freak."

I glance over at the other side of the room. Kya's right. It's even neater than hers.

"So," I tell her. "What do you normally do when you bring guys over?"

"I don't normally bring guys over. I don't hook up. I'm not like you and the other people on this campus. I want... something real if I ever get with a guy."

I raise an eyebrow. I'm no expert, but I'm pretty sure her swallowing my cum earlier counts as "getting with a guy".

"Shut up," she says. "That was blackmail. It doesn't count."

I don't know what about that little comment pisses me off.

"Life isn't a fairytale, Kya. People hook up. They fuck."

"Don't you think I know that? My dad's a serial cheater. I know that's all you misogynistic men care about."

I think she expects me to disagree with her because she visibly relaxes when I respond, "Yeah. My dad kinda sucks too."

"I love him, but… it's hard being his kid," she says. "I'm not a brat, I swear. It's just… I want something different. I don't want to spend every Thanksgiving following my husband in my sister's car to catch him cheating with his sidepiece. Who happens to be my daughter's fourth nanny in a row."

Damn. That was… specific.

I take a step closer to her. My heart is beating out of my chest like crazy. She's getting real with me. And I want to get real with her. It's easy to forget she's my servant and I'm only here to play a game with her. To control her. To humiliate her.

For a moment, I don't want that.

"I get it," I whisper. "There's a part of me that thinks if I make it… if I get into the NHL, he'll come back and everything will be okay again."

She gives me those serious brown eyes.

"Cole Seabrook getting real?"

"Yeah," I tell her. "I can get real."

She smirks at me.

"Would you really want your dad to come back just because you were rich and famous?"

I shrug. I've thought about that too. It's hard growing up without a dad, especially knowing that he could have been there. He just didn't want to.

"I don't know," I whisper. Words catch in my throat as I try not to spill them out and fuck things up. If I take one step in this direction, there's no going back. I can't change my mind once I go down this path and I've got a good thing going. I don't want to mess it up. Who else is going to do my laundry?

"You were perfect tonight, Kya."

"Perfect? Get a grip."

"Yeah. My mom's pretty special to me. I don't let people meet her and she normally hates all my friends."

"Your friends are assholes, so I don't blame her. And it's a good thing I'm not your friend."

"No," I whisper. "You're not. You're my servant. Mine."

I lean forward and kiss her. She resists at first and then she lets me do it. But when I put my tongue in her mouth, she pushes against my chest.

"No," she says, heightening her resistance and using more force than necessary against my chest. "We've already gone too far."

"Have we?"

"It is just a really bad idea if we have sex," she says. "That's what you want, right?"

Her eyes flicker to mine, tempting me and warning me away. I don't want to heed her warning. I don't care what anyone says. I want Kya Ambrose. I want her right now and I will do anything to have her. I wonder if she knows how much power she has over me.

I touch her cheek. "Yes."

I expect her body to shift away from mine, but she moves closer. She wants it. Maybe she can't admit it to herself or whatever. But it's just sex. Desire. We can't help it.

"We can't," she says. "Seriously, Cole. We don't even like each other."

"Who cares? This is animal lust, babe."

"I don't do animal lust."

Now I have to laugh.

"What about your kinky stories?"

"Those are fake," she insists. "In real life, I don't know what it would be like to just... not overthink everything and just have..."

"Animal sex?"

"Ew, can you stop calling it that?"

I grin, because annoying her is still pretty funny.

"What, are you scared of losing control or something?"

"Yes. That's exactly what it is."

"Then don't lose control, babe," I whisper, touching her cheek again. "Just give it to me."

"That would be so much better," she protests sarcastically. "Giving control of my sex life to an evil hockey guy."

"I already control your sex life, babe," I whisper. "Consider it part of the job."

She surprises me by taking a step closer. She tiptoes to my ear and whispers into it. "Have I ever told you that you're... disgusting?"

With her hand on my shoulder to balance herself, she's close enough that I can put my arm around her waist. Once I do that, she's pressing against me. Her heart is racing a million miles a minute. She's terrified.

"Yeah, all the time," I murmur. "I'll take it. I'm a filthy fucking—

Her lips stop mine. Kya grabs my face and kisses me. Holy fuck. She's so passionate that I nearly lose my balance. I stumble backward while holding onto her, my back slamming against her bedroom door. She doesn't stop.

My hands travel over her waist, down to her hips and I grip her there as she kisses me until temptation takes over and I run my palms over her incredible ass.

"Kya..." I whisper when she pulls away.

"Don't say anything," she says. "Just... take control."

"Got it, babe."

I lift her off the ground easily and we keep kissing against her bedroom door like that for a long time. I don't only enjoy her hips, but her full thighs wrapped around me and her breasts right where I can see them. She gets me hard instantly, but I've waited for her long enough. I can wait even longer to make her cum and make her really want me before I enter her.

Plus, Kya's a pretty small girl compared to me. I don't want to hurt her with my dick. I carry her over to her bed and we fall into the pink sheets. They smell delicious and so much like her that my dick struggles against the fabric at my crotch for release.

Her hair spreads out like a mane over her pillow, and I run my fingers through it.

"Your hair is so sexy."

"You hate my hair," she whispers back, running her fingers over my five o'clock shadow and making it hard to focus on anything other than my dick and how badly it wants her.

"No. I don't," I whisper. "I want to pull on it. I want to play with it. I fucking love it."

I kiss her neck and then run my fingers through the hair at the base of her neck, getting a good grip on her head. I move her head to kiss her where I please on her neck and collarbones. We need to get more clothes off…

"Get naked, babe. I'm gonna eat your pussy."

Before she can protest, I lift her shirt and kiss her bare stomach, wriggling between her legs as she slides her pants off. She's warm down there and totally soaked from our slow make-out session. Her juices glue her underwear to her inner thighs and to her lower lips. I can barely remember the first night I went down on her — too much to drink.

But I am totally sober and awake for this and it's the best gift a guy could ask for after scoring a hat trick. I spread her lower lips with my fingers and then use my tongue to make her moan. When she's close to climaxing, I add fingers between her thighs and massage her inner walls as my tongue enjoys every swirl and flavor of her tender nub.

"Cole..." she gasps my name as she climaxes and a gush of juices erupts from her thighs.

I go crazy with my tongue against those thighs, taking in every drop I can. My cheeks are red and my animal lust for her at a new peak when I pull away. I hurry back to her lips and kiss her properly. Kya runs her hand down my back, lingering at the largest muscles, stopping abruptly before her hand gets to my ass.

I don't want her to stop.

"Do I taste funny?" She asks.

"Huh?"

There she is, freaking out and thinking about stuff again. Maybe I waited too long to get my dick in her...

"Down there..."

"Babe, any guy who talks shit about pussy probably wants to suck dick instead."

"That is so offensive," she whispers.

"Yeah," I tell her. "That's why you hate me so much."

"Yeah," she snaps back. "That doesn't explain why you hate me."

"Hm... maybe I don't hate you?"

My dick definitely agrees with the words coming out of my mouth. I hope I don't come to my senses and regret what I'm saying after we have sex. Because that is definitely happening.

"You hate me enough to make me your personal slave."

"We agreed that you were my servant, babe. And I dunno. It's just fun…"

I kiss her, because if I let her go, my little parakeet won't stop talking and I don't want to talk right now. I want to give in to that animal lust Kya's so fucking scared of. I pull my dick out of my pants and it thwacks against her thigh, making a loud noise.

"Damn," she gasps. "Why is your dick so big?"

I rub the head between her bare lips and she whimpers. I love the twisted look of pleasure on her face as I tease her with it. I rub her clit with the head of my dick, getting myself even harder and watching her wriggle and moan.

"You're no virgin, right?"

"Everyone's a virgin to you with a dick that big," she grumbles.

Only Kya would complain about a cock that can make her cum until morning.

"Yeah, yeah. I normally go four or five rounds, babe. That okay?"

"Four or five?!"

She dramatically shifts her weight, sitting up so her breasts are basically in my face and her body pressed closer to mine.

"Yeah. Isn't that normal?"

"No, Cole. And I don't even believe you."

I chuckle because that's such a Kya response.

"Come on," I whisper. "It's going to take forever to get my dick in a pussy as tight as yours. Chill out."

I kiss her reassuringly and she lies back in her cute pink bed so I can put my dick in her. I tease her entrance open and kiss her slowly as I move an inch inside her. The girth of my dick surprises her and she moans into my mouth as we're kissing.

I stroke her hair, hoping I can calm her down before she has another freak out.

"Relax, babe…"

I push another inch inside her, enjoying her moaning again. I practically rip her shirt and bra off as I keep moving inside her. Fuck. I nearly burst with my dick halfway inside her when I see her nipples up close for the first time.

They're dark brown and look like giant chocolate chips with hard protruding tips, begging for my tongue. My face warms and I grunt as I move my hips *hard*, overtaken by lust. Kya screams as my swift movement buries the rest of my enormous cock in her unaccustomed pussy.

Fuck.

❧ 14 ❧

THE WHORE OF BABYLON

KYA AMBROSE

Cole's cheeks turn red as he buries his dick inside me. I scream louder than I mean to because he's enormous. I think it's going to hurt like hell and it does for a moment, but then I feel this phenomenal fullness and yearn for the sensation of his large body pinning me to my bed. Taking me.

I grab his cheeks, raking my fingers through the sprinkle of blond stubble, and kiss him. Cole kisses me back slowly and his kisses are the most romantic I've ever experienced in my life. It's weird that they're coming from Cole. Beyond weird — totally wrong.

But somehow that makes kissing him hotter. With my legs spread lewdly to accommodate his member, Cole eases his hips forward, thrusting even deeper. I moan and he kisses my neck, brushing his tongue just beneath my ear lobe before kissing me in that tender spot.

"You are… so hot," he whispers.

Then he moves his hips again and I can't come up with a sassy quip because he feels so damned good. He grunts and pushes his hips forward again. His body is incredible and my hands instinctively wander over his thick biceps and his back, coated in rippling muscles.

Underneath all those dumb hockey pads, Cole's body is immaculate. And now that he's growing his hair out, he looks like a sexy, wild man. I curve my fingers over his butt and he thrusts into me harder. I moan and pull him into me deeper.

I'm so close already that my body is fighting any ounce of common sense I might have and telling me to yield to Cole's desires. To let him have me. He moves faster, ardently thrusting me into my bed with heaving grunts between each stroke.

Then he moves his fingers between my legs and slowly massages my clit as he pounds me into my bed. I've never had both parts of me stimulated like this and I go crazy, bucking my hips to meet Cole's thrusting while I moan.

"Cum for me, babe," he whispers. "I want to watch you cum on my cock."

Oh. My. God. A wave crashes into me. Pleasure emanates from between my legs, spreading everywhere. I gush juices and excitement while Cole continues thrusting. The continuous stimulation makes my orgasm last longer and I can't stop crying out in pleasure, even when Cole kisses me to get me quieter.

We're in a dorm, after all. Anyone could hear us. I gasp for breath and try to push him off me. If he wants me quiet, he has to stop making me cum. Naturally, Cole doesn't move a muscle.

I push hair out of my face and press my palms against his chest as he quits moving his hips.

"I like watching you cum," he whispers. "That was pretty hot."

"We can't… I mean… What if people hear us?"

"Then they'll know I've got a pretty big dick."

"Is that all you care about?"

"No," Cole whispers, running his fingers through my curls. "I care about… hockey."

My throat clenches and then releases. I don't know why I expected him to say anything other than "hockey". Cole's obsessed with hockey. It's the only thing he cares about more than he cares about himself.

"Wow. So deep," I murmur sarcastically.

"Did you say deep, babe?" He smirks as he pushes his hips forward, making me moan even louder than before.

He's so deep that his dick feels like a tight knot just beneath my belly button, and I know Cole's slightest movement between my legs will make me cum ridiculously hard.

"You're such an asshole…"

He leans over, kissing me slowly before pressing his lips to my ears. "Don't tempt me," he whispers.

I wriggle and Cole grabs my arms, pinning me to the bed with those powerful biceps I just foolishly admired. I wriggle my hips again and only come dangerously close to making myself cum while Cole pins me down. His grin is danger-ously evil now and I know he's probably had some sick idea pop into his dumb jock brain.

"Now that would make you a proper servant," he whispers. "If I fucked you in the ass."

"I am not letting you do that."

"Why not? Scared?"

He runs his tongue over my neck again, making me whimper. I can feel my traitorous pussy soaking my thighs with desire for him and I know Cole can feel my response, too. I just wish he would move his dick and get it over with.

I gasp and move my hips desperately. He pins me down tighter with his hands and then uses his hips to pin me down.

"Promise me your ass," he says. "Not tonight. But soon."

"I won't do that."

"Do you want to cum?"

Again, my body betrays me. He pins me down with only one of his hands as he slowly moves the other between my legs and softly brushes his fingers against my clit. I moan desperately.

"That's a yes," He whispers. "You really want to cum. So I think you'll do what I say."

"I hate you," I gasp.

"Don't care," Cole whispers. "C'mon babe. Give me what I want."

"Fine," I gasp. "Do whatever you want to me. Just stop torturing me."

"Oh, I am so not done torturing you," he whispers. "But thanks for giving me that perfect asshole for dessert."

Before I can ask what he means by dessert, Cole moves his hips again and I explode after a few slow thrusts. Unsatisfied with giving me one measly orgasm from his gentle thrusting, he moves slowly, gazing into my eyes as he makes me cum again. And again.

He pins me to the bed and enters me slowly, taking his time with me and bringing me to each orgasm carefully.

I can tell from the evil smirk on his face that he enjoys how I melt against him, how I can't resist him even when I loathe everything he stands for. It's not my fault he's insanely hot. It's not my fault he's a great kisser who knows exactly what to do with his hands or that monster dick between his legs.

Any woman would be powerless against Cole. And what choice do I have? He's blackmailing me.

He pulls out of me after a few orgasms and kisses my forehead.

"Thanks," he whispers. "I think I'm ready for dessert."

My thighs feel empty and my body yearns for more of him. He hasn't finished yet. This is still round 1. I want to grab his body and drag him against me because now, I don't know if I have the stamina for this crazy athlete.

As I move toward him, Cole expects my movements and grabs my hips, flipping me onto my stomach before I can react. I make an awkward sound between a squeal and a squeak as my hot pink pillow squishes my breasts together.

Cole spreads my legs and then runs his thumb through the juices leaking over my thighs before swiftly pressing his thumb into my ass. I scream because holy shit, there's a giant thumb in my ass.

Cole laughs.

"Stay still."

"Your thumb is in my ass!" I scream, as if there's a chance Cole somehow got confused and didn't just put his finger in my ass on purpose.

"Yeah," he whispers. "It's pretty tight. Kinda hairy…"

"COLE!"

He moves his thumb deeper inside me and I make a noise halfway between a moan and a grunt as I adjust to him penetrating my resistant butt hole and feel a strange throbbing between my thighs.

"Ever put anything up there?" He whispers.

"No! Who puts stuff up their butt?!"

"I dunno," he whispers. "You look pretty good with a thumb up there."

I make a huffy little moan and try to wriggle away. Cole uses his palm to pin me down.

"Not so fast, servant. I like the idea of fucking my servant in the ass."

"Well, I hate the idea."

"You know that makes me like it more, right?"

"You're a sick freak."

"I don't get it. You write your dirty little stories about sticky butt sex, but you turn into a nun when I have a thumb in your ass."

"I don't know any nuns who let people put thumbs in their asses in the first place!" I huff. "And first I'm a slut, now I'm a nun? Make up your freaking mind."

"I did," Cole replies smugly. "I'm going to fuck your ass."

"Cole!" I plead, but he only pushes his thumb deeper.

"Fuck," he groans. "Your butt is going to swallow my dick."

"Your dick isn't going anywhere near my butt!"

I try to glance over my shoulder, but Cole continues pinning me down and the moment I protest, I hear a loud thwack as his dick smacks against my ass.

"Cole! Your dick is near my butt. Your dick is way too close to my butt."

"Maybe it's a cucumber," he whispers. "Or an eggplant."

He withdraws his finger from my ass and I breathe a sigh of relief, hoping that Cole has finally seen the light. My relief spreads when he removes his hand from my back.

"Any good lube in here?" He murmurs, crawling out of my bed and flinging my drawers open.

"Cole! There's no lube in here because I don't have butt sex with random guys."

"I'm not a random guy. I'm your master."

"That is so not funny."

"Chill out, Kya. Can I use this?"

"Can you use my Pattern Beauty $80 bottle of conditioner as lubricant?!" I shrill. "Are you on crack?!"

"Okay, fine. What about this?"

"That's my roommate's jojoba oil."

"Her what?" Cole replies like I just spoke a different language. White boys are so clueless. Another reason I shouldn't be letting him do this. There's definitely a rule book for women out there that says don't let someone clueless put his dick in your ass.

"It's a type of oil for black hair," I explain.

Cole perks up considerably.

"Does it work on black butt holes?"

Every single word that comes out of Cole's mouth makes me want to strangle him to death. But it's not like I can come back from this. We already had sex. And I've known Cole long enough to know that when he sets his dumb jock mind on something, he won't take no for an answer.

"Yeah. It's fine," I say. "But you need to pay my roommate back if you use that stuff."

"Whatever. Spread your ass cheeks, babe."

"Is there any way you could be less of an asshole?" I grumble.

"No."

He spreads my ass cheeks himself and takes Raven's jojoba oil dropper out of the bottle. I assume Cole's going to use one large drop on my ass, maybe two. Nope. He tosses the dropper onto Raven's desk and pours nearly half the bottle onto my asshole.

"COLE!"

"The more lube, the less it hurts. Plus, oil makes your ass look juicy."

He rubs the oil over my butt cheeks, enjoying himself a little too much and massaging me just enough that I forget that I'm supposed to be trying to get away from him.

Once he's satisfied my cheeks are covered in slippery oil, he rubs it all over my asshole and then slides his thumb into my back door again, laden with jojoba oil. This time his thumb enters my ass easily and I relax as the lubrication coats my entrance and makes it easier for him to move his thumb.

Cole moves his thumb back and forth until all the pain melts into these slippery and warm sensations of pleasure. I moan, and Cole chuckles.

"I knew you'd like it."

"Shut up."

"Why?"

"This is just another way of you calling me a slut."

He chuckles.

"Pretty sure if you were a slut, your ass wouldn't be this tight."

"That's still super misogyn—COLE!"

He removes his thumb, and I feel the large head of his dick pressing against his back door.

"What's a guy to do in a feminist world?" He whispers. "I have to take my chances."

"Surprising me with a dick in the ass?"

"It's not a surprise. You gave me your ass. Remember?"

He kisses the back of my neck as his warm body hovers over mine and his enormous dick presses against my back door.

"Yes," I whisper. "I remember."

I feel as defeated as I sound.

"Be gentle," I whisper.

"I wouldn't hurt you, babe," Cole whispers. And it's really weird that I think he means it, that somehow in his fucked up hockey player brain, he thinks putting his dick in my ass is romantic.

He slowly massages my back door open with the head of his dick and there's no pain as he slides the head in. Even with the size of his dick, there's enough lube that I only feel pleasure and a strange tightness as he puts the entire thing inside me. When our hips join again, Cole's cheeks are purple.

"Fuck," He whispers. "I've never done this before."

"You haven't?"

"No," he whispers. "But I read every one of your fucked up fantasies. You write pretty hot stuff, Kya."

"Thank you…" I moan. I don't know if I'm thanking him for the compliment or the pleasure mounting with his cock slowly moving into my ass.

"You gave me everything I need to know to make you cum," he whispers. "And fuck… it's hot."

He moves his hips again and I can't stop myself from climaxing. Cole's dick is so big that it's impossible for every nerve ending not to feel alight with an incredible fire for his body.

He kisses my neck and presses his cheek against mine as he takes large grunting thrusts into my ass. He moves his hands around the front of my body, sliding over my navel and stomach and fingering my clit as his dick plunges into my ass.

"Fuck," he whispers. "Cum for me, babe. Cum for me…"

With his cheeks pressed against mine, his scent fills my nostrils, and he's everywhere. He's on top of me, inside me, his scent's in my nose and his hands… I cum hard.

Cole groans and pulls my body against his.

"Yeah," he grunts. "Fuck… I'm…"

He groans before he can finish his sentence and I feel the thick ropes of his cum pumping into my ass. His weight collapses on mine and I squeak as the movement just pushes his dick deeper into my ass.

"I probably should have used a condom," he whispers.

It's like he has a handbook that just tells him the exact wrong thing to say. I whimper and move my hips back to push him off me, but I only end up taking his dick deeper and climaxing again.

Cole chuckles.

"Damn, you like butt sex, huh?"

"Shut up."

"Makes sense," he whispers. "I mean… you've got a big butt. It's basically an ad for butt sex."

"I am more than just a big butt."

"Duh," Cole whispers. "You're also a tight pussy and a big mouth."

He has literally no grasp on how to be a decent human being.

"Yeah," I grumble. "And you're just an asshole."

"Yup," he whispers. "I'm just an asshole."

He pulls out of me and my ass feels a little sore from accommodating Cole's dick.

"Give me a minute," he sighs. "I need a cuddle before round 2."

"Round 2?" I murmur in disbelief. "Are you sure?"

"Yeah," he whispers. "I'm sure. Come here, servant. Master needs a cuddle."

I elbow him in chest as he pulls me against him.

"It's a joke," he grumbles. "Getting you pissed is way too easy. You should work on that."

"Maybe work on not being an asshole."

"Asshole..." Cole murmurs, his fingers traveling back to my butt.

Sigh. What did I think he was going to do?

Round 2 with Cole turns into round 3 before I know what hit me. He's incredible in bed, better than he should be. I expect him to be a selfish asshole, who only wants to look at his abs in the mirror while jack-hammering me to death, but... he isn't like that at all.

He makes me cum so many times I lose track and when he finishes, he kisses me deeply and teases my nipples so much with gentle fingers that I almost want to beg him for round 4.

Almost…

"You are… really good at your job," he whispers.

"Shut up."

"You went above and beyond your call of duty as my personal servant… Well done."

"Didn't you hear me say shut up?"

Cole chuckles.

"Come on," he whispers. "Let me cuddle you to sleep, princess. You can bite my head off tomorrow."

"You can count on it."

"Uh huh," he whispers. "I know it."

Then his body covers mine like the warmest blanket in existence, and I fall asleep before I can think of another sassy retort. Unfortunately, I wake up to whispers. Loud whispers.

"There's a man in there."

"We should pepper spray him."

"Girl, what if we kill Kya?"

"I think it's the hockey guy?"

"Do you think he… you know…"

"Do rapists cuddle their victims?!" Raven whispers, and I hear footsteps inching toward the bed. Fuck. My roommate.

I open one sleepy eye and panic.

"Raven! What time is it?"

I thought they weren't supposed to be back until way later. Shit.

Of course, my moving wakes up Cole.

"Go back to sleep," he mutters, sitting up and wiping his eyes before actually waking up and noticing that he just got caught naked. In my bed. By my roommates.

He has the most irritating response ever. He grins.

"Hey, ladies."

The blanket falls away from his chest and Makeba can't help but let out a little squeak. My cheeks are completely hot with shame.

"COLE!" I shriek. "Get out of here."

"What?" He grumbles.

"I said, get out!"

"I just woke up, aren't you going to get me coffee or—

"GET. OUT!"

He scowls and gets into his clothes, trying to dress himself beneath my sheets without exposing more of his body to my roommates. It's a painfully awkward five minutes. Cole attempts to make his blond hair lie down flat, but gives up on taming the hockey flow after a few awkward seconds of trying to glimpse himself in Raven's mirror.

Before leaving, he leans over and kisses me on the lips.

"Be back before practice."

I don't respond to him. I'm just embarrassed like hell and my best friends are looking at me like I'm the whore of Babylon... *Crap.*

15

WASN'T ME

COLE SEABROOK

Kya Ambrose gets me so fucking pissed. Seriously. I can't imagine a woman who pisses me off more. I'm the one who kicks chicks out of my bed, not the other way around. She wouldn't even look at me. I can't get her out of my head, no matter how hard I try.

It doesn't bother me or anything. But I feel weird, like I need an extra workout. An extra skate. I text Dustin and Jayce, hoping we can work some shooting drills in before I half-ass my homework.

With an important game coming up, I can't afford to worry about drawing diagrams of animal cells or whatever. I definitely need to stop thinking about her. I need the guys to set me straight. To remind me that there are other chicks out there. Millions. Possibly even a billion. When I'm in the NHL, I can worry about girls. Before that, I have to focus on my game so I don't lose everything. Kya's just a big fucking distraction.

I can count on Dustin to show up for extra skating. He was already at the gym pumping iron. Jayce tries to make some lame excuse about studying for his science class, claiming it's the "hardest shit ever". I don't know why he doesn't just take an easier freaking class, but whatever.

Luckily, Dustin and I get to him and remind him that only pussies miss out on extra skating. Hanging out with the guys helps me forget my chick problems. I guess, my Kya problem. It's good to get my heart rate up and keep my body tight and strong for the season. This is no time to slack off and get flabby. I need to put these muscles to work. We're just messing around, skating and shooting on the empty net with a few pucks from the locker room.

"What's your deal, brah," Dustin says, slapping a corner shot into the net. "You weren't home last night. Everyone says you were out taking it up the ass."

Jayce laughs at Dustin's idiotic joke. I swear those knuckle-heads get on my last fucking nerve. I love them to death, but they're hockey guys. We're all fucking idiots.

"Yeah. Not exactly."

That only makes Dustin laugh harder.

"Where were you, bro?" Jayce asks, swerving toward the net and then tipping it in with a gentle tap before retrieving the puck and sending a dirty pass down the ice to Dustin.

"Kya."

"Woahhhhh," Dustin whoops, passing the puck to me. I hit it hard, and it slams into the back of the net.

"Shit. Did you bang her finally?" Jayce answers, sliding around me in a figure 8. I wouldn't normally mind telling girl stories to my guys, but I feel weird doing that with Kya. I mean… she's not just a hookup. What we have is a bit personal, because of the blackmail, not for any other reason or anything. I keep it short.

"Yeah."

"Was she good?" Dustin asks.

"Did she cry?" Jayce asks.

"Why would she cry?" I reply, mostly because I don't want to answer any of my idiot friends' questions.

"Because. Chicks do that," Jayce answers.

"Fucking virgin," Dustin snaps at him. "Now answer me. Was she good? Because I might try her out next."

"No, you fucking idiot."

"No, she sucked?"

"No, you can't try her out."

"Why not? She's your personal servant. I'm your best friend. She's already seen one of my snakes…"

I slam another frustrated shot into the goal and glare at Dustin, who doesn't seem to give a shit.

"It's not like that with her," I snap, and I feel so dumb for saying it. They're totally going to fucking make fun of me, and I deserve it. Whatever. It just came out and I guess a part of it is true. Kya and I have a different arrangement. The guys don't give a shit and still heckle me.

"OOoooooooohhh."

I swear, I hate both of those assholes so damn much.

"You guys are assholes."

"Yup," Dustin said. "And you are about to be... enemy number one on this campus. Everyone knows black guys hate when white guys fuck black girls. A bunch of seven foot tall basketball players are going to fuck you up the ass."

"Shut the fuck up, Dustin."

"It's true. It happened to Jayce."

Jayce throws the puck at his face and Dustin laughs hysterically, amused by his own shitty sense of humor.

"Shut the fuck up, Rathbone."

"Whatever, bro. I'm just saying it's a bad idea."

"I don't care. I just fucking want her."

Dustin and Jayce exchange glances and shrug. I guess they're deciding to help me. Or something.

Dustin begins, "You need to take control of the situation and make her yours."

"She's already mine."

"Yeah? Is that why you're sulking like a pussy about her kicking you out of her bed?" Dustin challenges.

Jayce chuckles. I hate those assholes.

"I'm not a pussy. Kya's just different from other chicks."

"Because she's black?" Jayce offers.

"No. I mean... yeah... I guess. But it's not just that."

"Is she like... a total sex freak?" Jayce asks. "Please... give me details. Positions. Nipple size. Whatever you got."

"Shut up, you sick fuck," I grumble.

"We need to treat this like a play," Dustin says, ignoring our brewing argument. I already told Jayce Dumb-fuck that Kya wasn't like that, and if he makes one more crack at her, I'm definitely going to kick his ass.

We leave the rink for the locker room and kick our skates off. Dustin rushes over to the blackboard and finds some leftover chalk that Tuck Murphy crumbled in his hands after our last practice.

Dustin scrawls on the blackboard in barely legible handwriting.

THE KYA PLAY

"Seriously?" I groan.

"Seriously," Dustin says proudly, underlining his work twice.

"Okay," Jayce chimes in, keeping us focused on the game. "What do you want? How do you get it?"

"You're going to talk shit about me if I tell you."

Bringing up Kya with these idiots was a total mistake. But it's almost too late to back out.

"Damn it, Cole. Tell us. Butthole? Pussy? Both? Threesome?" Dustin asks frantically.

Dustin's sex list has nothing to do with what I want from Kya Ambrose. We had sex. I expected everything between us to fizzle out after that. I guess it did for her now that we broke that crazy fucking tension between us.

But that's not what happened with me...

"I want her to be my girlfriend."

The locker room is way too fucking quiet. I regret saying anything to these stupid monkeys. What did I expect, Dustin Rathbone and Jayce Clutterbuck to understand?

"Does he have a fever?" Dustin whispers. "Check him."

"Touch me and I'll break your hand," I grumble, causing Jayce to retreat before he makes a critical mistake.

"No fever," Dustin whispers. "But how to trick her into actually liking your shitty personality? Now that's going to be a challenge."

"I don't want to trick her. And it doesn't matter. It's stupid. She definitely doesn't want that."

Dustin groans.

"If you give up this easily, you'll never play for Boston."

"Shut up."

"I'm serious! Make her want you. Force her."

"Have you ever had a girlfriend, Rathbone?" I snarl.

"Hey," Jayce says. "He gets laid."

"Yeah. I get laid. I don't need a girlfriend. I just need pussy. You're the one who wants a chick hanging onto your every move."

"Whatever. It's just not going to happen," I groan. This was definitely a mistake. My friends are better at hockey than pretty much anything else. They're definitely the worst people to get relationship advice from.

Dustin writes on the blackboard for a moment. It takes me a while to make out what he scratched onto the board.

Sex = like = more sex = love

Sex + Kya + more sex = Kya love Cole

He dusts his hands off and gazes at it proudly.

"I think I solved your problem," Dustin says.

"Shit. It might just work," Jayce murmurs, tilting his head to the side.

"That's your plan? Have more sex with her?"

"Butt stuff," Dustin says confidently. "Works every time."

"We already did butt stuff."

"Fingers only? Because you need to get the whole dick in there," Jayce says.

I'm in the world's most fucked up relationship counseling session. Dustin adds a bullet point.

- Get the whole dick in there.

"Thanks, but it's going to take more than my dick to win her over."

"I'm confused… are you small?" Dustin asks. "Or is she just used to black guys with like… monster cocks."

Kya would have loved giving Dustin a super annoying lesson about racist stereotypes and black cock. I know because she gave me the same one during round 2 or 3 of us having sex.

"It's not her. It's me. She thinks I'm an asshole."

"Women like assholes," Jayce said. "That's why we get laid."

"I need to show her I'm a good guy."

"Are you?" Dustin asks, twirling the chalk between his fingers.

"I'm okay." I shrug. That's the best I can do for them. I'm no angel. Dustin takes what he can get and runs with it.

"Then tell her about all the good stuff you do, brah."

Dustin adds another bullet point.

- Score hat tricks.

"You think more hat tricks will impress her?"

Dustin shrugs. "It will impress Tuck. And chicks like guys who win."

"True," Jayce answers. I don't know if he's just going along to be agreeable or if he really gives a shit.

Jayce grabs the chalk and writes his own bullet point.

- Expensive dates.

Dustin scowls. "Expensive dates?"

"Dude, that annoying chick is Dwayne Ambrose's daughter," Jayce reminds him. "Like the Dwayne Ambrose."

"Wait… the Dwayne Ambrose?" Dustin says.

"The one and only."

Dustin mutters, "Shit."

"Shit," Jayce replies.

"Fuck," I mutter under my breath. These idiots haven't helped at all.

"We need to rethink this," Dustin mutters. He circles expensive dates. Then he returns to score hat tricks. "Her dad's an athlete. You need to impress her. Show her you're strong, that you'll take care of her."

Jayce teases him. "Chill out, Dr Phil."

"Shut up. This is totally going to work."

"I don't know if working on my game is going to work on Kya."

"She's your servant, right? Make her watch you. Make her realize that she wants to eat, sleep, and breathe hockey players."

"Not all hockey players," Jayce corrects him. "Just you."

"Yeah. Totally."

"She's coming back to my room tonight. Maybe we should just... talk."

"Or you could talk," Dustin replies, shrugging. "But don't say anything dumb. Chicks never sleep with you after you say something dumb."

"It's true," Jayce answers solemnly. "They never do."

It's a good skate, but I want to get back to my room to mess things up a bit before Kya gets back. I have sweaty hockey pads at the gym, a couple uniforms that need a wash, and if I have enough time, I can borrow a couple of Dustin's tarantulas to hide in my desk drawer and scare the crap out of her.

Maybe I'll skip the tarantulas this time...

After a shower, I head back to Pesthouse from the gym. I can't stop thinking about our night together. Her skin was so soft. Her body was basically perfect. Her nipples are totally etched in my mind forever. I wonder what she'll say tonight. Judging by the way she chased me off this morning, she has me out of her system.

I don't even know if she'll be in my room waiting for me like I asked.

On my way down the hall, I hear muttered swearing and footsteps clomping around my room. She's there…

I fling my door open and holy shit.

"What the fuck did you do to my room?"

There's red paint everywhere. And I mean… everywhere. All over my bed, my hockey pads, my desk, my books… my freaking laptop.

"Kya, what the fuck!"

"I swear, I didn't do it! I just got here!"

I cross the room and grab her hand, coated in thick red paint.

"Your hands are red! I am literally catching you red-handed!"

"It's all over the floor too! I slipped. Look!"

She shows me the handprint on my desk, plus the drag marks on the floor where she clearly slipped. But that doesn't mean she's innocent. I know she's been trying to get back at me for a long time.

Only this time, she's gone too far.

"Where's the rest of the bucket?" I ask calmly.

"Cole, I swear! This wasn't me. Please…"

Fuck… she is so good at lying to my face. It makes me forget everything from last night in an instant. I look at those pouty lips and her large, sad eyes. She wants to manipulate me. That's probably the only reason she slept with me.

"Who did it then? You're the only one who has a key to my bedroom. So you can clean up. And what the fuck do you do? You destroy everything…"

"I didn't! Cole… I swear… Please… don't freak out. Don't send the stories to my dad."

"Is that all you care about?" I snarl. "Because if you genuinely gave a shit about that, you wouldn't have done this."

"But I didn't!"

I want to believe her so badly. But I don't know if I can…

16

RED PAINT

KYA AMBROSE

His eyes glaze over with rage as he surveys his bedroom and realizes just how much damage there is. A little sabotage is one thing, but does Cole really think I would be stupid enough to pour red paint into his skates or splatter it over his Wayne Gretzky poster? My heart's racing. I don't know how he'll react to this but I know whatever he does will be sadistic.

This isn't the way I wanted to get revenge on him. Sure, I got a little hit when he got all mad about how I kicked him out but… this isn't my style. It's too mean.

Cole Seabrook still has dirt on me. He can still ruin my life. Judging by the look in his eye, he's strongly considering ruining my life. I need to prove to him that I wasn't even here until a few minutes ago.

"I swear, Cole. I wouldn't do something like this."

"Then who would?"

Is Cole serious? I'm not the only person at Laguna Grove who thinks hockey players are assholes. They walk around this campus like they own the place all because they win a few games. Because of their stupid sport, they act like gods.

"Maybe it's that girl you kicked out of here the other night."

Cole scoffs. "I guess you'd know all about kicking people out."

Seriously? For a jock, Cole is petty. He knows exactly why I kicked him out of my bedroom and he knows exactly why he was there too. He doesn't get to act all offended like he's my boyfriend. Never!

"I didn't want my friends to know what happened between us. It's called privacy," I snap. I can't believe this actually hurts his feelings. He needs to grow up.

Cole doesn't back down. Not like I expect him to at this point.

"Pretty sure they figured it out when I climbed out of your bed in my boxers."

"That was humiliating…" I remind him. "So thanks."

"Yeah. I'm the worst," he says sarcastically. "Except for making you cum like seven hundred times."

He is so annoyingly arrogant. Why is he even bringing up my orgasms? Just because he made me cum doesn't mean he's not a complete dick.

"Um… it's not about that," I explain, because I have to remember, Cole is a hockey player. Sometimes, I need to explain things to him. "You're blackmailing me. You turned me into your personal slave and then we… you know…"

I mash my hands together in something that's supposed to be one of the weird sex positions Cole and I did. He smirks and then his smirk quickly falls away. I'm not in his good graces anymore. I don't even get that stupid cocky smirk plastered on his face. Ugh! He's probably going to take this out on me in all kinds of twisted ways.

But I really didn't do this. I would never risk getting paint on my own stuff and my books on Cole's desk are covered too. If he would stop talking for one second, I could explain that to him.

"So you decided to get revenge by fucking with my stuff?"

"No!"

"Can you honestly say you haven't been fucking up the past few days? You only sharpened one of my skates before practice on Wednesday, you stained my travel hockey t-shirt bright pink and you shrunk five sweaters. You've been messing with me. Trying to get back at me... even if I made you cum a bunch of times. Pretty messed up, Kya."

Great. So he was totally onto my sabotage. At least it messed with him a little.

"Okay, that stuff maybe I did, but I swear I didn't do this Cole. Last night..."

"Last night was a big mistake," Cole snaps. "Because I let my guard down around you and what does the big bad feminist do? She uses her pussy to manipulate me."

It's times like this I remember why I hate Cole. Manipulate him? He's the one manipulating me. It's the literal definition of blackmail. Ugh.

"Manipulate you!?"

Has Cole Seabrook seriously lost his mind? Why is he even acting all offended?

"It's not like you even like me!" I scream back at him when he doesn't respond. "You loathe me."

"Oh shut up with your fancy words."

"What are you doing?"

He finds one of his skates — filled with that stupid red paint — and he's just taking the laces off. Randomly. Or maybe not so randomly.

"I'm getting to the truth."

Okay... so he's searching for clues? Maybe Cole secretly enjoys true crime or something but I don't see what his dumb laces have to do with anything.

"Last night... you're right. It was a mistake," I offer. "We shouldn't have done that. And we definitely shouldn't have done it more than twice."

His gaze flickers angrily to mine. What the hell? Now he's mad that I'm agreeing with him? I am so not getting out of this. Cole has his laces free and before I can say anything else, he lunges at me and grabs my wrists.

"COLE! What the hell are you doing?!"

He's seriously strong and even as I fight back, I'm powerless against the giant, muscular hockey player. He pins me against the wall, getting paint in my hair and all over my shirt, not to mention his own hands and then he freaking ties me up with the laces from his skates.

His knots are surprisingly good and without my hands, I

basically can't fight back until he starts tying my feet together and I try kicking the shit out of him, which fails too.

"COLE!" I scream again. "Stop being insane!"

"Insane? Princess, you haven't seen insane yet."

He starts rifling around his desk, moving my text books into a half-dried puddle of the stupid paint.

"Cole, what are you doing!?"

He brandishes a pair of scissors and it hits me. He's going to stab me to death. Holy shit. He is into true crime after all and he's going to make this his crime scene. I start screaming bloody murder.

"HELP. HELP. HE'S GOING TO KILL ME!"

Cole doesn't say anything and he doesn't look me in the eye. He just dutifully takes the scissors and cuts my clothes off. He shreds my white Marc Jacobs crop top with the red heart in the middle and slices his way through my La Perla bra.

I shriek when he exposes my boobs and start trying to kick him again.

"Will you stop that?" He snaps after a while.

"You're trying to rape and kill me!" I shriek.

Cole snorts and then continues cutting my clothing off. He doesn't even bother denying it. Holy shit... I always knew Cole was a stupid and entitled jock, but I didn't think he'd actually murder a fellow college student in his bedroom. This is beyond frat house shenanigans.

"HELP!" I shriek again.

"If you don't shut up, I'm going to put a sock in your mouth," he snarls and he cuts my LuLu Lemon leggings off, the base of the scissors sliding so close to the skin on my thighs that I'm too scared to breathe. I don't exhale again until he cuts my thong off.

He rips the shredded designer clothing away from my body and then rests the scissors on his desk. He scoops me up and tosses me onto his bed. I roll over to face him. To try to look him in the eye and guilt trip him over whatever evil shit he's planning to do to me.

"This is low, Cole. Even for you."

"Can you shut up?"

"No! I'm not going to let you rape and kill me."

"Princess, rapists and murderers don't ask for permission."

I thrash as much as humanly possible, desperate to break free.

"HELP!"

"Can you chill?" Cole snaps furiously. "I'm not going to do that stuff. I just want you to be honest with me."

"I am being honest with you!" I shriek.

Cole gets close to me, close enough that I can smell him. And his hair. His hair has a separate smell, and it's delicious. Wait, no. He's evil. I'm not supposed to be thinking about his delicious blond hair.

"Did you fuck my bedroom up, Kya?" he whispers. A shiver travels down my spine.

"NO!"

His gaze falls to my boobs. Why the fuck did he strip my clothes off? With his gaze on my nipples, he continues his interrogation.

"Then who did? Give me a name? Was it one of your dumb friends?" he snaps.

"My friends aren't dumb by the way. And they're right about you."

"Whatever. I want to know why you did this," he growls. Why won't this idiot just believe the truth?

"I didn't! After last night… I thought… I thought things were different between us."

"Liar," Cole says. "Five minutes ago, you just said it was a mistake."

"That was only because you said it was a mistake, dumbass," I grumble.

"So, how did you feel about last night?" he says. "Don't lie to your master."

He runs his hands over my thighs slowly. I don't know if he's teasing me or just trying to piss me off, but I'm powerless to stop him and he's ignoring my glare and my thrashing. I want to kill him every time he calls himself that.

"Call yourself my master again and I will bite your dick off."

"It's a joke, princess," he whispers.

"Does that make every fucked up thing you say suddenly okay?"

"Yes."

There's seriously no reasoning with Cole. He's mentally deranged, unfortunately.

"Tell me," he whispers. "I want to know."

He rests his firm palm on my hips. I hate that I'm naked and I especially hate how much Cole seems to enjoy it. I stammer away like some idiot freshman who is way too excited about hooking up with a hot athlete.

"I mean… it was sex. I came a lot. It's messing with my head. Don't worry, I'll get over it when I remember your personality."

At least I hit him with a sassy comment to knock him down a peg.

Cole scoffs.

"Yeah. I know."

"You said it was a mistake," I remind him. "You weren't lying."

"It definitely was a mistake," Cole says. "Because we want different things, princess."

"Right, you want a woman to totally dominate and I want a real relationship, which trust me, I don't want with you."

"But you still want something with me?"

Cole has the magical ability to focus on all the wrong things. His hand takes a wrong turn and rests calmly on top of my mound. No way. That isn't happening here, and it isn't happening now with red paint coating his bedroom.

"Yes. I want you to freaking untie me!" I yell at him.

"Swear you didn't do this," he whispers. "Swear on your anal virginity."

I want to kill him sometimes. What kind of swear is that? Can't he act like a normal person for a change and pinky swear or something? Cole's fingers run over my nipples and he starts slowly pinching them, making it very easy for me to squeak out anything I think will get him to stop.

"I swear!"

His hands stop moving, but only because he's cupping my bare breast and staring into my eyes.

"What about your friends? Could they have done this?"

His tongue runs over his lips and I'm both terrified and excited about what he's going to do next. I'm also desperate to hide it from him. One night of sex doesn't mean everything between us is different. Cole just scared the crap out of me, and he doesn't even care. He just wants to touch me. To get me wet…

It's so hard to focus on his question. What about my friends?

"They're not talking to me over the whole you climbing out of my bed thing, so I don't think they'd vandalize your bedroom just to help me."

"Fuck. So what, you think I have enemies? Besides you, obviously."

"Yes, you definitely have enemies," I tell him. "Duh."

Cole is downright delusional if he thinks there aren't people who hate hockey boys and all athletes. I mean, hello Cole, I'm one of those people…

"Who?" he says, his fingers moving suspiciously close to my nipples again. I sense a chance to break free from my enslavement by giving Cole something that he wants — besides sex. If he wants information, I'll demand my freedom.

"Untie me," I tell him. "Then we'll talk."

"You strike a hard bargain, princess."

"Uh huh."

He frees me and I try swinging on him again, just in case I have enough luck to catch him off guard. I don't think I stood a chance. Cole catches my fist and presses it to his lips. His hands curl around my fist and he grins after the kiss.

"Careful, slave."

"I hate you," I whisper. "And I'm going to ruin you some day. Soon, hopefully."

"Sorry... it's just too funny to piss you off. And you're already ruining me babe."

What the hell does that mean? And wait... what did Cole say? It's funny to call me a slave?

"It's actually not funny that you call me a slave. It's racist. Can you spell that?"

Cole ignores my dig about his spelling again, although from the confused expression on his face, maybe he really isn't sure how to spell the word. He puts my hand down at my sides and continues staring at my boobs while we talk.

"What's racist about it? I like black people just fine."

"Do you even have any black friends?"

He gives the most obvious, idiotic answer. "You."

"We aren't friends," I scoff.

Is Cole deranged? We don't have a friendship. We have… nothing. And that totally doesn't make me feel weird. We have nothing in common. I guess we're both stubborn. But other than that…

"Oh yeah? If we aren't friends, then why am I giving you a shirt to cover your naked body?" Cole replies, smirking and tossing a giant white shirt with a hockey camp logo on the back over my head.

"That shirt was from your dirty laundry hamper."

I wriggle my way into it anyway, because I don't have much of a choice and I'd rather cover my boobs than have Cole keep staring at them.

"Everything's covered in paint here, princess. You need clothes that can get dirty so you can get this place clean."

He leans over and kisses me on the shoulder. I hope he gets a good whiff of his nasty ass shirt, but when he presses his face there, he only gets in closer to my neck and kisses me again on my neck. I push him off me. This is no time for neck kisses.

"You aren't seriously going to make me clean this up!?"

He's relentlessly entitled.

"I still own you, babe. Get to work. You can tell me your list of suspects once this place is clean."

"And um… where the hell do you think you're going?"

"I'm going to play video games with Dustin. When you're done, bring us lemonade."

"Lemonade? I'm not bringing you any damned lemonade."

"Fine. Bring your fine ass over in that shirt, then. I'll let Dustin decide what to do with you."

"That's sick," I snap. "And this is so degrading. If I have time… I might bring you lemonade. From the vending machine."

Cole nods approvingly and then cracks his knuckles.

"Wouldn't it be more degrading if I took my shirt back? You're welcome, by the way. And anyway, your ass looks great hanging out like that. So if you don't want to bring lemonade… that's fine with me."

"Wow, you're so generous."

"Thanks, babe."

Then he freaking kisses me, which only makes me want to spread the paint all over his pillow. He leaves his bedroom and I send a text to my friends' group chat. It's a long text apologizing for everything and telling them as much of the truth as I can fit in a brick of text. Hey, I'd rather text than get this room clean and Cole never said I have to rush. I hope they reply soon…

I wonder if any of them might know who did this. I wonder if they'll respond to me. They're pretty mad at me about Cole, and I don't even blame them. I'm furious with myself for giving in to him. After it's done, I feel all guilty and dumb, but in the moment, I just go for it like a horny idiot. Ugh. My friends deserve to roast me alive for this.

They think I should have mentioned the fact that we were having sex. They're right, of course. I need to make things better with them. And anyway, maybe they're right about Cole. There's nothing good behind those gorgeous blue eyes, only pure white male evil.

He pisses me off so much, but there's something there some-times. I can feel it. I just don't know how to put it into words. Maybe I just want him because I know I shouldn't.

Maybe with him, I'm just going to get hurt.

17

THE FAKE DATE: COLE'S CHAPTER

COLE SEABROOK

Kya makes the best lemonade. And after cleaning my room, her pout is wide enough to shake Pesthouse. She walks into Dustin's room and he accuses her bad vibes of scaring his tarantulas.

"Fuck your stupid spiders," Kya snarls as she slams the lemonade down in front of him.

"She didn't mean that, Pastrnak," Dustin whispers. The brown spider scuttles to its log.

"Kya," I say. "You're going with me on a date."

Dustin snickers, but it's cool. I'm taking his advice. I already put the whole dick inside her, and my next step is to treat her like a gentleman. It's Kya, so she would obviously never agree to a proper date with me, unless I blackmail her, which is exactly what I'm going to do.

"Um, no I'm not."

Dustin laughs. "Oh, yes you are, princess."

"Was I talking to you, Dustin?"

Dustin belches loudly in response, and Kya makes a disgusted noise.

"I'm ordering you on a date with me. We have Agent Night a couple towns over and I need a date. I'll take you to dinner before and we can go skating."

"That sounds like a horrible idea."

"Perfect, so you're going," Cole says. "Unless you want me to tell Dustin why you're so willing to be my —

"Okay, fine! I'll go with you."

She storms off back to my room and Dustin laughs as she slams the door.

"She likes you so bad."

"She definitely doesn't. But it's cool. She's fun."

Confessing that makes me feel weird, but Dustin doesn't even make fun of me, which is cool. Maybe he just gets it. Kya has been hanging around a lot and the guys have finally stopped picking on her as much.

"Are you kidding? She's probably just super guilty for liking a white guy. It's like… betrayal of her race, you know?"

"You are such a fucking idiot, Dustin."

"Yeah. Totally. Want to light up?"

"No. And you should stop smoking weed. We need to focus on getting agents and getting one step closer to recruitment."

"Whatever, Seabrook. And why is that chick so scared of you? What have you got on her?"

"You wouldn't believe me if I told you, bro."

Dustin laughs. "I bet I wouldn't."

I follow Kya because I feel a little guilty for ignoring the fact that she just spent three hours scrubbing my bedroom clean. When I walk into the room and flick the light on, she snaps, "I was sleeping."

"You look wide awake to me, servant. Thanks for cleaning up in here."

"Whatever! I'm sleeping, asshole."

She pulls the blanket over her head, but some of her puffy hair escapes.

"Where's your magic hair thing?"

"My scarf," she snaps at me with that tone she uses when she thinks I'm super fucking dumb.

"Yeah. Whatever."

"Date. It's tomorrow."

"Great. I don't want to go because I fucking hate you."

"Well, you're coming. I'll take you back to your room tomorrow to get your skates."

"I don't have skates. I don't skate. I'm black."

"Do you play basketball?"

"Huh? No."

"Why not?" I snap back. "You're black."

"Whatever, Cole."

"I'll get you skates," I tell her. "Then I'll teach you. Now scoot over. I'm coming to bed."

She scoots over, but she's in a huffy mood until she falls asleep. Whatever. At least she's going on a date with me. A fake date, but that doesn't matter. This is my chance to put my plan in motion and impress Kya Ambrose.

It's tough to impress a chick who has everything. It's even tougher to impress a chick who hates everything about you. It's a challenge. Like a corner shot when you're surrounded by three guys on the other team. Like slamming heads into the boards. Like flipping the puck to your side of the ice when you're down a point.

I don't know why I want the challenge. There are hundreds of girls on this campus who would give anything to sleep with me, date me, get a chance to pretend they're going all the way to the league with me. But I want this girl. Kya. The one girl who doesn't even give a shit about hockey.

There's definitely something wrong with me. Definitely. It's even worse because Kya hates my guts. I think. Dustin disagrees, but why the fuck should I trust a guy who keeps weird spiders as pets?

Kya gets ready for our date in her bedroom. Her roommates are at the library and still giving her the cold shoulder. I know she blames me for that, so I try not to bring it up.

"I don't want you watching me change."

"I watch you change every single day," I retort.

"And I tell you not to do that every day."

"Nothing I haven't seen before. Or sucked on…Or licked… or put my finger in…"

"Can you shut up, Cole? I can barely get into this dress."

She grunts and I turn around, ogling her body blatantly. I know she hates when I do that, but I'm just a red-blooded white American male and when I see something fucking gorgeous, I need to take a pretty good look.

I slide the zipper up her back easily and the dress lifts her breasts so her perfect pair gives me the perfect view of her cleavage.

"Whoa. Tits."

"What a complicated and intellectual response," she snaps.

"Nice tits."

"Cole!"

"You're going skating in that?"

"No, I'm going to change into jeans. Here, hold this."

She hands me a pink weekend bag that's heavy.

"What's in there, a dead body?"

She glowers at me, a look I'm coming to expect from my loud-mouthed parakeet.

"Actually, Cole, I borrowed skates from the gym while I was sharpening yours earlier today," she says. "And I have my second outfit, emergency third outfit, and overnight stuff. Plus a First-Aid kit and a rape whistle."

"A rape whistle?"

"You stripped me down and tied me up like a day ago. I'm staying woke."

"Whatever, Kya."

I don't know why she freaks out so much when I never hurt her. I don't think I could at this point. Whatever. My plan is definitely going to work. First, I win her heart on this date and after that, I win her heart on the ice. A girl like Kya wants to know a guy has a future, right? After Agent Night, she'll see that I'm going to be filthy rich one day because of hockey. She won't think I'm such a dumb jock after that…

At least her outfit looks hot. She always dresses hot, which is pretty chill.

"How do I look?" She asks, and then she catches herself. "I mean… I definitely don't care what you think, but do I have spinach in my teeth or something?"

"You look amazing, Kya. Like… drop dead gorgeous."

She gives me a funny look. I can't stop staring at her. If I could, I'd hold her in this moment forever, looking all awkward as I watch her check her body out in the mirror. She has freaking nothing to be insecure about.

"Come on," I tell her. "We'd better go."

"Where are you taking me to dinner?" She asks. "Just so you know, I don't eat meat. I'm vegan. That means I don't eat eggs. Or cheese. Or anything with a heartbeat or potential heartbeat."

"Yeah, you only mention it a thousand times a day. I remembered."

"And I prefer somewhere that has gluten-free options just in case my stomach feels funny."

"Do you want somewhere they make love to the salad before serving it, too?"

"You are so not funny," she grumbles.

I take her to my car, which I normally don't feel insecure about, but I realize that Kya's probably spent her life traveling in limos or G-wagons or some expensive fucking car that I've never even been near.

"This is mine," I tell her. I don't really drive it much to save on gas money, but it's Agent Night, and dating Kya night, so this is important.

"I didn't even know you had a car. Any demented white women waiting to maul me in the back seat?"

"Nope. Just hockey gear."

"Right."

I hold the door open for me and Kya raises an eyebrow as she's about to slide into her seat.

"I can open my own doors, you know."

"But why should you?" I tell her as she crosses in front of me, getting so close that I can smell her perfume and, of course, her hair.

"Um, because I'm strong and independent."

"So am I," I tell her. "And I respect a woman's time enough to treat her right when I take her out. Now, are you going to get in the damn car or will I have to throw you in?"

"Such a gentleman," she quips sarcastically as she slides into the car. At least my car isn't filthy.

She settles into the seats and suddenly she seems a little nervous.

"Hey," I whisper, leaning over to her. "It's not a real date. You can chill out."

"Obviously it's not a real date," she snaps. "And shut up, because I'm definitely chill."

It's so tempting to put my hand on her thigh as I'm driving, just to touch her, but I don't want to freak her out before we even get started on our night together. I don't know why I care so much. I guess teasing Kya and making her do stuff she doesn't want to do is pretty fun.

That must be it. We get to the restaurant, a couple miles away from our small liberal arts college, and Kya presses her face against the window.

"You're taking me to Club Cocoa for dinner?"

"Yeah. Problem?"

"Cole. This place is fancy. Like, every girl at Laguna Grove wants her boyfriend to take her here. But it's somewhere for anniversaries or birthdays, not a freaking fake date."

"Would you prefer I took you to McDonalds?"

"I never said that," Kya replies.

"Cool. Then pipe down and let's go in. I made reservations."

"You know how to use a phone?"

"Good thing your dumb jokes never get old..." I mutter.

"They don't," she says haughtily, proud of herself for at least getting one joke in.

I grab her door from the other side of the car before she can get to it and help her out of the car. I don't know why, but she looks even better here than in her dorm room.

"You're beautiful," I tell her. "Seriously."

"Fake date, Cole. It's a fake date."

"Yeah. I'm just playing my part super well. So play yours, princess, or I'll leak your stories before you can say daddy's money."

"Cheap shot," she snaps.

I put my arm in hers and grin down at her.

"Yeah, those are kinda your thing, huh?"

"Whatever. Let's go in. I still don't believe this isn't just some elaborate prank."

"I am way too hungry to even think about pranking you right now."

"And nervous?" She asks.

"Why the hell would you ask that?"

"Agent Night. It's a pretty big deal finding a good agent. You know… my dad."

I make a noise somewhere between a huff and a grunt and take Kya into the restaurant. Somehow, I'm less nervous when I'm around her and thinking up new ways to torture her. I haven't really thought about Agent Night. But Kya's not entirely wrong. I am nervous. Mostly because this date doesn't feel so fake to me. I really want to impress her. I just knew she'd never agree to a real date.

And that sucks. Chicks are always nervous around me, not the other way around.

The hostess (named DeShaunda) leads us to our seats and with a warm, friendly smile introduces us to our server, a nervous-looking kid who probably goes to Laguna Grove. Kya's smiling as she orders water with ice "on the side" and then a bottle of sparkling water.

"Is that too much?" She asks me worriedly (after she orders and sends the guy chasing down her fancy pants water).

"No. Get whatever you want."

"Cool," Kya says. "I can pay for half of this. Since it's not a real date."

"If you even dream about trying to pay for this, I'll make you hand wash my boxers all of next week."

"Ugh! That's disgusting. And I don't need a man to buy me dinner."

"What is it with you and that stuff? Do you just like hate men?"

"Why do you think that wanting to be independent means I hate you?"

"It's not about being independent. You're a pretty girl. I want to take you out. I'm paying. That's the whole deal."

"What about equality?"

"I'd say most relationships are pretty unequal, princess."

Kya smiles haughtily at me. Man, this chick loves being right.

"Finally. We agree."

"Women have to give birth, breast feed, take pay cuts to raise kids and a bunch of other bullshit. The least guys can do is pay for a fucking dinner," I tell her.

Kya stares at me like I have fifteen heads.

"I… never… thought of that."

"Sometimes it takes a dumb guy to make sense of things," I say, sounding way more bitter than I mean to.

"Well, I guess I'll let you pay. But you don't know how annoying it is for guys to infantilize you all the time."

"Maybe I don't. But I know it's my job to look after you when I take you out. That's all I need to do."

The server returns with the water and Kya pours her sparkling water into the empty cup, taking her side of ice and scooping precisely two cubes into the glass. She stirs furiously with her spoon until the ice melts and I gaze at her in a mixture of awe and confusion. She's a really weird girl… but I like it.

A lot.

"Can I get you dinner?"

"Can you list your vegan options?" Kya asks, prompting a fifteen minute list of vegan options which she asks detailed questions about. I start thinking about eating the tablecloth by the time she finishes her order. Finally.

"What about you, sir?"

"26 oz. sirloin. Medium-rare."

Kya's nose wrinkles as the guy walks away.

"What's your problem?"

"Medium-rare? Are you some type of wild beast?"

"Yup."

"White boys…"

I snicker. "You didn't seem to have a problem with white boys the night we… you know."

"Yeah, well, that was my body getting the better of me."

"I thought it was pretty fun."

"I thought you said it was a mistake?" She says. "So, which was it?"

❦ 18 ❦

THE FAKE DATE: KYA'S CHAPTER

KYA AMBROSE

My heart pounds as I ask Cole a terrifying question that I definitely don't really want to consider. I hate that I want him to say it wasn't a mistake. I mean, what could I really get out of Cole having feelings for me? Except my freedom, I guess.

"No. It wasn't a mistake," Cole says. He's staring at me again. He's been doing that a lot. When he looks at me like that it makes me feel weird. I don't really understand guys like Cole.

What does he want?

I thought he'd lose interest in this whole blackmail thing once we had sex. I thought Cole was the typical athlete at Laguna Grove, obsessed with adding notches to his belt. I mean, he's totally like that on some level, but he has what he wanted from me and he still hasn't even hinted at letting me go.

I don't know what to make of it.

"Cool."

"Cool?" He responds. Yeah. Cool like his crazy blue eyes. Cool like his skin before practice, right before he skates onto the ice.

"I mean. I had a good time."

"Trust me, princess, that wasn't a secret."

"You don't have to be so arrogant all the time."

"The word you're looking for is cocky." He wriggles his eyebrows and looks down. He is so annoying. I can't even call him out because his dick is… enormous.

"I hate you."

"I know. It's kind of what makes this fun."

"This is mostly fun for you. I'm the one getting blackmailed."

The server brings us our food. I try not to get too grossed out by Cole's basically raw food. Makeba's been trying to tell me for ages that white men eat raw meat. At least the vegan option is amazing — a black bean burger with quinoa and spices.

Cole seems really relaxed too, which is great because I'm nervous as hell.

This is supposed to be a fake date, but it's like my brain can't process the fake part and I'm worrying if Cole thinks my hair looks nice. Ugh, gross. I hate that I even care. I'm a modern woman. We're not supposed to care about that kind of stuff.

After dinner, I'm stuffed and Cole's grinning from ear to ear.

"Ready to go skating?"

"I already told you I don't skate... I only brought skates in case you stoop low enough to blackmail me onto the ice."

"I'm blackmailing you."

"Thanks for your mercy."

"Not really my thing, princess," Cole whispers and then he kisses my cheek. I feel my cheeks get really hot, which I definitely don't want him to notice.

"What the hell was that for?"

"For being a good servant," he whispers. "Duh."

Right. Still the same old annoying Cole. I give up on trying to see the human in him. I don't have much of a choice but to let him drag me across the ice right now, anyway. He drives me back to the rink. The lights are off and only the varsity hockey team has access back here after hours.

Cole got special permission just to take me here. He flicks the lights on and leads me excitedly toward the ice. I remind him that I have to change and he nods, pointing me to the men's locker room. When he sees my nervous expression, he reminds me that the boys aren't here and it's totally cool. I'll just have to be quick.

I change out of my dress into jeans and a top that suddenly feels way too low cut. I don't want Cole to get the wrong idea. I'm too scared to put my skates on and trudge all the way back to the ice, so I carry them and tiptoe over in my socks, lugging my weekend bag in one hand and the pair of skates in the other.

Cole's sitting on the bleachers, waiting for me when I get there. His face lights up once I appear. He's just so into this whole servant and fake date thing.

"Hey, your skating outfit looks pretty hot, too."

"I have another dress for the cocktail thing. Don't worry."

"Whatever. You look amazing. Ready to skate?"

"Um, are you ready for me to fall on my freaking ass?"

"You've got plenty of ass back there to fall on."

"Thanks, Cole."

He laughs and walks over to the ice. I meet him at the door and he sticks his hands out. I finally put my skates on and he sticks his hands out.

"Do you trust me?" He whispers, putting his hands in mine and suddenly sounding really sweet. Like the Cole I wish he was.

"Not really."

"Okay," he whispers back. "Well, you'll have to trust me now or you're going to wipe out. Be careful and step onto the ice. Your center of gravity is going to change a bit. I'll help you get used to it."

"I'm scared."

"I'm right here, Kya."

My eyes flicker up to meet his. Kya. Not babe. Princess. Servant. Not even his worst name — slave. I bite my lower lip and nod.

"Got it."

I take one step onto the ice and my leg wobbles. Cole grabs my forearms and I feel stable.

"One more step," he says. "Come on."

"Oh God… I'm going to die."

"No way, princess. I've got you."

I put my second skate onto the ice and wobble again. Cole's gripping me, but he can't help laughing at me.

"You're like a newborn," he says.

"When did you learn how to skate?"

"Before I could walk," Cole says. "My dad took me skating before we left. He used to play, but… he chose drugs over hockey. And drugs over me."

"Oh. I'm so sorry."

"Don't be sorry. Just feel around for where you're most stable and we can move."

"No way we can move," I say, clinging to him for dear life. "I'm going to fall."

"You're not," Cole says. "I promise. Take your time. Just… get a feel for it."

He moves slightly, and I shriek as I move forward. I wobble, but then I find a stable point and I can stand. Cole stops and holds onto me.

"See?"

"That was hardly skating."

"You'll get the hang of it. Come on. Let's try again…"

His body is really firm. He feels sturdy as I hold on to his arms and wobble like a baby deer again as Cole suavely skates backwards. I don't even know how he's holding onto me like that without letting me fall over.

"Think you're ready to handle it on your own?"

"No!"

"Okay," he says calmly. "Take your time. We'll cross the ice super slow."

"I swear I'm going to fall," I say, hating how shrill and annoying my voice sounds. Cole chuckles.

"I'll catch you before you hit the ice. Promise."

We move a little more and I feel myself getting less wobbly, almost like I'm getting the hang of this stupid skating thing. Cole's holding onto me a little less tightly, but that still makes me nervous.

"Don't you dare let go!"

"I won't," he says. "Not yet."

But then we only go a few feet forward before he lets go of me.

"COLE!"

"Relax. Find your balance. Come to me."

I relax and try to find my stupid freaking balance, which eventually happens.

"Oh, my God. I'm not falling."

"See? Now come."

"Oh, God…"

I try to skate forward and it actually works.

"Oh my God! I'm doing it!"

Cole grins, and I move a little forward. Then I stop getting it. I screech and lurch forward. Before I can fall, Cole catches me. I slam face first into his chest as he grabs my hips.

"I've got you," he whispers. "Just like I said."

I shriek and stabilize myself against his chest, hating the up close and personal reminder of how firm and chiseled his body is. I cling to his shirt and pull myself up.

"Totally fine," I say, trying to play it cool.

"You were great."

"You can let go of me now."

"Don't think so, babe," he whispers.

Then he kisses me. I try to push him away, but it doesn't work. I end up clinging to his shirt and pulling him in deeper. Cole's grasp on my hips tightens, and he lifts me up. I don't know how he balances holding onto me and wearing skates, but he moves backward, clinging to me until his back slams into the boards. I rake my fingers through his hair and Cole chuckles.

"Fuck," he whispers. "I promised myself I wouldn't do this."

"Shut up," I whisper back to him.

"Got it, babe."

He shuts up and kisses me — and the kiss is perfect.

❧ 19 ❧

THE FAKE DATE: THE FINALE

COLE SEABROOK

Kya looks amazing in her last outfit for the night. Cocktails with sports agents, recruiters and a bunch of major league fat cats looking to recruit ought to be the perfect end to this date. Kya will finally see that I'm serious about hockey and I'm serious about becoming the kind of guy she wants to date. You know, a guy who can afford to impress a girl like her.

"Are you nervous?" She asks me.

I can't help but feel like she's the nervous one, but yeah, I'm finally nervous.

"It's only my future. Nothing to be nervous about."

"Your future? You really take hockey that seriously?"

"Isn't your dad an athlete? You get it."

"I mean, yeah, but... that's basketball. This is... different. What about brain injuries?"

"According to you, I'm pretty stupid. I don't see how a few brain injuries could make that worse."

I glance over at her sitting there in the passenger seat of my car, fidgeting with her dress and avoiding my gaze. She always looks away when I look at her, which is pretty annoying. But then again, I guess I like that she's pretty annoying.

"You're not stupid," Kya says, sounding like someone's holding her at gunpoint and forcing her to say it.

"Yeah, right. You made it pretty clear how you feel about me. It's cool."

"Wait. Stop," she says. "I mean it. You're not stupid. I... I was wrong."

"Holy shit. Did Kya Ambrose just admit she was wrong?"

"Shut up. And thanks for teaching me how to skate."

"We can practice whenever you want."

"After I'm done doing your sweaty laundry and hunting down Dustin's escaped pets in your bedroom, I doubt I'll have much time for skating. But thanks."

She cracks me up. I link arms with her, fighting the desire to kiss her or worse, make some dumb confession.

"Come on. We'd better go in there."

"Right. And I'm just your arm candy..."

"No way, babe. You're a little more than that."

"Um... what does that mean?"

"Never mind. I need a drink. Let's go."

I got so freaking close to getting real with Kya and that's the last thing I need right now. It's Agent Night and I can't think about feelings when I need to think about something way more important. Money. Hockey. My future.

I help Kya out of the car and maybe she's more than arm candy to me, but she's definitely also arm candy. She looks so hot in that dress. I know some of the guys may give me shit for showing up with her, but... I don't really care. They wouldn't get it.

Our names are both on the list and Kya seems surprised that I would show up anywhere that had a list.

"This is fancy."

"I told you, Agent Night."

As soon as we walk in the door together, someone practically shouts across the room.

"Kya Ambrose? Is that you?"

Kya glances over her shoulder. A tall black guy — not basketball tall, but a little taller than me — outstretches his arms and looks at her with a big smile on his face. I hate myself for the tiny (yet inescapable) pang of jealousy. Who the fuck is this guy?

"Oh my God! Dylan!"

Dylan. I already hate Dylan. Kya bounces over to him — I don't think she can help the bouncing between her great ass and her curly hair — and wraps her arms around him.

"What are you doing here?" Kya asks.

"Looking for good athletes. What about you?"

"I'm here with my... friend... Cole Seabrook."

She pulls away from this Dylan guy, who gives me a nod.

"Seabrook. I recognize that name. Hat trick guy?"

"The one and only."

"Wow. Kya. I hope you know you're in the presence of a college hockey legend."

"Dylan, stop. You don't want his head to get too big."

"I'd love to talk to you if you have a chance, Cole. I've heard a lot about your college record."

"I'm going to get a drink," Kya says. "You two talk."

I don't want her to leave my side, and not just because I worry that she'll bolt out of here. Dylan talks to me for a while about hockey, who he normally represents, and then he gives me his number. Kya takes a suspiciously long time to return, but she interrupts me in a conversation with another agent. This guy, a Mike Emmanuel, knows Kya too.

"How's your dad?"

"He's good. Still doing his thing in LA. He's busy."

"This guy your friend?"

"Uh huh," she says, sipping some champagne. Mike (who Kya calls "Mikey") takes more of an interest in me once he realizes I know Kya Ambrose. We talk for a while and when I finally get his business card too, Kya's nowhere to be seen. Shit...

I should be thinking about getting more contacts, not tracking her down. I walk back towards the champagne, guessing that she's hunkered down there somewhere getting her drink on. I run into Jayce and Dustin, chatting with a tall white guy with a blond bowl cut I recognize from the American Hockey League infomercials.

They grab my arms and introduce me to the guy, who is pretty keen on talking to me. I chat for a bit, but I still can't get Kya out of my mind.

I grab Jayce's sleeve and ask if he's seen her.

"I think she went outside for some air."

"Shit. She probably bolted," I grumble, regretting letting her out of my sight.

"No way, dude."

Jayce is just trying to make me feel better. At least I have a couple business cards and agents that are definitely interested. I walk outside and catch Kya holding onto…

"Since when do you smoke?"

She coughs dramatically and drops the cigarette on the ground.

"I don't. It's gross. Dylan gave it to me and I thought it would make me mysterious."

She coughs again and steps on the cigarette.

"What the hell is going on?" I ask her. "You disappeared and now you're smoking?"

"I figured out why you brought me here, that's all. I'm just beating myself up for letting my guard down. Again."

"Kya, make sense."

"You're using me. For my connections. Obviously. I thought you wanted me here because—

"Using you?" I interrupt because the idea is ridiculous. How was I supposed to know Kya knew every sports agent on the East Coast? How could I have possibly known such a specific detail?

"I was right about you. You're not stupid, but you're a manipulator. I actually thought tonight was fun, but then it hit me... you want my connections. This is all about your stupid career."

"That's not true."

"Isn't it? I know all the agents in there."

"How the hell would I have known that?" I snap back. Kya seriously gets on my nerves, but this is the worst thing she's said to me.

Use her? I'm trying to freaking impress her. And it's definitely not working, which gets me more pissed off.

"I don't know, Cole. But it's what you do. You use people. You literally use me as your servant and I don't even care if you blackmail me anymore."

"Fine," I snap. "You are seriously so annoying."

"You're one to talk! You annoy me with your dumb skates and your dumb blond hair."

"I have annoying hair? Says the chick who sheds all over my pillow."

"Ugh!" Kya shrieks. "Do you ever shut up?"

"Kya, relax," I sigh, sticking my hands in my pockets and fighting the urge to mess with her even more. "Tonight wasn't about using you. I wanted to take you out. For real. Like a date."

"You forced me to go."

"Yeah, because I knew you wouldn't say yes."

She gives me a haughty expression.

"I wouldn't," she says. "You're right."

"Whatever," I tell her. "Point is, at some point over the past few weeks, I actually… Oh, fuck. Never mind."

"No, wait. Tell me," she says, tilting her head to the side and giving me a sharp look with those gorgeous brown eyes.

"I fucking like you, Kya. Duh."

"What? No, you don't! You definitely don't like me and here's why. First of all—"

"Do you have to argue with everything I say?"

"I'm not arguing, I'm just explaining that it's impossible for you to like me because—"

I clamp my hand over her mouth.

"You never shut up," I whisper. "And it drives me fucking crazy, but… I want to be with you."

I drop my hand away, waiting for a response.

"Well, you can't," she says, a little too quickly for my tastes. "You're blackmailing me in case you forgot."

Shit. I actually forgot. I got so caught up in my feelings for this annoying little parakeet that I totally forgot.

"Fine," I whisper. "Then I'll prove how I feel about you. No more blackmail. I'll leave you alone. I just want you to give me a chance tonight."

"Just tonight?"

"Yes."

"Then I'm free to go?"

"Yeah," I whisper. "But I don't want you to go far, Kya. I want you."

"Cole…"

"Shut up," I whisper, raking my fingers through her curls and grabbing her cheeks before kissing her.

Kissing her feels amazing, and once I start, I don't want to stop. She presses her body against mine and lets me kiss her. I don't want to stop. But I also don't want to keep standing here because I want to bring Kya back to my place. Or wherever.

She pulls away far too soon and licks her lips.

"We should go back in there."

"I want to take you home."

"I know," she says. "But it's Agent Night. Let's go in there and get you an agent."

"Uh… do you plan on helping with that?"

"Yes, stupid," she says.

"You don't owe me anything," I tell her. "I think I've been enough of an asshole."

"Come on, dumbass," she says. "Before I change my mind."

Her smile is fucking contagious and the next thing I know, I'm holding onto her hand and letting her champagne tipsy ass drag me back into the party. Kya snags five more agent business cards for me before the night is out.

She went pretty hard working her connections and talking me up. She actually knows shit about my game, which surprises me, since she glares at me every time I force her to do something hockey related.

It's almost midnight when we're both exhausted, but I'm not too tired to take her home. It's the only thing on my mind when she's tipsy and giggling her way out of the party.

"Hey hat trick guy," she teases. "Take me back to my room. I want to sleep in a bed that doesn't have a snake in it."

"Ovie was only trying to hug you."

"He was trying to eat me, Cole, and you know it."

"What about your friends?"

Kya bites her lip. "Right."

"Listen. We don't have to… you know… have sex. I just want to hold you tonight."

"Um… now you're scaring me."

"Why?"

"Because five minutes ago you were blackmailing me and now you apparently like me and want to cuddle without sex. It's highly suspicious."

"Only because you're drunk."

"You're drunk too," she accuses.

"Yeah. I definitely shouldn't be driving right now."

Kya glances over her shoulder.

"We could sober up in the back seat of your car and watch like… cat videos on your phone."

"Or hockey videos," I tell her.

Kya raises an eyebrow. "Or cat videos."

"Or hockey videos."

"Are we always going to fight like this?" she asks.

"Always?"

"I'm drunk," she says quickly. "I didn't mean that."

"I kinda wish you did," I whisper. "Because… I kinda want to fight with you. A lot."

"Back seat," Kya commands. "We need to sober up."

Yeah. Like there's any way I'll get Kya in the back seat of my car and act like a responsible adult male. It's just never going to happen. She's been too perfect tonight, and it feels like all the bullshit between us is finally going away.

I scramble into the back seat behind her. I want to make her mine tonight. 100% mine.

COLE'S CRAZY QUESTION

KYA AMBROSE

I don't know what the hell I'm doing in the back seat of Cole's car, my fancy dress clinging to my thighs and his eyes clinging to my body with equal eagerness. I never expected myself to get close enough to Cole to be one of those girls, one of the hockey groupies who would climb into the back seat of Cole Seabrook's car without so much as a second thought.

He puts his hand on my shoulder, turning my body to face his.

"I like you, Kya," he says. "For real."

"We're both drunk. We should just sober up and try not to do anything stupid."

Cole chuckles — of course he does. He seems to get bizarre entertainment from doing stupid things. Like blackmailing me. Or kissing me. Or eating me out. Or sleeping with me. This man is absolutely full of bad decisions.

"What if I want to do something stupid?" He whispers.

"Of course you want to do something stupid."

I know I'm unnecessarily harsh with him, but I don't know how else I can stop this from happening. We're both drunk. We already kissed. We've even slept together. I'm at an incredibly high risk of exercising poor judgment, which I know Cole would enjoy in his own sick, perverted way.

"If kissing you is the dumbest thing ever, then I'm proud to be an idiot."

"Stop…" I sigh, throwing my head back against the seat and waiting for a clear thought to enter my mind. Cole seizes his opportunity and kisses me. I want to be the better person, but kissing him has always been one of my weaknesses. I let his kisses trail from my lips to my neck before I rake my fingers through his blond hair and attempt to push his head away from me.

"No," Cole whispers. "Let it happen, babe."

"Why?" I murmur. "So you can stop calling me babe and start calling me a slut?"

He laughs.

"You are… funny."

"I don't think what I said was very funny."

"You're not a slut," he murmurs. "I think you're the hardest chick to get into bed I've ever met."

"You realize we already had sex."

"That was because I was blackmailing you. This time, it's because you want to."

He sounds so cocky and that pisses me off, but it's hard to stay mad with his lips pressed against my neck again. I try pushing his head away again, but he doesn't want me to and suddenly I can't get a good grasp of this dumb hockey player's big head and all I can do is let him kiss me and kiss me.

Cole pats his palms on his lap and encourages me to climb on top of him. His kisses are good enough to compromise my reason, already previously compromised by champagne, and I nervously straddle him. As I sink my hips against his, Cole groans.

"You are so hot, babe," he whispers. "Seriously."

"Shut up."

"I mean it."

"Great. I think there are better compliments than hot."

"Frustrating?" He grumbles.

"That's not a compliment."

"Really?" he murmurs, planting kisses on my neck. "Don't you have a quote... Frustrating women make history or something?"

"Well-behaved women seldom make history," I correct him, as if he won't forget my correction entirely in the next ten minutes.

"Oh," he whispers. "I guess that means you're going to have to be pretty bad-behaved to make the history books."

"Is that the best pickup line you can come up with?" I grumble between kisses.

Cole chuckles. "What's a guy to do in a feminist world?"

"Ugh. Shut. Up."

"Okay," Cole whispers. But he only gets quiet because he has other plans for me. Plans that involve working his hand up my thigh and under my clothes.

"Cole…"

"Shh," he whispers. "Let it happen."

His hand slides over my tights and into my underwear. I gasp as he touches me down there and makes a low pleasurable grunt in the back of his throat.

"I want to rip those tights off," he murmurs.

"Great idea, except for the part where I freeze my ass off."

"You'll be fine," he whispers back. "Plus, isn't this part of your dirty fantasies?"

Before I can respond and push Cole for getting dangerously close to blackmailing me after promising me he wouldn't, he rips my tights all the way off.

"Cole!"

He rips again, getting the rest of them and dragging the sheer fabric away from my thighs.

"Perfect," he whispers, his hands returning to my underwear again. He rubs my mound from the outside and then slides my underwear over his lower lips, his fingers probing the apex of my thighs. I grind my hips forward, leaning into Cole's grasp. With his nose pressed into my neck, he slides his fingers into my underwear and past my entrance, thrusting two fingers inside me and catching me by surprise. My hips buck forward out of surprise and I let out an unwilling moan, which Cole enjoys.

"Gotcha," he whispers.

"I… I'm…"

"Shhh," he whispers back. "Cum all over my hands, babe."

He moves his fingers in the same rhythm I move my hips, making it extremely pleasurable to have his hands working me between my thighs. I push my hips forward as Cole's fingers plunge into me more roughly, massaging my G spot and my clit as I move my hips against him. I moan as he uses his hands, and each time he discovers a new spot that brings me crazy pleasure, he stays there and pushes me close to an orgasm. It's like Cole can tell when I'm about to cum, because every time I get close, he pulls away.

After the seventh almost-orgasm, I shove his chest. Hard.

"What is wrong with you?" I gasp. Cole laughs.

"I was wondering when you would say anything," he says, removing his hands from my underwear and frustratingly sticking his fingers into his mouth and licking me off his hands. My cheeks flush.

"What are you doing?"

"Tasting you."

"I want… Ugh!"

Cole keeps licking his fingers, getting his tongue all between his fingers.

"What do you want, babe?"

"You know what I want. You're just taking some kind of sick pleasure out of—

"Teasing you?"

"Yes!"

"Then tell me what you want," Cole whispers, propping his head up on his hands. "And maybe I'll give it to you."

"Maybe? Haven't you ever heard that the woman is supposed to cum first? The orgasm gap is almost as serious as the wage gap."

"I don't know what wage gap you're talking about," Cole answers calmly. "But don't worry. You're gonna cum first. After you beg for it."

I shove his chest again, which naturally only makes him laugh harder.

"Come on," Cole insists. "Beg for it."

"Do you still have to take pleasure out of humiliating me?"

"Nope," he whispers. "Just making sure I've got your enthusiastic consent."

I take Cole's stupid hand and slowly move it into my underwear. He smirks as I brace his hand against my mound.

"Is this enthusiastic enough for you?"

"I'd rather hear you beg," he replies, spreading my lower lips apart and teasing my clit again. He is pure evil. Seriously. I don't know how I can stand him and then I remind myself that I can't. But if I want to make Cole's annoying personality tolerable again, I'll need to have an orgasm. It's the only way to work out the insane pent up frustration between us.

"Please…" I gasp. "Can you stop being an asshole for ten seconds and make me cum?"

"That's not a very nice way to talk to a guy about to give you an orgasm."

"Orgasm first," I whisper. "Then I'll be nice."

I should have known Cole would have gone about it in the most frustrating way possible. He slowly massages my clit, taking his time until I'm close. I'm so freaked out that he's going to pull away that I push my hips forward and make sure I cum. Hard. My weight collapses against Cole's chest, and his free hand strokes my hair as he keeps massaging my clit.

Holy shit.

I'm gasping for breath and making all these pathetic whimpering sounds as he removes his fingers from my underwear and again licks them clean. My underwear is totally soaked and I'm trembling from desire. I want more than one orgasm. I grab Cole's cheeks, ready to kiss him, and he dodges me.

"What the hell?"

"Taste yourself first," he says, holding his fingers up to my face.

"Um, I'm not doing that."

"Aren't you a feminist?"

"What the hell does that have to do with tasting my own pussy?"

Cole shrugs. "Women's rights."

I open my mouth to protest and realize I should have seen Cole's next move coming. He pushes his fingers into my mouth and makes me taste myself. I suck on his fingers, mostly because I'm considering biting down as hard as possible, but he withdraws them as I sink my teeth into his hand.

"Sorry, babe," he whispers. "No biting this time."

"Asshole."

"You taste good," he says. "I don't know why you're so uptight."

"I am not uptight."

"Okay," he whispers. "Whatever you say. Now take my cock out."

He's still so bossy and demanding. I want to smack him in the face instead of taking his dick out, but I can feel it about to burst through his formal pants. He's so big when he's hard, it's like he's got that dumb snake Ovie in there. I run my hands over his dick slowly. Cole groans. Ha. I can tease him just as much as he can tease me. Teasing him feels amazing, obviously.

Cole grunts as I undo his belt buckle and then sit back.

"What are you waiting for?"

"Who says I'm waiting for anything?"

"I get it. A taste of my own medicine," Cole grumbles. "I guess I deserve it."

His palms cup my ass, and he draws me close.

"Take your time, princess. Your pussy is worth it."

I feel a wave of desire surging through me and wonder if Cole means what he's saying or if he just wants me to ease his dick out of his pants faster. I tease his belt open more and his dick practically attempts to jump out of his pants, flinching like a monstrous predator beneath the fabric.

"He's excited," I whisper, stroking Cole again through his pants, still enjoying how good it feels to tease him.

"Yeah," he whispers. "You're pretty fucking exciting."

Without my help, his zipper travels over his bulge, and Cole's dick releases itself from his pants, but not his boxers. From here, I can feel his warmth pulsing from the giant member, yearning for escape. I wrap my hands around it, getting as much of his girth in my palms as I can manage. He's so big, I can barely wrap my hands all the way around. Cole shudders, and goose flesh breaks out over his skin as I touch his dick through his boxers.

"How did it get so big?" I whisper, because those types of stupid questions pop into your head any time you see an unusually large penis. It's only natural.

Cole shrugs. "It's probably why I'm so cocky."

"You are not funny," I whisper, my hands mindlessly stroking his shaft through his boxers.

"Yeah," he says. "I know. But I'm pretty fucking hard and I want you, Kya. Now."

I can't resist him any longer. I'm not as good at teasing as Cole is. I take his dick out of his boxers and Cole slides my dress over my hips.

"Crazy thing is," he whispers. "I've never felt more sober than I do now."

"You don't smell sober," I whisper, taking full grasp of his member and sliding it against my entrance. Cole groans.

Teasing him like this is fun. I use his big dick like a toy for a minute, rubbing my clit and sliding it between my lips as Cole gets harder and harder. I know he wants more from me. I know he wants to get inside me and knowing that just drives me wilder as I tease him. I make myself cum on his dick without getting it inside me. He cups my ass and holds me close as I climax, and before I can catch my breath, he sneaks the head of his cock against my entrance and pushes.

"Cole!"

"Can't wait anymore. Sorry."

He doesn't sound very sorry as he slides the full length of his dick between my legs. Holy shit, he is huge and I wish he would enter me more slowly. Teasing Cole has its downsides, as he's tired of waiting and working his giant dick between my legs is painful. I cry out as he thrusts his hips up. I'm soaked, but his big white boy dick is still a tight squeeze.

As I move my hips, he works his way in deeper and I cry out loudly when he buries his dick inside me to the hilt. Holy shit. Cole grins once he has me balanced precariously on top of him, totally at the mercy of his dick.

"Like that?" Cole murmurs, pushing hair away from my neck as he kisses me.

"Yes," I whisper, moving my hips and nearly exploding from his big dick between my legs.

"Good girl," he whispers. "I like how you feel around my dick. So tight."

He grabs my ass and moves me over his dick again. The slightest movement pushes me over the edge. Cole's dick brings orgasms, whether I'm ready or not. I cum hard and Cole pushes deeper as I'm cumming. I swivel my hips and move on his dick as he teases my clit with his fingers again, entertained by me having yet another orgasm.

As I climax again, Cole grunts.

"Fuck," he mutters. "What are you doing with your body, girl? It feels good."

"Yeah," I whimper, moving my hips more and bringing myself to another orgasm. Now that I have Cole's dick inside me, I don't want to think about anything else. I just want to feel him between my legs and enjoy him without thinking about his personality or any annoying thing that might snap me back into reality.

"Cum for me," he murmurs. "Come on."

I keep moving my hips until I cum again and Cole groans.

"Yeah, it's that," he whispers. "You are great with these hips."

"Black girl magic," I whisper back, leaning forward and kissing him as my hair falls over his chest. Cole pushes hair out of my face and chuckles.

"Black pussy magic," he whispers back. It feels totally inappropriate to let him say something like this, but the next time I move, I can't even sharply chastise him because I cum way too hard. Fuck. How does he have this effect on me?

"Shut up…"

"I love it, you know," he whispers. "Being with a black girl. It's awesome."

"Cole, that is so inappropriate," I say, struggling not to whimper as my hips move again.

"Come on," he teases. "What's wrong with liking black girls? Sounds a bit racist, Kya."

I grab his dumb cheeks and kiss him, because kissing Cole is apparently the best (and possibly the only) way to shut him up. As I kiss him and move on top Cole slowly, I cum again and he grabs my ass, pulling my body against his and groaning as his fingers sink into my butt cheeks.

"Your ass is insane," he murmurs. "Fucking hot."

I cum again and Cole kisses my neck, moving faster between my legs. I can tell he's close. I run my hands down his back, appreciating the thick muscles holding his athletic body together. When my hand gets to his ass, it's so incredibly round and muscular. Hockey guys have crazy butts. I run my fingers over Cole's ass and cup him close to me. He groans as I touch him and pull him close.

"I love your hands," he whispers. "Touch me."

I squeeze his butt, and Cole's hips move deeper into me. Holy shit. He feels incredible and I know I'm going to cum again. Climaxing with Cole is effortless, and he holds my sweaty body against his, kissing me softly until he's finally ready to release. His hips rock forward one last time and he groans with satisfaction as he finishes inside me. I feel his dick tremble and explode between my legs. My thighs wrap around his and our lips find each other easily.

"I want you," he murmurs. "I fucking want you, Kya."

"You already have what you want," I whisper.

"That's not what I mean, princess. I want a girlfriend."

"Is sleeping with your former servant the best way to do that?"

Cole chuckles.

"Kya, I'm serious."

"About what?"

"I'm asking you a question, stupid," he says, making fun of the way I call him stupid all the time. "Will you be my girlfriend?"

❧ 21 ❧

ARE YOU RACIST?

COLE SEABROOK

Kya shifts her body over mine, her little hips wriggling and her soft butt cheeks nestling against my thigh. I miss her pussy already and the little wet spot she's making on my leg only makes me want her crazy ass even more. She's fucking everything. I don't want to pretend that I hate her guts anymore. It's just way too hard. The problem is, she has every reason to hate my guts and every fucking reason to say no to me. I run my thumbs over her dark brown nipples as I wait for a response, enjoying the way the goosebumps look across her medium-brown skin.

"I can't believe you're asking me this," she whispers, which totally doesn't answer my question.

"Believe it."

"Why? Is this some trick where the cameras are going to come out and expose me?"

"Uh... no."

My eyes flicker to hers. She acts better when I'm looking at her. Sweet. Shy. The girl she tries to hide with the arguments and the loud mouth.

"So, why are you asking me?"

"Because I like you. Duh. That's what people do."

"Do you really think we make sense as a couple?"

"Who cares?"

"Um… we should care?"

"You're overthinking it," I tell her, because that's basically what she does. Of course, this gets her all puffed up with annoyance. Even her hair gets puffier when she's mad… I swear.

"No. I'm not."

"You like me," I tell her. "Don't deny it."

"Like you? How dare you assume—

"My hand's been on your tit for the past five minutes and you haven't complained. Pretty sure you like me."

"Shut. Up."

I squeeze her cute ass boob and Kya pouts, pushing against my chest.

"You're annoying."

"Cool. So we're dating then."

Kya scowls. She has really thick natural brows that scrunch up when she gets all angry with me, which, you know, happens several times a day.

"When the hell did I say that?"

"I'm tired of waiting for an answer, Kya. We're dating."

"You are so sexist, Cole. You can't just announce we're dating. I'm a woman. I have feelings. I get a choice…"

Oh, God. Somehow, I set her off. I don't know how I got this deep, but I have to find the right thing to say to stop Kya's rant. It keeps going for a few more minutes.

"… what's next? You're going to tell me that I can't leave the house without a chaperone?"

I clamp my hand over her mouth, silencing her elaborate squawking.

"MMMHMMHM!"

"Are you my fucking girlfriend, yes or no? Nod or shake!"

She nods. I remove my hand from her mouth.

"I still hate you," she says.

"Sure," I whisper. "Whatever you say, princess."

I lean forward and kiss her. She allows me to, so I guess she's not too mad. I grin when I pull away. She's mine.

"What are you smiling at?" She asks, her hand running over my chest.

"My black girlfriend."

"Ugh, Cole. Don't make that a thing. It's totally not a thing."

"I've never had a black girlfriend."

"Maybe it's your attitude."

She climbs off me and starts finding her clothes. Yeah. We're definitely sober enough to head back to campus now. Draining my balls always helps sober me up. I don't know why. I watch her dress in the backseat, my heart racing a million miles a minute. I did it. I got her. She's mine. I want to take her again, right here in the car's backseat, but she's right... we need to get back to campus.

As I scramble into the front seat in just my boxers, Kya shrieks.

"What? Just climb up here."

"Cole! There's someone outside the window!"

She ditches the leggings and scrambles to get her dress on. I squint and look out the window. Fuck. Those idiots... Dustin and Jayce bang on the door and window.

Jayce yells, "SEABROOK'S GETTING LAID!"

"Woo! Finally losing that virginity, brah!" Dustin says, pounding on the door in a drunken excitement.

"I'm going to go out there and tell them off," Kya says.

I glance over my shoulder at her and suddenly feel grateful that I have child locks on the back doors of my car. The last thing she wants is to get into a screaming match with my teammates. They don't have my tendency toward mercy.

"Kya, get up front."

I turn the car on, and she listens to me, which is a total fucking surprise. I roll the windows down, which only makes Dustin and Jayce whoop with laughter as they crowd around the window.

"You smell like whiskey," I tell them. Dustin sticks his head and the car and reaches for Kya.

"Hey, princess. Wanna do the entire team?"

Jayce laughs loudly and elbows him.

"You drunk idiots better shut the fuck up or I'll kick your ass."

"Ohhhhh," Jayce teases. "Cole has a crush."

Dustin laughs hysterically, even if this is only moderately funny — and mostly just annoying as fuck.

"Hey, can you assholes shut it? Kya's my girlfriend, so stop acting like dicks. I mean it."

I roll the window up and Kya's gazing at me like I have two heads.

"What the hell is happening to me?" She says slowly.

"What?"

"Did you just stand up for me?"

"Yes. I'm not an asshole. You're my girl. That means looking out for you."

"Yesterday you asked me to send a bikini pic to Dustin because he needed a new home screen pic."

"That was then. This is now."

"Less than 24 hours?"

"Look, Kya. You're my girlfriend now. That means something to me."

"Oh yeah? You have big deep feelings suddenly?"

"Maybe I do."

I drive us back to campus. I know Kya's feelings about my rape den, so I agree to take her back to my dorm.

"What about your friends?" I ask her on the way up the stairs. "Are you going to tell them about us?"

"I mean… I wouldn't keep you a secret. I guess. But they're going to be confused since I tried to slip laxatives into your protein shake last week."

"You did what?"

"Don't worry," she sighs. "I'm the one who drank it accidentally. Those things are pretty good, by the way."

"Is that why you were all cranky last Wednesday?"

"Can you shut up?"

"You told me it was a second surprise period."

"Is it my fault you're too dumb to know anything about periods?"

"I know plenty about periods."

"Whatever, Cole. I don't want to talk about my periods."

We're right outside my bedroom door and before I can kill the period talk, Makeba swings the door open and glances between us with a weird look on her face.

"Periods? Who's talking about periods? And why'd you bring the white boy back?"

"Hey Makeba," I greet her with a bright smile on my face, hoping it dulls the effect of Kya's friends going ape-shit when they find out we're dating. They both give me a look like they didn't expect me to know Makeba's name. I know all Kya's friends. I've spent the past few weeks learning everything about her. Falling for her. Or whatever.

"Seriously? You brought the white boy?" Makeba whispers, like I'm not standing right there.

"Um… you're also dating a white boy," Kya hisses. "BJ!"

"BJ isn't that type of white boy."

"And what type of white boy is that?" I ask, leaning in the doorway and grinning at Makeba's extremely suspicious expression.

"The dumb kind."

"Makeba!" Kya says. "Cole is not dumb."

"You called him dumb in a text message to me seven hours ago."

Kya glares at her and puts her hands on her hips.

"Well, he's my boyfriend now. So I've changed my mind."

Makeba gags dramatically. "Both of you get in here. We need a tribunal."

"A tribunal?!" Kya complains. Makeba drags us by the wrists and slams the door behind us. I don't have a fucking idea what my crazy little parakeet is getting me into, but I have a feeling I'm going to be entertained by her weird little friends. Raven takes her headphones off and finally acknowledges us from her desk. She's bent over a book called Outlander and she slams it shut when she notices me staring at it.

"What is that white boy doing back here?"

"Hanging out with a black girl," I reply with a grin. "That's still legal, right?"

"Was that a race joke?" Makeba mutters. "I'm taking note…"

Kya shoots me a glare, and then she softens and puts her hand in mine.

"Cole and I are dating now. Makeba thinks this somehow warrants a tribunal."

"We had a tribunal when I wore that blonde wig," Raven says. "We can have one now."

"Fuck..." Kya mutters, genuinely meaning it.

Makeba pulls a desk chair into the center of the room.

"Sit down, Mr. Seabrook."

"Are you ladies serious?"

"Sit the fuck down," Makeba says sharply, reminding me of this totally scary hockey coach I had as a kid. Okay, then. I guess I'm doing this shit. I sit down, spreading my stance wide.

"He's manspreading," Raven whispers as she stands in front of me with Makeba, both of them looking like they're going to give me a beat down.

"Should we tie him up?" Makeba suggests.

Thankfully, Kya intervenes.

"There's no need to tie him up! Can't we just talk to him like normal people? You guys are embarrassing me... I mean, I know I deserve it but..."

"Girl, you're totally dickmatized," Makeba says calmly. "We need to intervene and make sure he's a decent guy."

"Cole... I am so sorry for this."

"I don't mind. Subject me to your tribunal, ladies."

"What is that black woman's name?" Raven asks, scrutinizing me coldly.

"Kya Ambrose."

"Star sign?!" Makeba asks.

Kya presses her hand to her forehead.

"Pisces."

"Wait, is that right?" Makeba whispers to Kya.

"Yes. It's right."

Raven shakes her head and folds her arms.

"Do you think you have what it takes to date a black woman?" Raven asks me.

"What the hell does that mean?" I ask, feeling a little red around the ears now. These chicks are freaking serious and they're scaring the crap out of me. I've never sat down and had two black women yelling at me, but it's scary as hell.

"It means... are you like aware of black women and our struggles?" Makeba explains in that tone Kya uses when she thinks I'm really stupid. My ears get redder and I can't find the words I'm looking for the way I should be able to. Kya puts her hands on my shoulders and thankfully interjects.

"Guys, he's fine. Cole and I... we reached an understanding. We've overcome our differences."

"So he's not blackmailing you anymore?" Raven asks.

"No. I'm not," I tell them. "Happy?"

"I don't know if we're happy," Makeba says. "Are you racist?"

"Why would anyone answer that question with a yes?"

Makeba strokes her chin dramatically. "Fair point, white boy."

"But are you racist?" Raven asks. "Because Kya's black."

"I noticed."

"Okay, guys," Kya intervenes. "That's enough. Cole stood up for me tonight with his friends. He took me on the best first date I've ever been on. We're giving it a shot. That's all you need to worry about. I can handle myself."

"We will die for that girl," Raven threatens me. "Don't make us have to."

"Damn, Raven. Relax!" Kya says. "I thought y'all were still mad, anyway."

Raven winks at her, but then turns her wicked glare back at me.

"I'm not afraid to give a white boy a beat down," Makeba says. "We're watching you."

"You don't have to worry about Kya. She can definitely handle me."

"Okay. Okay," Raven says, relenting and finally unfolding her arms. "Are you over 21?"

"Huh?"

"We're too young to buy alcohol and we want to throw a party this weekend with our club."

"Uh, I can help with that. Sure."

"Great," Raven says.

Kya relaxes, like she's happy I finally won them over. Of course I won them over. I'm awesome…

"Am I invited?"

"It's kind of a black people on campus thing," Kya interjects. "It's not really a hockey guy type of place."

"What does that mean?"

"No kegs. No shirtless white guys peeing in trash cans. No vandalism. No breaking glass. No fighting. No white girls doing body shots on pong tables. It's a kickback."

"A what?"

Makeba giggles, but I don't really know what's so funny about what I said.

"So, am I invited, or what?"

Kya sighs. "It's technically open to everyone because it's a campus event, so yeah."

"Can you imagine how crazy it would be if he showed up," Raven says, stifling a laugh.

"That would like… end racism on this campus just a lil' bit," Makeba agrees.

Kya doesn't seem quite so happy. But she shrugs and appears to give up fighting for once.

"Cool. I have a game after, though."

"Oh, we're definitely coming to that," Raven says grinning. "Go Vipers!"

I guess I passed the tribunal.

❦ 22 ❦

THE WHALER'S GAME

KYA AMBROSE

"How do I look?" I ask my friends as I twirl in front of my standard issue full-length mirror.

Raven answers way too quickly for my tastes. "Like a puck slut." At least she's smiling when she says it, so it's probably mostly a joke.

"Thanks, Raven," I respond sarcastically. "That's exactly what I want to hear from my best friend."

"I meant it as a compliment," Raven covers quickly. She turns her nose down to her book, sneaking in a few more pages while we get ready. I don't mind her shady comment. I totally deserve it for how long I kept Cole a secret from them.

"Fine," I grumble. "I know I deserve it."

"For lying?" Makeba says. "Uh huh."

"I know. I know. I'm the worst. Can I promise to make it up to you guys?"

Makeba and Raven nod eagerly. At least they're giving me a chance, but that doesn't mean they've stopped making comments about Cole. My friends have been throwing shade about me and this new relationship all week. Our first week officially dating. Ugh. I have mixed feelings about the whole thing and they're not wrong to be wary.

It's not really Cole's fault. He's been great as a boyfriend. He's a much better guy when he's not bossing me around or making me clean his stupid, dirty boxers. I don't even know how I got here…

I can't exactly blame my friends for not trusting our relationship. I started off by telling them I wanted to rip Cole's heart out with my bare hands, and now I can't stop talking about the sweet text messages he sends me or our magical first date. Ugh. Feelings are complicated.

Cole texts me every morning during our first week "together" and we have dinner together after hockey practice every night. I learned about the first hockey game he went to, how hard he worked to get his scholarship to Laguna Grove, and then tons of stories about his teammates and coaches — all the guys who made it easy for him to forget that his dad left. Cole listens attentively and asks tons of questions about my life. He doesn't even seem to care about my dad too much, which is nice. He just asks what it was like for me growing up with my dad's mistresses always around the corner or listening to him fight with my mom.

"I never want to be like that with you," he says.

He scares me when he says stuff like that, because Cole almost sounds serious. There's still a part of me that can't believe he would care about anything other than sex or hockey. I don't hold back telling him that and he laughs.

"Maybe after we're dating a while, you'll realize I'm not such an evil misogynistic pig or whatever."

He listens patiently to my lecture on that comment and then tells me my rants distract him from how freaked out he is over the game. Raven and Makeba aren't nervous at all. They're just excited we got great seats in the student section thanks to Cole and that there's a chance they could meet some cute guys there. Makeba has a boyfriend, but Raven is still looking for her cute guy. (And Raven's convinced Makeba needs to toss BJ back into the sea, but we're trying to support her new bae.)

It's a big game for Cole because three of the agents we met on Agent Night are going to be there watching him. Dylan and Mike will both be there and they're really into Cole's game. It's a big game for me because I need my friends to know that I'm not totally different because I have a boyfriend now. I'm still the same old Kya.

Tonight, Cole insists that I wear something special to support him, and even if he's not blackmailing me anymore, I agree, which makes Cole's freaking day.

I'm wearing a jersey from his first season at Laguna Grove with SEABROOK on the back and Cole's number. He's always been #59 no matter where he's played and this vintage jersey replica looks pretty cute, even if it's enormous on me. It's forest green with silver trim, a giant open-mouthed viper on the front and #59 on the sleeves and back. I spin around in the mirror, admiring the jersey which I've paired with a pair of Dolce & Gabbana leggings plus Tory Burch black boots. I wear a black turtleneck from Prada underneath so the itchy jersey material doesn't mess with my skin.

"This had better be fun," Makeba sighs. "I'm still a stupid virgin and BJ is getting on my last nerve. He's seriously the worst boyfriend ever."

"Why don't you dump him!"

"I'm close to having sex with him," Makeba says. "I can tell."

"Couldn't you find another guy who wants to have sex like… ASAP?" Raven points out.

"When has banging an asshole ever worked out for a character in your novels?" Makeba shoots back.

I wonder privately who claimed BJ wasn't an asshole. He hasn't weirded me out or anything, but I've never taken to his vibe. My friends think I just don't like white people, but I like Cole just fine. And I have white friends back in L.A. they don't even know about. Some people just have a vibe.

Raven's response flies off the tip of her tongue. "Actually, banging the asshole pretty much works out 100% of the time. Look at Kya."

"Cole isn't an asshole!"

"He is," Makeba says. "He's just your asshole now."

"He used half my bottle of jojoba oil," Raven says. "That makes him an asshole. But Makeba's right and hey… according to you, he has a pretty big wiener."

"Raven!"

Raven and Makeba enjoy laughter at my expense. I don't worry about saving my reputation because Cole actually replaced Raven's jojoba oil. I'm the one who forgot to give it to her.

I tell Raven that I'm the one at fault and set the brand new bottle on her dresser. My cheeks grow hot remembering the nasty things Cole and I did with that oil. I wonder if he bought a spare bottle for us to use just in case…

"Do we have anything better to do on a Friday night?" I tell Makeba. "Even if BJ's being an asshole, you deserve to go out and have fun. He's not planning dates or inviting you anywhere. Maybe he needs to learn that there's a risk of losing you."

Makeba twists her hair back and pins it together with a brown crab clip. Her cheekbones look phenomenal with her hair up, but she refuses to dress up like a super fan for the hockey game, sticking with flared navy jeans and an oversized Laguna Grove hoodie with a hole in it. Makeba doesn't care about fashion at all. It's such a change compared to people from L.A.

"Kya's right," Raven sighs with frustration. "I'm tired of being single. Maybe I'll meet a guy at the game."

Raven's definitely dressed like she's trying to meet a guy and I don't have the heart to tell her that meeting a guy she'll actually like in the bleachers of the hockey game is fairly unlikely. Maybe at the hockey after party she'll have some luck. She wears this adorable black velvet dress with leggings and a pair of champagne riding boots with high knee socks to handle the rink's icy chill.

"To meet a guy at the game, we actually have to get there," Makeba says. "Can we take a picture and get out of here? BJ still hasn't texted me back from hours ago."

My friends and I take a picture together, then Raven and I sympathize with Makeba for her boy problems. We look great. I hope this is a night we remember forever. After our picture, I cheer Raven and Makeba up about their boy problems by describing my latest escapade with one of Dustin's escaped tarantulas while I was lying in Cole's bed. We all enjoy shrieking about weird white boys and their exotic pets.

I don't want to rub in how happy I am to be with Cole, but it's honestly all I can think about as we prepare to walk over to the rink. We're still in that exciting new phase where I don't know what's going to happen next, but this is his first game where we're officially dating. It feels automatically special and I'm in a hurry to get to our seats.

Raven and Makeba oblige my desire to rush, gossiping about the boys they've met on the hockey team as we walk over. Makeba says Jayce Clutterbuck is in one of her classes, but she doesn't know him well. Raven still thinks all the guys on the team are assholes.

"Except Cole," she says reassuringly.

We walk over together to the Laguna Grove U. hockey rink with our fly ass outfits and homemade fan signs. I made signs for both my friends and then one that says GO SEABROOK #59.

"So," Raven says. "We're officially Laguna Grove girls. Going to a hockey game instead of watching TV in a back room."

"Don't let fame change you, Kya," Makeba warns with a bemused tone of voice.

"I'm not famous, and neither is Cole. Trust me, I'm not different because we're going to a hockey game."

"Don't let him change you," Makeba says. "That's all we're saying."

"And make sure he isn't just tricking you to blackmail you again," Raven says. "He could be faking everything."

That accusation burns my cheeks, but I don't want Raven to know her words are getting to me. I don't want to think Cole is faking our entire relationship. What we have definitely feels real. Then again, he ate me out the first night I climbed into his bed. I guess he could be faking.

"I won't let him change me. And I won't let him use me. I promise. Now let's go have fun!"

My friends don't notice how Raven's comment immediately soured my mood. At least Raven changes the subject to her more pressing concern — online dating. I think her romance novel addiction is finally getting to her head, because she wants a boyfriend now and it's driving her crazy.

Raven pulls her phone out and opens up this new app she's into Flinger, casually glancing at profiles with a disinterested look on her face. I guess she isn't seeing anything or anyone inspiring. Raven exhales dramatically.

"All this relationship talk is making me wish I wasn't single," Raven says. "Maybe I'm just jealous."

"Stop it! You are not jealous. You're looking out for me."

"Nah, she's jealous," Makeba said. "At least I have a man. I don't know about her."

Makeba says this with a smirk on her face — she has a dark sense of humor — and Raven smacks our mischievous friend with a cellphone.

"Dating BJ doesn't count as having a man," Raven says sharply.

"Whatever. Don't be dissing my man," Makeba responds defensively.

Speaking of BJ...

"Where is BJ? Didn't you at least try to invite him tonight? He is your boyfriend after all."

I definitely didn't want Makeba to feel like we weren't supporting her new relationship, although Raven is explicitly not supporting her new relationship.

"He didn't want to come. He has a gaming thing with his buddies."

"Oh. But it's Friday night!? You're dating!"

"Yeah."

Makeba looks really sad, so I elbow Raven. She glances up from her phone and gives Makeba a confused look.

"Wait, is everything okay with you and BJ?"

"I don't know," Makeba answers. "I've never had a boyfriend before, so I don't really know what's normal. I don't want you guys to judge me."

"So? I won't judge you. I've never had a boyfriend either. And the guys on Flinger are all weird," Raven says, at least doing her best to offer some hope.

"Kya? Promise you won't judge? You're dating like... one of the hottest guys on campus."

"Why would I judge? You're our best friend, Makeba. We're here to give you guy advice. You both accepted Cole. I'm loyal."

"Fine," Makeba relents. "I just feel weird with BJ. I mean... I asked him out. He said yes. But he doesn't really do boyfriend stuff."

"Have you guys hooked up?" I ask, trying to gauge the situation between them. Maybe he's one of those guys who takes things slow, or maybe he's only looking for sex and Makeba should get out before she gets in too deep.

Makeba shrugs. "I guess. Kind of?"

I don't know what that answer means precisely. Can you 'kind of' hook up? Before I can give a rational answer, Raven intervenes.

"Wait, sex?!" Raven shrieks, with the kind of aggressive disbelief that earns her a glare from Makeba.

"Can you not scream that at the entire hockey rink? And no, we haven't had sex."

"So then... how did you hook up?" I ask. I'm trying to get as much information as possible out of Makeba, and it's not like her to be so secretive about stuff. This is the girl who has no problem changing in front of us or making me help her do a sniff test on her socks. We're tight. Makeba covers her face with her hands and tries desperately to explain "the BJ hookup situation".

"I sort of pounced on him and we made out, and then he said he wanted us to date more before he did anything."

"Maybe he's gay," Raven suggests with far too much glee in her voice, like she's forgotten this is our best friend we're talking about and not some character in a romance novel. I elbow her.

"BJ is not gay. Have you tried talking to him?" I suggest to Makeba, giving her something to work with as a replacement for Raven's cynicism.

"He doesn't really like talking about our relationship. I mean, he likes video games and we play those sometimes, but he just shuts me down if I bring up sex. I don't know. I keep trying, but he won't even come out on the weekends with me. Is having a boyfriend supposed to be this hard?"

Raven and I exchange glances because we both know that having a boyfriend is definitely not supposed to be that hard. Raven tries not to say "I told you so", but she warned Makeba a hundred times about going after BJ. At least now, she steps up to defend our bestie.

"He's being an asshole," Raven says. "I'll text him.'

"No! That would be embarrassing," Makeba says, snatching Raven's phone, apparently prematurely. Makeba gawks at the phone, which apparently contains something horrific on the screen.

The pre-game skate starts, but I don't bother looking for Cole on the ice yet. I'll have plenty of time to watch him play when the game starts. Right now, I have a Raven-related emergency to attend to.

"Please tell me you did not heart this guy," Makeba says desperately, sufficiently distracted from her BJ problems.

Makeba thrusts the phone in my face. A picture of a rotund, bearded man named Bubba M. holding a fish and wearing sunglasses greets me. His Flinger app bio states, I'm looking for a girl who likes one wipe poops, camping trips in the deep woods, low-maintenance dates and isn't a total bitch. If you think you're worthy of my time, hit me up. No sluts.

I recoil instinctively. These can't be the men Raven is subjecting herself to. I guess Flinger is explicitly for flings, but the only "fling" I want to have with this Bubba character involves "flinging" him into a nearby trash can. Raven definitely deserves better.

"Give me that!" Raven says, her copper cheeks darkening with embarrassment.

"No way. Please tell me you are not going to talk to this guy," I plead with her. It's officially time for an intervention.

"Of course not!"

I still won't give Raven her phone back. The next guy to pop up has a literal hate symbol tattooed on his neck. As Raven grabs for her phone, I hastily delete Flinger.

"Hey! Why did you delete it? I need that to meet guys!"

I raise my eyebrow suspiciously. Come on, Raven.

"Because," I tell her. "You're not going to meet a decent guy on that app. And Makeba, you deserve way better than BJ. I know he's our friend and I know he seems cool, but... you deserve a guy who will move the sun and the stars for you."

Makeba groans and covers her face. "I'm not like you, Kya. I can't just attract hot guys. I'm basic. I'm plain. I'm simple. I study too much, read too much and I never leave my room. And anyway, guys at Laguna Grove don't like dark-skinned girls."

"I'm not that light!" I say.

"Um, yeah, you are," Raven says, even if she's not much darker than me, just more copper colored than a deep walnut. Now my friends are getting on my nerves. It's just a complete lie that dark-skinned women can't find love.

"Love has nothing to do with my color. If some guy doesn't want to date you because you're dark skinned, he's trash. Seriously. And there are plenty of guys who aren't trash."

"Since when do you believe that?" Makeba asks.

"You know what… maybe I've had a temporary, almost sort of change of heart. And you are not the problem either, Makeba. It's the bad men out there who insist on wasting our time while we search for our Prince Charming."

Makeba gives me a quizzical look as if she never considered the fact that the guys might be the problem and not us. Before I can give her more reassurance, the game buzzer sounds around the rink. I've been so busy chatting with my friends that I haven't kept up with what's happening on the ice. Oops.

"Oh shit, it's starting," Raven says, snatching her phone back from me more successfully this time. "Let's watch."

The start of the game is relatively quiet as we all try to figure out what's going on. Raven and Makeba scan the ice for the puck, but I just want to see Cole… I know this game is important to him and he's totally been freaking out in his dumb Cole way.

"Look, he has the round thing!" Makeba says excitedly. "Go Cole!"

Cole passes to Hargreaves, who skates around a player from the Westbrook Whalers (the opposing team) and then gets slammed into the board by one of their defensemen, who looks about a foot taller than the tallest guy on our team. The crowd makes a dramatic sound of disappointment as Hargreaves lands on his back and slides across the ice, relinquishing the puck to a guy on the other team. That guy is a brutally fast skater and the Vipers have a hard time keeping up with the passes for a bit. Great. Now I'm worried about the game.

After a hard battle, which Cole is mostly uninvolved in as an offensive player, the Whalers tap in the first point. The rink is dead silent with disappointment as the score flips 1-0 in the Whalers' favor. I can tell from looking at Cole's face beneath his helmet that he's furious. The Whalers are ranked dead last in our school league. There's no way they should be able to get a point past the Laguna Grove goalie.

Ugh, look at me. A few minutes of dating Cole and I'm already talking about his stupid sport like I care.

"GO COLE!" Raven screams when he slams a Whaler into the boards. I guess she's getting into hockey, so I have no reason not to do the same. Fueled by rage, Cole grabs the puck and skates around #14 for the Whalers. Holy shit. He's doing it... he has a breakaway.

The crowd goes wild as Cole shoots on the goal and scores for our team. I stand up and bang on the boards, pressing my sign against the clear plexiglass as Cole pumps his fists and then fist bumps his teammates. This game is heating up and I see men in suits watching from the other side of the ice. Dylan's here and he can't keep his eyes off Cole. He worked with my dad's friend, Duke Trent, a freshman pro-basketball player on his team.

The score stays tied after the first period. Cole looks red when he skates off the ice. He must be tired from playing most of the period. During the break, Raven and Makeba eagerly return to chatting about Raven's online dating prospects.

"Did you even find one decent guy on there?"

"Yes," Raven answers defensively. "Tom."

"Who the hell is Tom?" Makeba asks.

"He's a bricklayer currently out of work who unfortunately had his Dodge Ram repossessed because his crazy ex-girlfriend made him pay too much in child support and he couldn't afford it. I could tell he had a good heart."

Makeba and I exchange suspicious glances.

"What if I set you up with someone?" I ask her, desperate to have Raven to talk to someone normal, who goes to our freaking school and maybe doesn't have a dead deer (or God knows what else) in his freezer?

"Who would you set me up with? The only guy you know is Cole."

"Ouch. I also know guys on Cole's team."

"I'd have a better time dating Tom," Raven answers pessimistically. We get nowhere with her dating troubles when the second period starts. Cole isn't in the starting line this time, but I can't help watching him leaning over the boards, staring fiercely at the players on the ice. While Cole is on the bench, Jayce Clutterbuck nearly scores twice, sending the crowd on the Laguna Grove side of the rink crazy. But nearly goals don't count and we need to win this.

Halfway through the second period, a miracle happens. Hargreaves grabs the puck from a Whaler's player on a breakaway and quickly flips it out of Vipers' ice. The crowd erupts as he passes to Jayce, who finally makes a goal. It's 2-1. We're winning! I leap into the air with my friends as we cheer along with the rest of the crowd. As we're cheering, I notice Cole's mom entering the rink. Her seat is behind ours. Once she sees me, her face lights up. The first time we met, Cole lied and told her I was his girlfriend. Now that it's the truth, she's all caught up.

"Kya Ambrose! You look more beautiful than the first day I met you. Come here, hun."

Makeba and Raven have no idea what's going on, but they stare on curiously as I hug this blond white woman.

"New highlights?" I ask her. Cole's mom beams.

"You noticed! And I noticed your curls are moisturizing and luscious. Are these ladies your friends?"

Before long, Cole's mom has us chatting, and she gives Raven the phone number of a woman who does amazing braids in her city. Apparently, the hair stylist circuit is tight. We finish watching the second period together, although the game has another shift away from the Vipers' favor. A West-brook freshman scores again and we're heading into the third period with a 2-2 score. During the break between the second and third period, Cole's mom shows us her clients' before and after pictures on her phone and tells us the story of her most famous client yet...

"Sebastian Jefferson moved to our town," she gushes. "I picked his latest shade of platinum."

"Shut the front door," Makeba gasps. (She loves Rebel Blood.)

Our excited conversation only peters out when the third period starts and Cole's back on the ice. His mom watches him with rapt attention. I know how much he loves her and I get it. She's cool. Really cool.

The third period is slower than we all want. No one scores. But games don't end with a tie in hockey, apparently. I asked

Cole why once, and he acted like I'd asked him why the sky was blue. It incensed him. Now, I can see why. The pressure's up during overtime. Cole's not on the ice for most of overtime, but he's nervous. The game goes all the way to a shootout.

I've never actually seen one of these "shootouts" but according to Cole, it's the "worst fucking thing you'll ever experience as a player". I asked him if getting gonorrhea from random girls in his bed might be worse and he tickled me nearly to death. That was before we were dating. Before feelings. Or maybe those were our feelings coming out in our weird fucked up way.

The announcer tells us who will shoot for each time. Only one name sticks out in my head. Cole Seabrook. The first shooter for the Vipers is this sophomore kid named Benji Coyle, who has slept with half the white girls in our year. I don't know him well, but his distinct wheat-colored hockey flow sticks out the back of his helmet, earning hushed gasps from several of his paramours in the crowd. He makes the shot. Our school goes wild with pride, but Cole's mom is silent. She knows hockey better than any of us. This game could easily tip in the Whalers' favor. The crazy thing about Cole's career is he's not the only one who affects it. The entire team matters.

The Whalers make their first shot too. Cole's mom unconsciously taps on her black purse, her well-manicured nails picking at some of the worn leather. The next shooter for Laguna Grove is Dustin Rathbone. For once, I'm thinking something positive about Dustin. I spent most of the season finding his gross exotic pets scampering around Pesthouse. He smokes so much weed that he has to be psychically linked to Snoop Dogg.

I cross my fingers and I hope he makes it in. There's fancy footwork and then a tap into the corner of the net. He fucking made it! The crowd goes wild again and we go even wilder when the Whalers miss their next shot. This is it. The last shot on goal. If Cole makes it in, Laguna Grove wins the game 3-2 and he'll probably secure an offer to play professional hockey. Everything comes down to this moment.

You can do this, Cole.

He skates toward the net almost casually. You could hear a pin drop in the rink. When he whacks the puck with his stick, you can hear the power behind the shot ringing around the room. It's in the dead center of the net. He made it. Cole won the game.

Everyone goes crazy. Everyone knows how important this game is to our standing in our school's league, and I know just how important this game is for Cole. Cole's mom grabs my hand and rushes toward the ice.

"Come on, we have to see him!"

I wave a quick goodbye to Makeba and Raven, who understand that I don't really have a choice but to follow Cole's mom over to him. The doors to the ice open and the boys skate toward the exit, cheering their victory. Cole comes off the ice, his cheeks red hot and his hair sticking to his neck. He smells gross, obviously, but he's just played the hardest hour of his life and I can tell. He grins once he sees us.

My heart does that weird flip in my stomach — like everything's perfect, but I'm still nervous Cole will turn this all around and write my sex stories on the bathroom wall in Sharpie.

"Hey, ladies," Cole greets us. His smile is so contagious.

Cole's mom doesn't care that he's covered in sweat. She wraps him in a big hug and Cole hugs her back, looking more like a little boy than the monster I observed in our women's studies class. His mom promises to wait for him outside so she can take him to dinner — their hockey game tradition — and she leaves the two of us alone. Well, as alone as you can be in a hallway with other hockey players, coaches, agents and students milling about.

"You were amazing!"

Cole grins. "You weren't on your phone the whole time."

"No way! That was amazing."

"Thanks for coming, babe."

I can't help myself. I lunge for him and wrap my arms around Cole's sweaty body. He hugs me, laughing as he takes his gloves off.

"I thought I was gross after games?"

"Did I say that?"

"Yes. You said I was the nastiest white boy you'd ever met."

"Well, I don't remember that."

"Let me kiss you, then," Cole teases, running his sweaty finger over my lips. His hands smell like his disgusting hockey gloves and his fingers taste like salt. But beneath all that is Cole — warm, handsome, sexy ass, annoying ass Cole.

"Cole, ew!"

I squeal dramatically, but I'm not that grossed out because I want to kiss him really badly. I don't mind the salt on his lips when he kisses me. I just love tasting him. Touching him. Belonging to him. Everyone's congratulating Cole as they walk by and he just has his arm around me and his eyes on mine. Another pair of eyes seek us out in the hall.

Tuck Murphy. He's a Laguna Grove legend, but he scares the crap out of me. Cole's hockey coach (and Laguna Grove alumnus) storms over to Cole with a scowl on his face.

"Where the hell have you been, Seabrook? Get back here. There's some serious shit we need to talk about. Come on. Now."

࿐   23   ࿐

CHRISTMAS EVE

COLE SEABROOK

It all worked out. Two months ago, I signed an agent — Dylan — with Tuck Murphy sternly looking on and congratulating me.

Once this season's over, if I keep playing well, I'll have a gig lined up. A big time gig. Several million dollar contracts.

A way to take care of my mom and Kya. I want it so fucking bad it hurts. But I still need to wait… I still need to play like a fucking beast. I can't screw up.

Two months ago, after the game, I asked Kya to spend Christmas vacation with me. It's the first time I'll be mostly off the ice before we continue the season. I finally have time for her… the girl I love. I haven't told her that or anything. It's only been two months of dating, a little longer if you count the time she was my servant. (She chooses not to count it, I don't know why.)

Kya agreed to the Christmas vacation thing and my mom clearly spent the past two months going crazy setting up the house for her guest. She loves Kya and won't stop dropping hints. My last text from my mom just said, "Get married." She pretended like she meant it for someone else, but I'm pretty sure that was her way of sending a subtle message. I like this one.

"I gotta warn you, Ambrose, I don't live in a big fancy mansion like you're used to."

"Mansions are overrated. I prefer penthouses."

"You are so annoying."

"What's annoying about that?"

Seriously, Kya is freaking clueless sometimes. I love her, though. I guess it happened the night of the Whaler's game. I totally loved her before that, but after the game, I saw her there with that big smile on her face and she let me kiss her and smell that pretty head of hair. Yup, I got what I wanted and now I'm in love.

On Christmas Eve, I'll tell her. I have it all planned out and it'll be a huge surprise for Kya.

When I pull my car up to our modest small town family home, Kya's grinning. I can't really tell what's making her smile. Mom doesn't get home until 7 from the salon, so we have the place to ourselves for a couple hours.

I approach the front door and let myself in, my duffel and three of Kya's slung over my shoulders.

"Are you sure you don't mind carrying everything?" She chirps behind me as she searches for some lip gloss or whatever in her purse.

"This is only half your stuff," I remind her. "And I don't mind."

"Will your mom let us sleep in the same bed?"

"I'm 21. I can do what I want."

Kya looks at me like I'm crazy, but I don't get it. I point to the little flight of stairs. Before we can make it upstairs, the dogs are going crazy. Mom keeps them on one side of the house so they don't eat her shoes while she's at work. I open the dining-room door. Champ, our golden retriever, runs straight to a shrieking Kya with his tail wagging like crazy.

"Hey, Champ," I say as I hear Oochie wheezing behind him. Once Champ settles his paws on Kya's lap, Oochie finally makes it to the foyer. Our old chihuahua waddles like crazy but can still get around. The only problem is her drool. And her humping problem. Mom says she never quite learned that she was a girl. I don't know what her problem is. Oochie runs straight for Kya's sneaker and begins humping her.

"Cole!" Kya shrieks. "Your dog is humping me!"

"Oochie recognizes a beautiful girl when she sees one."

"Cole!"

I pick Oochie up and give her a little kiss, to Kya's utter dismay. Jealous of the attention I'm doting on Oochie, Champ barks like crazy. Kya pets him to calm him down and Champ responds well to her, sitting and acting like a good boy. I set Oochie down and she immediately starts humping Kya's purse. I wrestle the purse away from Oochie and point upstairs.

"Let's take your stuff to the bedroom."

"Is this a cheap ploy to get me into your room?"

"I think we've already been down that road," I point out. "It's up this way."

We walk upstairs together with Champ and Oochie disappearing into the kitchen, hoping for either food or a walk. I push the door open to my bedroom and feel like a kid again. Kya giggles hysterically.

"Oh. My. God. You are such a boy."

She immediately points to the poster of a hot chick wearing nothing but hockey pads, and I turn red.

"That's just a dumb joke. You weren't supposed to see that."

My mom could have helped me out by taking that down, considering she bought me four freaking scented candles and condoms.

"I can't believe I'm dating… you."

"What's that supposed to mean."

"We're just different, Cole. Doesn't that bother you?"

"No. Maybe I like different."

"Guys like you don't like different. You like… blondes in hockey pads. With fake boobs, by the way. No real woman looks like that."

I laugh and drop her stuff on my bed. Yeah, I know. Chicks in hockey pads are cool, but real women are way cooler. I hope Kya knows that. Whatever. I can always show her and teach her another lesson. She moves her body against mine and my hands grip her waist instinctively. We're here. In my bedroom. And every part of me definitely wants to take her to bed right now.

"Hey, princess," I whisper. "I can like both. And I like this… way more. A real girl. My girl. A girl I have feelings for."

"It's still weird when you get sentimental."

"Maybe because you assumed a lot of awful shit about me," I tell her. "Don't worry. I'll prove you wrong over the holiday."

"I'm just glad I don't have to spend the holidays alone. My dad's always busy training. I guess it'll be the same for you once you get an offer."

"Yeah. I guess. But I'll always make time for you, princess. Always."

I kiss her because I fucking mean that more than anything. Kya's reluctant to kiss me this time. Maybe my kid bedroom's making her feel weird. I can fix that. I shut the lights off and rake my fingers through her gorgeous mass of curly hair. My heart quickens once I feel the smooth strands sliding against my hands. I love that hair. God, it makes me hard just to touch it, especially with her lips against mine.

"Kya," I whisper, on the verge of putting my fancy plans behind me and just telling her the truth.

"What?"

"I… want to fuck you so bad."

The magic words. Kya rolls her eyes.

"So romantic, Cole."

"I want to fuck you… tenderly."

I kiss her and she lets me this time. I love kissing her. Disappearing into her scent. I want to take her to my bed, but I'd take her against the closet too if that was too weird.

"Please tell me you didn't lose your virginity in that bed," she whispers. "That would be weird."

"I lost it in my car. Don't worry."

Kya's fingers tangle with my hair and she pushes me backward onto the bed, climbing on top of me slowly. I love stroking her thighs. They're full and thick. Her hips are perfect to cling to and her hair falls over my chest, making my heart beat faster. I want her more than I've wanted any girl. I think from the second I saw her, part of what pissed me off was knowing a girl like her could never end up with a dude like me. That she wouldn't. She was too prissy. Too pretty. Too different.

"Hey puck head," she whispers. "Don't stop kissing me."

"Sorry."

"Lost in thought?"

"Yeah."

Kya laughs. She still thinks I'm pretty dumb, but that's okay. As long as she likes me, I don't care. Hell, maybe she's right. Maybe I'm dumb as fuck. Again, don't care. I just want Kya.

"We should probably take our clothes off. We're hooking up like high schoolers."

It's my turn to laugh.

"Trust me, none of my high school girlfriends were half as hot as you."

I roll her onto her back and take her clothes off. Once she's mostly naked, I need to taste her. Kya reluctantly spreads her thighs. She's eager for us to make love, but I want her to slow down. I want her to feel my tongue making her cum several times before I even think about putting my dick in her. Kya loves my tongue between her legs. She cums several times before she gives in and starts begging for my dick.

"I just think we need to hurry," she explains in her haughty voice, but I can feel her hips wriggling desperately beneath me and I know she's just horny. I kiss her neck, slowing down even more and feeling her getting hot beneath me.

"No," I whisper. "I want to take my time with you. Always."

Eventually, she yields to my pace, allowing me to kiss her, tease her and enjoy her body with my tongue a few more times before I enter her. Kya makes the most perfect sound when I enter her. I clutch her hips and pull her against me, sinking into her deeper and enjoying her tightness gripping me. Her body lights on fire in my arms and she doesn't take long to orgasm. When she cums, her moans get high-pitched and desperate. I hold her against me so her hard little nipples graze my chest and her thick thighs wrap around me, drawing my pale body close to hers.

Mine. She's finally mine. This is what I wanted all along.

We make love three more times before we hear my mom's car pulling into the garage. Kya tries to dress quickly, which I make more difficult for her by stealing her bra and thong, laughing hysterically while she tries to grab both from my hands. We get dressed in plenty of time to see my mom dragging in groceries and a funny story about a new stylist who works at her salon.

She's ecstatic to see Kya again and they immediately make plans to bake sugar cookies together. It's nice seeing them together. My mom doesn't get much company out here. She's dated no one my entire life. She's made it all about me. I never thought I could date a girl that didn't get along with my mom, but now I'm a little worried they'll start plotting against me.

Kya helps my mom with dinner while I take the dogs for a walk and work on fixing a couple things around the house that have fallen apart since I've been at school. I can hear them laughing and talking about my last game. That first night we have dinner and I can't stop staring at Kya Ambrose. I'm more sure about her than I've been about anyone. I want to tell her I love her. It sucks to have to wait until Christmas Eve. The crazy thing about Kya is that she's definitely worth the wait.

On December 23rd, Kya confesses the truth. She forgot to get me a Christmas gift and please, she needs to go Christmas shopping. She wakes me up at 7 a.m. with an anxious urgency.

"You don't have to get me anything," I mumble. "It's fine."

"Yes, I do! You got me something."

"Yeah. I did. Doesn't matter. Will you come back to bed?"

"Do you do anything besides sleep and skate?! Wake up, Cole!"

Then my girlfriend throws a pillow at my head. Sigh. I get out of bed reluctantly and slide into grey sweatpants and a hoodie.

"Okay. Christmas shopping. On the day before Christmas Eve. Have I ever mentioned how high-maintenance you are?"

"Are black women supposed to be low-maintenance?" She shoots back aggressively.

I'm just sorry I said anything.

"I don't know. I've never dated any black women."

"Ugh, don't remind me."

"What's so wrong with that?"

"I don't want to compete with a bunch of Becky's. That's all. We don't have to talk about it."

"I guess you've dated tons of white guys."

She gets quiet, which is what Kya normally does when I've caught her up in one of her smart chick confusions.

"No. I haven't. But that's not the point."

"What is the point?"

"Whatever, Cole. I can't expect some white guy to get it."

I grab her hand and pull her against me, which surprises her enough that she's not sure if she wants to hit me. I hold her hand against my chest, keeping her pressed to me.

"You aren't competing with anyone, princess. You might be my first black girl, but I want you to be the only one."

"Cole…"

"Don't say anything, princess. We're going shopping."

She makes a huffy noise, but she wrangles her hair back with a clip and slips into her Ugg boots, ready to go. There's a nice mall in Silver Hollow which Kya finds acceptable.

"You can wait for me at the food court," she says, prancing away pretty much the second we get there. I guess I'm waiting at the food court. When she's gone for over two hours, I see why she pranced off without giving me a choice. She also ignored all my texts. She returns laden with shopping bags.

"Uh… what's all that?"

"Christmas presents! I got nothing for your mom, Champ, or Oochie. Plus, I needed to get something for Makeba and Raven when I get back to school."

"I feel glued to this chair."

"You were so patient, Cole. Thanks."

Then she kisses me on the cheek and suddenly I feel like I could wait another two hours in that chair just for another kiss. I carry her bags to the car and get her one of her insane coffee orders at the drive thru.

"Want a taste?"

"It's coffee. Why is it white?"

"The sugar," Kya says, slurping as much as she possibly can in one gulp. Yeah, I don't get her. But whatever. It's almost Christmas, which means it's almost time for me to tell her how I feel. Once we're home, she heads upstairs to take a shower and my mom corners me in the kitchen.

"Cole! Come help me with the… with chopping the potatoes."

"Sure, mom."

I can always tell when my mom wants to tell me something. We're pretty close because we had to be. All those years without my dad and all we had was each other.

"Kya's a very sweet girl."

"I'm glad you like her."

"She's beautiful. She's smart. She's funny. She's not like any of your previous girlfriends."

"I thought you liked Jessica."

"Vicodin Jessica?"

"She had a little problem."

"Well, Kya doesn't have any problems. So please do me a favor and don't screw this up? I want you to have someone, Cole. I mean it."

"What about you?"

My mom smirks. "I do have someone."

"What? Since when?"

"Oh, that's none of your business. But he's a good guy. That's all you need to know."

"If you need me to kick his ass, I'll do it."

"I can handle myself. You need to handle yourself. You're my son. I know you better than I know anyone. You care about hockey and you care about Kya. Just remember that your life off the ice is important too."

"I get it."

"Don't screw up."

"I won't."

"Good. Now get out."

"I thought you needed help?"

"Oh. That was an excuse I made to get you in here. Run along. Shoo!"

After dinner on the 23rd, Kya and I watch some chick Hallmark movie together. It's not as bad as I thought it would be.

Kya curls up on my lap and her hair spreads out on my shoulders as she leans against my chest.

"I love romantic movies at Christmas," she whispers. "It's just… everything."

"Are you seriously crying?"

"No! I'm not crying. Those are from onions. In the shower."

"Onions in the shower?"

"Shut up."

"You are… such a goof."

"Thanks, Cole."

"I mean it."

"Again. Thanks," she grumbles.

"Come here, goof."

She lets me kiss her, so maybe she's not that mad at me. On the morning of Christmas Eve, I am losing my shit. Tonight, I'm telling Kya how I feel after dinner. My mom has a party with her coworkers so tonight, dinner's on me. Kya seems skeptical that I can cook, but I didn't grow up with a single mom and not learn how to cook.

After the best Christmas Eve ever, Kya's words, not mine, I get ready to make us a roast with seared asparagus, potatoes and a couple other sides. Kya plays with Champ in the kitchen while I'm working on the food.

"Are you sure you don't want help?"

"I'm cooking you a special dinner. Can you let me work?"

"No. I'm a control freak, in case you hadn't noticed."

"Control this."

I swipe flour on her nose.

"Cole!"

"Wow, are you wearing white face? That's pretty offensive Kya..."

"Cole! You are so not funny." She brushes the flour off her nose and hops onto the counter with the mug of coffee I made her a few minutes ago. She looks all cute, bent over sipping from it. Soon. I can't wait to see the look on her face when I tell her I love her. We've spent all week watching romantic movies and I've basically made it really obvious.

Once everything's in the oven, Kya looks especially cute perched on my counter. I want to have her there. We make out for a bit, but then it gets so hard not to sleep with her that I have to remind myself sleeping with her now will ruin everything and I need tonight to be perfect. Her thighs wrap around me and she rakes her fingers through my hair.

"It's so silky," she whispers. "I never thought I'd like white boy hair."

"Ouch."

"Sorry," she says. "It's just... exotic."

"Exotic?!"

"Yeah. It's weird."

"I'm going to report you to the woke police."

"Shut up, Cole."

"Anything for you, baby."

I send Kya upstairs to get ready for dinner and I quickly change in our guest bathroom downstairs. I want to look good for her. Formal pants. A white shirt. A little gel in my hair. Whatever. I never put in an effort like this for anyone but for Kya it feels right. When she comes downstairs, we meet in the dining room. Oochie trails behind Kya, eager to hump her leg now that she has a new outfit and new perfume.

"Oochie, down!" Kya shrieks, her heels tapping aggressively as she runs toward me. She nearly slips, but I catch her before she falls.

"Thank you," Kya says huffily, pulling away and fluffing out her hair.

"You look great, babe."

"So do you."

"Dinner is served."

"This is elaborate. But we'll have to taste it."

"What, don't think a guy can throw down in the kitchen?"

"Well, I'm not sexist Cole," she says and starts off on one of her little lectures. It goes on for a while as I pour her some wine. I'll need plenty of wine myself if I'm going to make it through this dinner. I'm so nervous. More nervous than any hockey game I've ever played. My mom's right. Maybe it's time for me to think about something other than hockey too.

Halfway through dinner, Kya clears her throat.

"What?"

"I have never heard you this quiet."

"I could say the same to you, babe."

"Cole, stop messing around. What's going on? You're acting all weird and romantic. It's freaking me out."

"Can't a guy treat his girlfriend on Christmas Eve?"

"Yes. But you're not even teasing me. Calling me a parakeet or whatever."

"Oh, you're definitely still like a parakeet."

"Then what the hell is going on with you?"

"I did all this tonight because I have to tell you something, Kya. Something huge."

"You're gay!?" Kya blurts out, slamming her hands on the table.

"What? Why would you assume I'm gay?"

"Sorry. Just paranoid. Holidays are always weird at my house."

I raise an eyebrow, but judging by some of her crazy stories, I believe her.

"Listen, babe. I know we had a weird start. Truth is, I can't keep this from you anymore."

"Oh my God… you knocked up another girl."

"Can you pipe down and let me finish?"

"Pipe down?" Kya shrills. "A man telling a woman to pipe down? Does that sound progressive to you, Cole? Does it sound—

"Damn it, Kya. I love you, okay? I fucking love you. I love your hair. I love your smile. I love the way you get me so pissed off. I love the way you can't ever stop fucking talking. I love it, okay? I fucking love you."

This catches her off guard. I can tell. But I don't care. I can't look at Kya anymore in that sexy dress, with her perfect curves and curls for days without saying anything. My mom's right. I always put hockey first. I always put myself first. This time, I can't screw up. This time, I have to do something different and let Kya know that I'm not going anywhere.

But why isn't she saying anything back? Why the hell is my noisy little parakeet so freaking quiet for a change?

THE LOVE QUESTION

KYA AMBROSE

My heart has never raced so fast before. I never expected to be in this position. I'm sitting across from one of Laguna Grove's hottest guys and he's telling me that he loves me. But this doesn't make any sense. A few months ago, Cole kidnapped me. He kept me in his bedroom as a servant for his own selfish gratification. Now, after a few short months, he's claiming to love me?

I know the fear pulsing throughout me means something. It has to mean something and I decide that it means Cole is pulling the wool over my eyes. His cruel joke never stopped, and he's finally taken it all the way to the edge so he can secure my complete humiliation. I keep trying to read whatever's behind those demonic blue eyes, but I can't see anything there that doesn't scare the crap out of me.

"Y-you love me?"

I don't sound like myself. But I'm trying to act like myself quickly. I need to prove to Cole he's wrong. I need to tell him the fifteen thousand reasons why he can't possibly love me. Everything about our Christmas holiday has been suspiciously perfect. Too perfect. Even this night is too crazy to be real. This stuff just doesn't happen in college. You don't meet an asshole athlete with a perfect body who makes you his servant and then falls in love with you.

I'm way too smart to fall for this obvious trick.

"Yes," Cole answers. "Duh. I love you, Kya. I mean… look at all this. Would I do this if I didn't love you?"

He's right that the dining room is beautiful. Dinner was perfect. He even brought out candles that flicker slowly, filling the room with a warm, penetrating glow. The smell of the roast and veggies seared in olive oil still fills the room. Then there's the red wine. Not only does it smell amazing, but over the course of our dinner, the wine only added to my warmth. I yearn for it. Obviously. But if there's one thing I know about love, it's that you have to be careful.

Really careful. And if I really think about it… all this is suspiciously perfect. Love isn't like this. It's messy. It's cheating and fighting. It's evil men fucking with you. Men don't just straighten up and act all perfect because it's Christmas Eve.

"You don't love me," I tell him. "This is just part of your blackmail, isn't it?"

"What? Kya, you can't be serious."

"Of course I'm serious. Come on, Cole. You almost had me. The past few months, you've been laying it on thick and this is all just part of your grand plan, isn't it?"

"What? What grand plan?" He answers, his voice steeling. I know I'm about to draw the truth out of him.

"Your grand plan to trick me into falling for you so that you can humiliate me."

"You think I would date you for months just to trick you?"

I hate that he sounds offended. Stupid Cole has no right to be offended. He's only mad that he got caught in the act of his stupid plan to trick me. That has to be the best explanation.

"Yes," I said. "And now, I've caught you."

"I put on a collared shirt."

"And?"

"Kya, I fucking love you."

Every girl would want to believe him in my position, which is exactly why I mustn't. Cole's a player. A douche bag. An athlete who calls women "sluts" or "babe". He's not the guy I end up with. He's not a guy I should fall in love with. Every girl wants to believe there's a beauty behind the beast. Maybe they're wrong. Sometimes, a beast is just a beast, believe it or not.

"I don't believe you."

"Is that why you won't say it back?"

I stand up, ready to leave dinner, although I don't know where I'm going. Tomorrow is Christmas Day. I haven't heard from my parents at all, not like I really expect to. Christmas is the anniversary of my mom finding out about my dad's side piece — the one who got pregnant — and it hasn't been the same since. Cole wants me to feel all warm and fuzzy, but I just can't. I don't know how.

"That's not why. I won't say it back because I don't want you to win."

"I'm not trying to win anything," Cole snaps, getting up too. Shit. If he catches on that I'm about to escape, I'm in trouble. I glance at the door and quickly come up with a strategy. I can bolt, let Champ out into the foyer, and then run outside. This place is sort of in the middle of nowhere, but I can get a taxi to the airport and just… escape.

"Yes, you are."

I take a step toward the door and before I know it, Cole's standing in front of me. I can't run now. He'll grab me. Subdue me. I know enough about Cole to predict that much about his behavior.

"Fucking hell, Kya. What's going on with you? I did all this because I care. I planned this for weeks. I love you. And I don't know what I have to do to prove it to you, but I will win your trust. I don't like losing. Especially not that."

He's giving me the most intense look I've seen on Cole's face ever and it scares the ever living crap out of me.

"Cole…"

"What the hell are you afraid of, babe?"

"Nothing."

"Bullshit. I know you. And nothing you say to me could scare me away. Nothing."

"Stop to, Cole…"

"Talk," he whispers. "Or I'm not letting you out of this room."

He puts his hands on my hips and pulls my body against his. I feel this wellspring of emotion that I've never expressed bubbling to the surface and as tears come to my eyes, I feel so small, pathetic and weak. I've never cried in front of Cole, and I don't really cry in front of everyone. I definitely don't tell anyone about my complicated, stupid NBA family.

"Your house is so warm," I murmur and the acknowledgement makes the tears fall. "I grew up in the nicest parts of America, but everything was always so cold. So distant. It's what I liked about you at first... you were cold. And it was just so familiar... and then... you became... something else."

Cole stops my lips with his. It's a kiss that tells me I'm not scaring him away with my big, wild emotions that just spill out of me. That he isn't going anywhere. I pull away from him and shudder, my palms pressed to his chest fill me with desire and nerves in equal measure.

"I'm right here," he whispers.

"I've never had a warm home. My dad provides for me, my mom tries, but... she's mostly busy chasing down my dad's mistresses. I love that you play hockey, but I know where this ends. I'm going to be your sad, lonely wife while you chase women up and down the country. That's where love ends."

"That's not true, Kya," he whispers. Fuck. Why do I want to believe him so badly? Am I really that weak?

When I'm quiet for too long, Cole whispers again. "I love you. And I'm not your dad. I will not cheat. I will not leave you in a big, cold house all alone. I don't care what I have to do. My dad was a pretty big dick. I promised myself a long time ago that I'd never be like him. Never."

"You have no idea what life you're going to have," I remind him. "You have no idea how much temptation you'll have."

Cole grins, which is a totally irritating response, considering how freaking serious I am.

"Temptation?" He whispers. "There isn't a woman alive who could tempt me away from you, Ambrose. I am head over heels in love and I've never felt this way before. I know I'm not going to feel this way again. A man knows what he wants."

"Women know what they want too," I protest, mostly because I don't want Cole thinking he's won any victories against my feminism.

"Fine," he says. "Can this woman tell me what she wants? Because I love you, but… you confuse me, Ambrose. One minute you hate my guts, the next minute you're all over me. So tell me what you want. Now."

"I want… I want to trust you. I want to be with you."

"Then be with me, babe. 'Cause I'm not going anywhere."

"You don't understand… I love you, Cole. And that's the scariest thing in the world to me."

"Don't worry, babe. It scares the crap out of me, too. Now come here…"

He tilts my chin up to face him and he gazes into my eyes. His eyes are so intense. I never really gave white guys the time of day and I've definitely never been the type to get all obsessed with a guy because his eyes are blue, but Cole's eyes are different. They're like the entire Midwestern sky captured in two perfect circles. My breath catches as he kisses me softly.

"I love you, Kya Ambrose. I promise you, everything I feel is real."

"I love you too."

Cole's chest shudders.

"Finally."

"Finally?"

"You make me work so fucking hard for everything."

"Yeah, that's what you're supposed to do hat trick," I reply, teasing his five o'clock shadow with my fingers, allowing myself to touch him and allowing my heart to crack open just enough that Cole Seabrook can weasel his way in. I want him so badly... and I badly want this to be real.

Cole grins.

"You are definitely worth the hard work," he whispers. "Definitely."

His hands stray from my hips to my butt. Cole has always had an obsession with my butt that he's terrible at trying to hide. His hands grope as much of me as he can fit in two wide palms and he kisses me passionately until we fall against the dining room wall in our embrace.

"Ow," I murmur, but I can't stop myself kissing him long enough to move and get comfortable.

Cole lifts me off the ground effortlessly and walks me to the foot of the stairs. He sits me on one of the stairs and climbs between my legs to kiss me.

"Really?" I murmur. "Here."

"We're getting to the bed," he murmurs back. "I'm just… hard. Impatient. I want you."

I wrap my arms around his neck and pull Cole against me. I ease back against the stairs, leaning on them for support as crazy Cole makes out with me hard. I can feel his hardness straining through his pants too, desperate to come out. I run my hands over the outside of his trousers. Damn, he's so big.

I grab his lower back and pull him against me, roughly attempting to strip his clothes off. I know I can't have sex with Cole right here on his staircase, but my logical brain is completely turned off. I love him. I want him. It doesn't matter where I have him, as long as we can press our bodies together and indulge in our feelings for each other.

"Cole," I whisper. "I want you. I want you now."

"Good," he whispers. "Because I don't think I can wait."

He hikes my dress up and eagerly removes his cock. I part my thighs and feel Cole's firm hands sliding along my inner thighs and slowing down once he gets to my lower lips. I moan as he rubs them, his fingers quickly finding my clit as he stirs me awake. It doesn't take much to arouse me. I already want to feel Cole between my legs. His fingers slide into my wetness and I moan as Cole buries his index finger in me up to the last knuckle.

"Fuck," he groans. "You have the best pussy."

I edge my hips forward, nearly slamming my ass down onto a lower step. Cole catches me deftly and slides me back as he removes his hardness from his formal trousers. It unfurls almost like a snake and juts forward. Large veins wrap around his blush pink cock and my chest heaves with anticipation from having him inside me again. Cole has always had an incredible dick. Even when I wanted to deny every ounce of emotion I felt for him, I couldn't deny that his cock was perfect. It's not just that it's long, it's thick too and has these incredible ridges of veins. His dick almost looks… muscular?

I shiver with anticipation as I feel the warm head probing against my soft and wet lower lips. Cole kisses my neck.

"Easy, babe," he whispers. "We're just fucking on my stairs. It's hot. Super hot. Like one of your fantasies."

"Shut up," I grumble, mostly because I forgot that stupid Cole has a catalog of all the erotica I've ever written practically memorized in his dumb hockey player head. He coaxes my hips closer and then eases the head between my legs. Cole slides into my softness slowly, easing his way in and appreciating every inch he slides in. I push my hips toward him, closing the gap between us and taking Cole as deeply as possible.

I moan with pleasure as our bodies press together, finally joined as Cole buries himself in me to the hilt on the stairs. More. I want more. I tilt my head back so my hips move forward and allow Cole to enter me deeper. He grunts and thrusts forward, clutching my back to steady my body as he enters me.

"I want to fuck you hard," he murmurs. "I want to fuck you hard, babe."

"Yes," I whimper. "Please, Cole. Don't stop."

We make love on the stairs until I cum. Cole moves me up a couple stairs and then spreads my legs wide so his tongue can drive me crazy. After making me cum a few times with his tongue, we're finally at the top of the stairs. We make love on the floor, right there at the top of the stairs until Oochie's ragged breathing emerges from downstairs and Cole's ancient chihuahua begins his hot pursuit of us. Cole drags me up from the floor and we're finally in his bedroom again.

Finally, ready for more.

When Cole slips into his bed with me, I pull him close and I don't want to let go. It's Christmas Eve and for the first time in a while, I'm not sitting alone in some "minimalist" luxury apartment. I'm in a warm, cozy home with a guy I love and every moment feels perfect. We climax together a few more times before Cole's mom comes home and we cuddle silently in bed until it's officially Christmas. I love him. Saying it out loud felt so dangerous at first, but Cole's here. He means it. I trust him.

On Christmas morning, Cole's mom opens presents with us before making an incredible breakfast. Cole loves my gifts to him. I got him a cashmere sweater in the same shade of forest green as his Laguna Grove hockey uniform. I got his mom a set of pearl earrings that she almost refuses. I won't let her refuse them. She doesn't know how much her hospitality means to me during the holidays.

She's so sweet. Not like my mom at all. No offense to my mom, but she spends Christmas Day tracking down whichever of my dad's mistresses gave a well-timed statement to TMZ. Last year I learned about another half-sibling (I have twelve) and my mom smashed all the china from their wedding while listening to Whitney Houston. That's her version of a family holiday tradition — a crazy ass meltdown.

Cole and his mom give me incredible gifts, too. Cole's mom gives me a set of salon hair care for my type of hair. She asked some of her clients with a similar hair type what their favorites were and tracked down some giant bottles typically only available for hair stylists to purchase. I can't wait to give my hair a much needed deep condition with the eucalyptus mint scents. Cole gives me the perfect gift. It's a white gold charm bracelet with a bunch of little charms on it. One has a black girl's Afro, another charm is shaped like a hockey puck with a 'C' carved into it, then he has a Los Angeles themed charm and a feminist power fist.

"You can add more charms like whenever," he mumbles, turning red as I gush over this gift and ask his mom for help to put it on. I never want to take the bracelet off. It's so sweet and it looks really expensive. I appreciate it so much.

Neither of my parents remember to call me on Christmas Eve or Christmas Day and neither of them reply to my texts. I try not to let it bother me, but I think Cole notices I'm a little down because he's extremely romantic on Christmas Day. Seriously.

Christmas Day is even better than Christmas Eve. After breakfast with his mom, Cole takes me out ice skating at the Silver Hollow outdoor rink. I haven't improved at skating since our first date at the rink and I give Cole several warnings. He is cool about it. Effortlessly cool. That's how he is about everything. Nothing I say or do upsets his cool control. I guess when you have to deal with pucks flying at your head faster than Teslas down the highway, you learn to steel your nerves.

At the rink, Cole helps me get into my skates, and he keeps his body close to mine as we step onto the rink. There's a sweet biracial kid and her mom on the other end of the rink. The little girl takes off, chasing something, and her mother shrieks, "Callie, no!"

As they whiz past us, I nearly lose my balance and collapse into Cole's firm chest.

"Careful, babe," he whispers.

I regain my balance, and eventually I get the hang of things again. The little girl reunites with her mother, who gives her "time to calm down" off the ice. This place is so sweet. After spending my life in big cities, I thought I could never imagine enjoying a small town like Silver Hollow. But this place is incredible. After skating, Cole brings me back to his place and we take Oochie and Champ for a walk together. I volunteer to walk Champ. Oochie can only walk a few steps without gasping for breath and coughing until she's carried, so I let Cole handle his horny chihuahua and her excessive drool production while I stick with the overly excited Golden.

We have Christmas dinner with Cole's mom and two of his aunts from out of town. They arrive with their husbands and kids. Cole has a couple cousins our age — a pretty blond named Ginger and a pair of red-headed twins, Duke and Daniel. They seem surprised that Cole's dating anyone and give him shit for spending Christmas with them for once instead of dashing off to skate.

"I see you've tamed him," Ginger says with a slight Southern twang to her voice. "Good for you."

Cole turns red as they tease him. I love seeing his sweet side. He's so different from the gruff, arrogant hockey player I remember from my classes. Maybe I just got him all wrong. After dinner, I'm stuffed with surprisingly delicious cooking. I'm used to restaurant food at Christmas. Well, usually only my pho place is open on Christmas Day in our neighborhood — if we're even there.

As the day winds down, Cole takes me to see the Christmas lights in downtown Silver Hollow and we walk amongst the ice sculptures holding hands. He asks me questions about my life growing up, about Los Angeles, about having a famous dad and he listens carefully, holding me tightly against him and gently touching me so I know he cares.

When we're back at his house, we make love slowly in his bed, peeling off our clothes and our layers of separation until our skin presses together and we join in the most perfect way. I yearn for more of Cole when we're done. I can finally admit to myself how badly I want him. How attractive he is. I don't know when the switch flipped, and I realized that I didn't completely hate him... but I'm glad it did.

We spend all our days like that until it's time to get back to school. New Year is low key, but we see fireworks together downtown. Then he has to skate like crazy before the semester starts, so I hang out with his mom at her salon and even spot a couple of her celebrity clients. By the time Cole has to drive us back to Laguna Grove, I don't want to leave. I even cry when I say goodbye to Oochie, who won't stop humping my pink suitcase as I'm sobbing and desperately trying to pry it away.

Cole teases me a little for crying, but I can tell he finds it endearing because he kisses me and cuddles me until I stop. Then we get in the car for our long drive to Laguna Grove. I keep my phone off for most of the drive so I can chill with Cole and pretend I don't have to get back into a new schedule with new classes. I pretend that I can live like this forever, in this beautiful romantic space I have with Cole Seabrook. At least away from school, we don't have to care what other people think. He doesn't have to act like an asshole to fit in with other hockey players, and I don't have to pretend I hate him just because he's an annoying white guy.

I think I like him because he's an annoying white guy. Whatever.

I turn my phone on as we get closer to campus, and suddenly, reality smashes into me. I have seventeen missed calls and nearly a hundred text messages from my friends and from our group chat. What the hell is going on?

I scroll through until I get to the pertinent message describing the emergency.

Holy shit, Kya. Your DAD is in our room. DWAYNE AMBROSE IS IN OUR ROOM.

I wasn't expecting that.

❧ 25 ❧

WE NEED TO TALK

COLE SEABROOK

We need to talk. It's been a day since we got back to campus. She hurried out of my car and wouldn't even let me carry her stuff to her dorm room. I tried to push and get involved, but Kya was stern and insisted on going back alone. I didn't think anything when I didn't hear from Kya after dropping her off. That's just who she is… sometimes, she wants to push me away, and I let her. As long as she knows, I'm always coming back.

But I let her scamper off all nervous and weird because she has her nerd friends and her 'black girl talk' to get into. I don't understand the black girl talk thing, but she tells me to mind my white business any time I ask, so I let it go. When I get those four little words… I wonder how I messed up.

I thought Christmas was perfect. I know it was perfect. I loved her before we got there but I fell deeper in love with Kya as I watched her bake sugar cookies with my mom, stumble across the ice like a baby deer, cuddle up under the blankets watching her favorite chick movies with just that mop of fluffy hair sticking out. I'm already pissed I had to spend a night without her in my bed. I rolled over, forgetting she wasn't there, to find stupid fucking Ovie sliding into my bed next to me. That escape artist snake is going to meet his match one day.

I text her that I'm at practice and we can meet up after, but she doesn't reply with her list of demands or even a suggestion about where we should meet. What the hell... this is just so not like Kya.

Whatever. I have practice to worry about for now and if I don't get my shit together, Tuck Murphy is going to drag me naked across the ice with a hockey stick shoved up my you know where. At least, according to him. Anijah's super pregnant and I swear she's been leaking her hormones into coach's coffee because he's more stressed than he was before the holidays. I have an agent. I just need to keep playing. I have more motivation now than ever before.

Over Christmas Break, I listened to Kya. I swear, I never wanted to know so much about a girl before. Every night she cuddled up next to me. I couldn't get enough of breathing in the scent of her hair and listening to her stories about her fancy pants life. She's the coolest chick I know, but she's more humble than I thought. She's quick to point out the truth behind the glamor of an almost-celebrity life. She's just... way more down to earth than I thought.

I like it. And fuck, I enjoy holding her.

My cousins are right. I've never cared about something that isn't hockey this much. I know one day I want to marry her, but Kya probably thinks marriage means "women are property" or whatever stuff she's always talking about from her chick classes. I bet she still wants a big fancy ring. I'll use my first paycheck from the NHL to get it for her. Diamonds. I know she wants lots of diamonds. Someday soon, she'll have them. I want to say yes to her crazy.

Maybe when we talk, I'll tell her. I know it's early, but I've always known what I wanted out of life and I've always gone after it. We should wait. It only makes sense. She'll still be in college when I'm in the league. She's already given me a thousand lectures about how she's never dropping out of school, especially not for a man.

But one day, I'm definitely going to marry Kya Ambrose. I never thought I'd fall for a nerdy black chick with big hair and a bigger mouth, but life is full of surprises. Just like hockey.

One surprise comes flying at my face. A shitty shot by Clutterbuck smacks into the side of my helmet and the surprise sends me off balance, careening into the boards. I need to pay attention more. The whack on my head hurts like hell.

"Shit! Sorry." Jayce grins, like he's not that sorry and skates around me in an irritating figure 8. My friends are fucking assholes.

"You fucking idiot," I snarl, clutching the side of my head, grateful that shit didn't land on my neck or something.

"You were supposed to get that pass," Jayce says, like this is my fault and not his.

"It was a shitty pass," I snap as he continues making that figure 8, waiting for me to tap the puck back. Jayce needs a fucking hobby. Or maybe a fucking girlfriend.

The offending puck lies at my feet. I whack it back across the ice to Jayce, who smirks and hits it into the net. Our goalie catches the shot. He's been getting better, which we really need when we play the Worcester War Hogs in a week. We're getting into the meat of the season and our game needs to be incredible if we want a shot at making it to the playoffs. If we don't make it to the playoffs, I might as well kiss my professional career goodbye.

I practice shooting with Jayce and correct Hargreaves' high stick before we work on speed drills as a team together. For a moment, I forget all about Kya's ominous text message. There can't be anything wrong. I'm in love and I'm playing like it. Nothing can shake me off my high after practice except Kya waiting for me in the hallway outside the rink, swollen and red with tears. Her face contorts in rage, which I don't understand. Someone hurt her. I don't know who, but whoever it is… I'll kill him.

Her face tightens with greater anger as I approach her. What the hell is going on?

In front of everyone on my team, the moment I'm within earshot, she takes her phone and throws it at my head. Hard.

"SCREW YOU, COLE!"

What. The. Fuck. Okay, I like a little crazy. Let's be honest, Kya's brand of crazy is kinda my thing. I like a chick with a little fight in her — okay, a lot of fight in her. But this is just…

"What the hell is going on?" I ask her.

"You screwed up my life!" She yells. "You promised… you… you're a fucking LIAR!"

Everyone on my team is watching. I wish I could care about what the fuck they think, but what I want to know is why my girlfriend's screaming at me like a crazy person.

"What the hell are you talking about?"

"You know what I'm talking about. God, Cole. I can't believe I ever trusted you."

"Babe… Can we talk after I get out of my skates?"

Okay. This has to be the worst thing I could say to a woman. Apparently. Because Kya loses her fucking mind.

"No! We're talking right now, Cole. You betrayed me. I gave you my heart, and you screwed me over. I don't want to talk to you anymore. Ever."

"Kya… I don't know what the hell you're talking about."

"Fuck you, Cole. Just… fuck you."

She storms off and everyone just stares at the spot where she was just standing. Shit. I know I'm a pretty dumb guy, but I still keep track of my fuckups. In the past 24 hours, I haven't done anything to make Kya go fucking postal on my ass. Tuck thumps my shoulder. Hard.

"Seabrook. My office."

"What the fuck did I do?"

Everyone on the team snickers and talks shit. Whatever. I care way less about what the guys on my team have to say than whatever the hell has pissed Kya off. She means more to me than anyone. I don't know what I did to screw up with her, but my fucking God, I'm going to fix everything — right after this meeting with Tuck Murphy, where he's probably going to kick my ass.

I get my clothes off in the locker room, throwing dirty looks at anyone who tries to comment on the situation. Those guys don't know Kya. I don't care what they think about her and I don't give a shit if Dustin hassles me for liking "crazy" chicks. Listen, Kya might be the hot kind of crazy, but she's also a real smart girl. She wouldn't go this far unless I fucked up. Somehow.

Once I change into sweatpants and a hoodie, without bothering to take a shower, I rush to Tuck's office. The faster I get this over with, the faster I can head back to Kya and find out what the fuck is going on with her. Tuck's not in his office when I open the door, though. His very pregnant (and very black) wife sits in his chair with her feet on the desk, singing some song by Beyoncé. (Kya listens to Beyoncé all the time, so now I know every single album and a bunch of other chick stuff about Beyoncé I never thought I'd give a shit about.)

"Cole!" she says, practically squeaking and rearranging herself into a more appropriate seating position. "Tuck's on his way back with some coffee. Don't worry."

"Can I sit?"

"Go ahead," Anijah says.

"Fuck…"

Anijah gives me a really weird smile.

"What?"

"I'm just enjoying watching you in pain."

"Uh… why?"

Tuck Murphy's got a really sick chick at his side. Can't say I'm surprised.

"You know what you did. You leaked Kya's crazy sex stories to her dad. He was waiting for her in her dorm when she came back and everything became... fucked up beyond all recognition?"

"I didn't do that!"

"Um... pretty sure you did," Anijah says in that sing-song voice. I swear, Tuck must have a thing for difficult women because I can tell Anijah's... difficult. But this is about Kya and some shit I didn't do... Is that why she's out for blood now? Because of a lie?

"Is that what she's so fucking mad about? I gotta get out of here..."

"Not so fast, Seabrook," Tuck says, pushing the door open and dutifully handing Anijah a mug of decaffeinated coffee.

"Decaf for my baby," he whispers, kissing her on the forehead. She squirms with bratty levels of excitement as she sniffs the mug.

"Did you remember my six pumps of caramel? I have cravings, Tuck. Cravings."

"Yes, I remembered," he says, siting on the edge of his desk and turning his cruel stare upon me. "Seabrook. We have to talk."

"Yeah, everyone wants to fuckin' talk to me today."

"Cut the shit, Seabrook."

"Yes, coach."

I don't want to fuck with Tuck Murphy. Not just because he scares the crap out of me, but because I respect him. He cares about the team and he cares about the guys. He cares about hockey. He's the one dude I know who loves the game as much as I do. Jayce loves fighting more. Dustin just loves being a fucking creep. But Tuck Murphy eats sleeps and breathes the ice. He's like the big brother I never had.

"What happened out there was unacceptable."

"It won't happen again."

"How much time did you waste blackmailing some chick you don't even like?"

Fuck. I thought I could get this poor conduct talk out of the way and brush shit off, but clearly Tuck knows more about what happened than he's letting on. Anijah sips her coffee and avoids eye contact with me. Sneaky. I suspect Tuck's source of information into my personal life is the pregnant black woman sitting in his office pretending to be more interested in checking out her hair in the reflection on her phone.

"That's not what happened."

"Really? Because she sure looks like some sick fuck broke her heart."

"Come on, Cole. Chicks act wild all the time. I'm not the only guy on the team to have girl problems."

"Girl problems? You fucked with Dwayne Ambrose's daughter. She might be a quiet chick, but everyone at this school knows her dad. Everyone in the professional sports world knows her dad. Your agent knows her dad. If you show terrible judgment like this now, they'll pick a recruit who knows the difference between his ass and his elbow."

"Coach, I swear… I know how bad this looks, but I wouldn't hurt Kya. I just wouldn't."

"Then what happened, Seabrook? Because right now, I'm looking at the top player on my team like I don't even know him. You still have weaknesses. You might still lose your chance to play. If you don't get your fucking act together—

"Coach, I'm going to get my act together. I promise. And I promise I didn't fuck with my future like this."

"Fix this, Cole. Fix it now, or I swear, you'll lose everything. I know that's not what you want."

I leave the meeting feeling like shit. No. This isn't possible. I never would have leaked Kya's sex stories. I forgot about those dumb sex stories a long time ago. I stopped caring about those stories when I fell for the annoying black chick with the big hair and the loud mouth. I love her. I wouldn't hurt her. How the fuck could Kya believe I would after everything I did?

She must think I'm such a piece of shit and it gets me hot with rage. I confessed my feelings to her. I gave her a piece of my heart and she couldn't even trust me enough to give me a chance. I hate that it hurts. I hate that she humiliated me. I hate that the only thing I care about now is getting her back. But she's ignoring my calls and when I walk to her bedroom, her two dweeb friends answer the door and tell me Kya's not home, when I can definitely smell her shampoo and hear her sniffling in her bed.

Raven calls me an "asshole" before slamming the door in my face, which is the icing on the fucking cake. Damn it, I need a new plan to get to her because I can't let Kya go over this. She has to know the truth. And hey, since I didn't leak the stories, that means someone else did. Possibly someone she trusts.

Anyone who would hurt her that badly is definitely signing up for an ass kicking. This won't be easy with Tuck on my ass. He's going to keep a closer watch on me and he'll probably have the other guys on the team watching me even closer, so I don't fuck up. We have the War Hogs game to worry about. I have to stay focused...

But fuck, how can I stay focused without her? How can I pretend to give a shit about anything with Kya Ambrose pissed off at me? I head back to my room after a couple hours. I need to regroup. Strategize. Come up with a new play. It's what I do, right?

But my bed feels so fucking lonely without her that I can hardly think without my chest caving in and getting all tight. Fuck, she would make so much fun of me for how much I care about her. I feel like the dude in one of those chick movies Kya likes. All emotional. It sucks. Nothing I do helps me to fall asleep. I need good sleep for our morning skate, but I also can't skip the morning skate.

Dustin reminds me of that when he comes banging at my door like a crazy person. I open my door, ready to chew his head off when he gets to me first.

"Anyone tell you that you look like shit?"

"Thanks."

"Game in two days. Skates on, brother."

"Fuck hockey."

Dustin looks like I just smacked him in the face. He presses one hand to my forehead and when I let my guard down, his other hand smacks me hard across the face. Fuck.

"Fuck off!"

"Pull yourself together, Seabrook."

"I can't."

"Is it about that chick with the… you know… the ass?"

"Kya's more than an ass."

"Yeah. She's got hair too. Not on her ass. I mean, maybe…"

"Can you shut the fuck up, Dustin?"

"Sure, man. Come on."

"I'm quitting. I'm not skating right now. I have bigger problems."

Dustin groans.

"Coach said you might be like this."

"And what did he tell you to do?"

"Punch you in the face."

"Thanks, Tuck."

"Listen, I won't do that. Go to the morning skate and I'll help you get your chick back. I can be very convincing."

Dustin isn't convincing me at all, but I don't want to get punched in the face and he's right about skating. The ice will make me feel better. And after practice…

I'll get my fucking girl back.

❧ 26 ❧

AT THEIR MERCY

KYA AMBROSE

Makeba moved into her new room at the start of the semester after Christmas, and it has officially become our new gossip spot since Raven and I share a double and Makeba has one as a single all to herself — and if we don't visit her daily, her messy room descends into complete chaos. Raven's folding her shirts while Makeba burns some leaves from her dead plant in her new scented candle, completely distracted by the flames. We love our little weirdo.

And I especially love my friends for helping me with my breakup ritual.

"So," Raven says. "We're on day three of the breakup. Is this the part where you hook up with a much hotter guy."

"No! I'm not hooking up with anyone else. I'm never having sex ever again."

My friends offer me a sympathetic look. At least whoever leaked the stories didn't send them to TMZ, which is honestly an exceedingly small comfort considering my dad confronted me about the blackmail he received with all my sex stories attached. And he read them. All of them. Along with his lawyer. I was honestly so embarrassed, I could have died on the spot.

And that was before his I'm so disappointed in you, Kya lecture. The first time he talks to me in like a month and that's what we have to talk about. It's totally humiliating. It's worse when he reads excerpts out loud to me and asks me if he raised me to be a slut. I'm still reeling from all of it. He left as suddenly as he came. I know we probably won't talk for months. He was furious with me and his threats clarified that if I allow these stories to leak, he'll make my life hell and maybe even stop paying for college. I tried arguing with my dad about women and their education, and how it wasn't fair, but he told me that college girls were mostly sluts anyway and that he was rethinking the entire operation.

I couldn't believe he would say that to me.

This is the type of stuff I'd normally vent to Cole about. He's the only person I've ever opened up to about my weird ass relationship with my parents. I had to come clean with my friends at least about the erotica and they're trying to be supportive, but I can tell they secretly think I'm some kind of sex freak or something. After burning her dry plant leaf into oblivion, Makeba glances at me with a worried look on her face.

"Never again? You sound like BJ…"

"How is that going? Did you guys… you know?"

"No. Your breakup is inspiring me, though. Maybe I need to dump him."

"Good," I reply bitterly. "Guys are not to be trusted."

Raven sighs. "Girl, not all guys. Cole was an asshole from the start. I mean… he leaked your stories just like he said he would. Why are you surprised? He's just a hockey player. You're better than him."

"I'm just surprised he denied it. He lied to my face. Sure, Cole's an asshole, I knew that. But I didn't think he was a liar."

"Maybe he wasn't lying," Makeba says. I glare at her.

"This is breakup week. You're not taking his side," I grumble.

Makeba shrugs. "Whatever, I mean… you said yourself he looked really surprised. And that he did all that romantic stuff for you at Christmas. He didn't have to do all of that."

"He's a totally twisted psychopath, Makeba. Obviously."

She exchanges a glance with Raven that they both think I don't notice. What the hell was that little look about? Raven gives Makeba a little nod, and she changes the subject. They don't want me feeling too awful about Cole.

"BJ's still acting weird," Makeba says. "He's just… I don't know."

Raven folds her arms and scowls at her. "Dump him. Listen, he's my friend and all, but I hate the way he treats you. You need someone excited about you… like the guy in Stormfire."

Raven holds up one of her dark little bodice rippers. It's my turn to exchange glances with Makeba. We don't know if she should be taking relationship advice from books where half the heroes are literal kidnappers.

"Listen, I'll dump him for you," I tell Makeba. "Give me your phone."

She hands me her phone and Raven crowds around it with me. The three of us try to come up with a break up text, but instead of sending it, Makeba insists we try good old faithful. "We need to talk". BJ doesn't respond right away, so Makeba chucks her phone on her bed and hugs me.

"Break up ritual. Let's do it."

"Okay. I want to go throw eggs at his car."

Raven laughs. "That sounds funny, but… um… child… Cole is crazy. I'm not gonna have him running after me looking for ways to blackmail me."

My gut reaction is defending him by telling her that Cole isn't really like that, but I'm pretty sure he just proved he is like that in all the worst ways.

"Okay, well, what do I do?"

"I found this spell on Instagram," Raven says. "It attracts bad vibes to your subject."

"Sounds risky, Raven."

"All you need is a few of his toenails and some pepper."

I wrinkle my nose in disgust.

"Please tell me you aren't using a spell involving toenails to get a man now."

"No, just my jojoba oil still."

"Well, be careful," Makeba grumbles. "I tried getting a boyfriend, and it sucks. All BJ cares about is hanging out on the internet all day. We've never even had sex. Or kissed. Or been on a real date."

Poor Makeba. She gave it her best shot with BJ. I don't know why he doesn't appreciate her. Or why he said yes to dating her if he wasn't even going to move off the couch to do it.

"Don't worry," I tell her. "You'll dump him soon and join me in single land. Trust me, it's great."

I know I don't sound very convincing.

Makeba's still comforting. "Sorry, Kya. Don't egg Cole's car, but maybe we can do something else to get over him?"

"I don't know. I guess I thought we had closure, but now… I'm not sure and it's messing with my head. I've never struggled to get over a guy like this," I admit.

"Maybe there's something left there," Raven says with a romantic tone in her voice. I swear she's thinking of her romance novels again and not real life.

"He gave my erotica to my dad. I don't think there's anything left between us."

"Unless…" Raven says. "Someone else stole your erotica."

I glare at her, because I'm not in the mood to hear anyone defend that idiotic hockey player. It was my fault for letting him into my life.

"No one else knew about it," I said. "It couldn't have been anyone else."

Raven shrugs. "Then he's an asshole. We'll cheer for the War Hogs at their next game. That'll piss him off."

I just groan. Cole's mom is going to be at her next game. It seems dumb, but I'm going to miss her. Too bad her son is such an asshole. After spending so much time with them, I really thought Cole was different, that he was tough and cold because he had to be without a dad. I thought there was some sweet part of him deep down. Deep down? He's a stone cold bastard with no redeemable qualities whatsoever. That's the hard truth I need to face — and it sucks.

"The real part of my breakup ritual right now is calling my mom. She loves when I go through breakups."

"Weird thing for a mom to love," Raven says.

"It makes her feel better about how shitty my dad is. But this time, I'm not in the mood for a men ain't shit talk. Guys… I'm being a downer. I should just head out for a walk or something."

"I can go with you!" Makeba offers.

"No, you deal with the BJ thing. I've got this."

"I'll help her deal with the BJ thing," Raven offers. "And take her trash out."

"It's not even that bad," Makeba complains as a fruit fly emerges from the pile of banana peels in her bin. Raven has the right idea about helping her. I hug them goodbye and leave Makeba's room. I don't want to drag my friends down any more than I already have. I don't want to be like my mom, always whining over a man…

It's freezing out and everywhere is covered in a thin layer of snow which makes me think of ice, which makes me think of hockey, which makes me think of Cole Seabrook and his impossibly blue eyes.

Kya, I didn't do this.

He keeps trying to talk to me. He keeps pleading with me about his innocence, but he's almost cost me everything. I had to beg my dad to keep paying my tuition, and I had to cry to beg him not to drag me back to Los Angeles. I'm basically on lockdown now. My dad threatened to have a security guard follow me all over campus, aka a spy, to keep me out of trouble. It's already bad enough having a famous dad. I convinced him I was safe out here without all that.

My very normal friends wouldn't want to be around me if he made good on his threat. Cole… I can't stop thinking about him. I can't stop thinking about Christmas. Why would he have planned such a perfect Christmas Eve when he had already gone behind my back? God, he must have taken so much pleasure out of making a fool out of me. How had it all felt so real?

And his poor mom… how could he let her think I was going to be a part of his life only to pull this crap? It doesn't make sense. My walk is supposed to be clearing my head, but it's just making me feel like I'm tangled up in this really strange web.

Cole's eyes flash into my head again. So icy. So freaking blue. I hated how much I loved those eyes. The second he walked into my women's studies class, I stared at him. He didn't notice because he was probably hungover from late practice or binge drinking in Pesthouse. I'd never seen eyes that brilliant blue, and his hair was just golden. Even in his dumb sweatpants, I thought he was insanely hot. I mean, I knew he would be a total asshole because of it, but he was still gorgeous to look at. A gorgeous fucking mess.

"Hey, Kya!"

What the fuck? Who was that? I turn around, looking over my shoulder to see who just called my name, but I don't see anyone. I hear someone calling from the other direction.

"Kya Ambrose, over here!"

"Um… who are you?"

I turn around and scream. There's a guy standing right behind me with a hockey mask like the one from Friday the 13th. Obviously someone on Cole's team. Or a fucking serial killer. I can't tell which, so I scream and cover all my bases.

"Calm down, it's Dustin."

"What? Dustin? Ha ha, very funny. I'm not dating Cole anymore, so I don't have time for your little—

I feel a hard thump to the back of my head and then everything goes to black like, immediately. What the hell!? I remember hoping I don't get a black eye when I hit the ground.

I don't know when I wake up, but I know I'm tied up and in the back of a truck. Dustin Rathbone has a truck, a douche-y Ford F-150 Super Duty truck with insane lifts and an extremely loud engine. I don't know where I'm going. I don't know why Dustin Rathbone has me in his truck. And I definitely don't know what he plans to do with me. I'm sure he's not up to anything good. I have to escape from this truck, except I'm tied up and possibly under a blanket!? Shit…

It's pretty dark out, so I don't know how long I've been unconscious, but it could be anywhere from one hour to four hours. Don't these idiots have a freaking game today? Makeba and Raven might not even notice that I'm gone. And I'm utterly at this idiot hockey player's mercy… Shit.

27

ROCKS AT THE WINDOW

COLE SEABROOK

I throw rocks at her window for about five minutes before one of her friends sticks her head out.

"What the hell do you want?"

I think this one is Raven. She's the shortest in the friend group — even shorter than Kya, which I didn't even think was possible.

"Hey. Is Kya home?"

"She doesn't want to talk to you, Cole," Raven says. "Go away."

"I can't! Listen, can you get her to come to the window? I can explain everything."

The other friend sticks her head out of the window next. Great. I have to face the tribunal of Kya's nerdy friends before I get anywhere. This is super annoying. I only have a couple hours before I need to be on the ice... I don't have time for this.

"She can't come to the window," Makeba says. "She's occupied."

"I need to talk to her. Please..."

"She's not here," Raven finally admits. "Okay? So go away and distract yourself with some stupid puck bunny. Stop trying to break out friend's heart."

My chest tightens. I would never do anything to break Kya's heart. I wouldn't hurt her like that. Maybe before I knew her. Maybe before I fell in love with her. But definitely not now.

"Where the hell is she? I have a game in a couple hours and I need to fix things."

Makeba and Raven exchange glances.

"We don't know where she is."

"What?!"

Then why the hell did they waste so much of my time?

"Library?" I suggest.

They both shrug.

"She's been gone for like two hours and she won't answer her phone," Makeba blurts out, until Raven elbows her and stops giving me the valuable information that I need. "She said she went for a walk."

"Do you have any idea where she might be?"

"Maybe she's with her dad," Makeba whispers to Raven, but loudly enough so I can hear.

"Her dad's still around?" I ask from beneath the window.

Raven glares at Makeba, who shrugs and mutters something close to an apology.

"Yes. He's at the Regency."

There's only one hotel in town and it's fancy enough that the rich people who send their kids to Laguna Grove are willing to stay there. My mom stays a couple towns over at a modest inn when she comes to visit. I've never been to the Regency… but I know exactly where it is.

"Thank you!"

"Wait! You can't go over there, you freaking traitor!" Raven screams at me.

I turn to say something back to her and then a black high heel comes sailing out the window, smacking me in the face and taking me by surprise. I drop my stupid car keys when I grab my face. As I scream out in pain, Raven and Makeba shriek as if they're the ones who took a fucking high heel to the jaw.

"Oh my God, Raven! You killed him!" Makeba hisses.

Unsympathetically, Raven mutters, "He's a white boy, he'll be fine."

Maybe I'll be fine, but I don't see what being a white boy has to do with that. There's a little blood on my lip. Not much, but it hurts like hell when I touch it. Fuck.

"Ouch!"

Raven yells down at me before shutting her window, "We're coming with you!"

"No, you're not!" I yell back. I clutch my face again. I've taken rough hits on the ice, but man, that chick can fling a shoe. I have to get out of here before those dorks get downstairs. Sigh. I guess they aren't really dorks. They're Kya's best friends and they care that she's MIA too.

As long as I get back before the game... I guess I can drag them along. I find my keys long after they get downstairs and I pick up Raven's heel. As she approaches, she glances at it warily.

"Don't throw it back," she says nervously.

"I won't," I grumble, handing it to her.

"Sorry," she says.

"Are you?"

"That depends. Did you send Kya's freaky sex tales to her dad or not?" Raven asks.

"Tell us the truth," Makeba says. "Raven's a witch. She'll put a spell on you."

Raven glares at Makeba, but I glance between both of them, uncertain how much of what Makeba's saying is real and how much of it is a big joke. I don't understand Kya's friends. They communicate without talking to each other — with gestures and facial expressions. It's weird. But I guess they're cool enough.

"I didn't," I say. "I swear. And I know you chicks have no reason to believe me, but... I love Kya Ambrose."

Raven and Makeba's eyes practically swim.

"You love her," Raven says dreamily. "That is so romantic."

Makeba rolls her eyes.

"I don't believe you. But if you're dumb enough to lie to Dwayne Ambrose's face… I have to see it up close."

"Then I guess I'm driving."

Raven and Makeba exchange another incomprehensible glance and I mutter awkward directions to the spot where I parked my car. They're whispering to each other and I feel like I should say something, but I don't even know what to say to them. They're… intimidating.

"I have a game soon, so I can't be long."

"We know," Raven replies smugly. "We have great seats, thanks to Kya. She gave us all of hers."

"Great."

My cheeks darken with embarrassment. She's so over me that she already gave her seats away. Even if I can get to the bottom of this and convince her that this was all a complete mistake… maybe Kya won't ever forgive me. Fuck, I feel like shit just thinking about that. It hurts like hell.

When we arrive at the Regency, I have this moment where I feel like this is a totally dumb idea. Like… a completely dumb idea. Kya's dad isn't just some guy I can talk to. He's Dwayne Ambrose. He's a fucking big shot.

"So um… no offense, but… what's your plan?" Raven whispers to me as I approach the front desk.

"Does he look like he has a plan?" Makeba whispers to her. "He has white man confidence. He'll be fine."

Before I can ask her what the hell white man confidence is — and how it differs from any other kind of confidence — the chipper chick at the front desk interrupts with a sing-song voice.

"Welcome to the Laguna Grove Regency! How may I help you this evening?!"

Here goes nothing.

"Hi… Uh… I need to speak to a Mr. Dwayne Ambrose. I heard he's uh… staying here. I'm a uh… I'm a friend of his daughter's."

Front desk girl smiles at me, her broad smile betraying nothing about whether she's going to help me or not. She taps away at her computer screen for a few seconds before finally agreeing to place a call to Mr. Ambrose's room.

I step away from the desk where Raven and Makeba are whispering to each other, probably talking about how annoying white guys are or something like that. I try to play it cool around them.

"I think she's gonna get him."

"Do you think he'll come talk to you?"

"I don't know. Kya probably told him about me, right? I'll just explain who I am and we can get down to business."

"He's a black father," Raven says.

I wrinkle my nose and tilt my head to the side.

"Yeah. I know that."

Kya probably told these chicks I was super dumb or something, because I don't know why else I would need a reminder that my black girlfriend's dad is… also black. I hear the elevator and before I see the 6'10" tall dark-skinned man in a navy suit rounding the corner. It has to be him. He has Kya's thick eyebrows and her scowl set on his face. I'd recognize that scowl anywhere. He comes straight toward the front desk, but I don't want him to get to Ms Chipper before he gets to me.

I'm the one who wants to talk to him and even if I probably should be, I'm not scared. This is about Kya. Not my feelings.

"Mr. Ambrose!"

When I call his name, he looks at me and his face, at first twisted in anger, settles once he sees Makeba and Raven next to me. I guess I made the right choice letting those two tag along.

"Makeba! Raven!"

"Hi, Mr. Ambrose," they respond dutifully, sounding way more innocent than the chicks who lobbed a freaking stiletto at my head.

"Mr. Ambrose, I'm Cole Seabrook."

I step forward and stick out my hand to shake his. Dwayne Ambrose glances down at my hand then looks me in the eye before squeezing the shit out of it with the strongest, most terrifying handshake I've ever felt. I don't break eye contact with him once.

"Cole Seabrook. I don't recognize that name."

Ouch. I guess Kya hasn't told him about me.

"I'm a friend of Kya's. I'm here to talk about… what she's going through."

Dwayne Ambrose is clean cut, and he's wearing a navy suit. I can smell his cologne standing next to him and it's hard to miss the quarter-million dollar watch on his wrist. Who the fuck am I talking to a guy like that? His face twists in confusion.

"What about Kya?"

"I need to know who sent you... that stuff about her."

Dwayne Ambrose's back stiffens, and now he looks more like a bulldog than a man.

"Who sent you? Are you from the press? Because I swear, I ain't above putting a hole in—

"Mr. Ambrose!" Raven interrupts (thank fuck), "He's from our school. He ain't lying."

"About that..." Makeba mutters distrustfully.

"Who are you then? And why are you asking questions about my daughter?"

Fuck... Here goes nothing.

28

DOES HE STAND A CHANCE?

KYA AMBROSE

Cole's idiot friends are idiots. I know, I know. I'm just repeating myself. But things get pretty boring when you're tied up in the back of a Ford F-150 parked behind the fucking hockey rink. When dumb Cole wouldn't answer their dumb calls, Dustin and Jayce came up with the brilliant — just kidding, it was obviously dumb — idea to leave me tied up in the back of Dustin's truck while they played against the War Hogs.

The truck's behind the hockey rink, where no one in their right fucking mind would dream of looking. I guess that part was smart enough, but the rest of their little plan to capture me and win me back for their buddy is turning out to be a complete failure. I'm tied up, trapped in the back of a stupid truck and all I can think about is a bunch of dumb revenge plans once they finally set me free. Hockey games last like three hours. I'll be here for a while... Idiots!

This is one of the last ones for the season, so they'll probably have a post-game party. These freaking losers plan on leaving me back here all night. They even took my phone. Actually, Dustin took my phone. I tried a good old Cole Seabrook tactic and shoved it into my underwear the second I could, but Jayce tickled me until it fell down the leg of my sweatpants.

Why the fuck didn't I think of that before? I hate being tickled. I also hate being outsmarted by idiot hockey players.

It's not like I haven't been screaming my head off back there in the off-chance someone walks by. But my throat hurts. And I only have one good scream in me left. We're probably halfway through the first period by now, so I know no one will hear me, but I have to try something.

"HELP! SOMEONE HELP ME!!!!"

There's an unexpected thump on the truck's chassis. OMG. Could it be real help?!

"Help!" I whimper, my voice sounding valley-girl-fried.

"Kya? Are you in Dustin's truck?"

I hear another thump and recognize the sound as Cole's hand touching the truck body. His voice... What the hell? What the hell is Cole Seabrook doing here?! He has a game right now. An important game. Whatever. At least he's here so he can set me free and I can kick his fucking ass for letting his moron friends kidnap me.

"Yes! It's me! LET ME OUT!"

"What the fuck are you doing in there?"

"I'm tied up! Let me out! NOW!"

Cole flings the door open and I wriggle like a stupid worm because, well, I'm tied up. Wriggling is all I can manage.

"What the fuck is going on?"

"Untie me! Your dumb friends kidnapped me!"

"Shit…"

Cole scrambles into the truck and starts working the knots tying me down. I hate that my body responds to his closeness even in a moment like this. He leans over me to reach for the knot behind my back.

"Working as quick as I can, babe."

"I'm not your babe!"

"I'm rescuing you, Kya. Can't I at least call you babe while I do the damn work?" He grumbles.

Cole is like the world champion of missing the freaking point.

"I don't need you to rescue me!"

He keeps working at the knots, ignoring my shrieking and wriggling until I'm free. He pulls me out of the truck and brushes the dust off my jeans, picking a twig or two from the floor of Dustin's truck out of my hair, which probably looks like a freaking mess since Dustin and Jayce didn't even have the decency to drop a silk pillowcase on the floor of the truck before tossing me in there.

"I'm sorry," Cole says, before I can open my mouth and say anything else. And when I do open my mouth, he covers it with his hands.

"I went through a lot of trouble to get the proof I needed, but I got it. From your dad. Here."

Cole hands me my cellphone.

"Proof? Proof of what? And what the hell happened to your face? Don't you have a game right now?"

My words come out as "MMMMPPHFHFDFD" because Cole's hand is still pressed over my mouth. He moves it away and I repeat my sentence.

"The black eye? That was your dad. And yes, I have a game right now. But I have somewhere more important to be. Right here."

"Are you crazy?! Your agent is at that game, Cole. This is it. This is your one shot to get into the NHL and you're standing over here talking to me."

Cole gives me this frustrated little look which is very annoying. Frustrated looks are my thing.

"You're worth it, Kya," he says, almost aggressively. "I'd rather lose hockey than lose you."

"Stop it," I hiss. "Stop that right now."

"Look at your phone. Now. I went through a lot of trouble to get this."

I glance down and open it. There's a text from my dad. It's not a happy text necessarily, because Cole apparently opened his big mouth and told my dad we were dating, but it proves everything Cole said. The message never came from him. He didn't send my dad my erotica.

I still don't know who did, but in that moment, the only thing that matters to me is that Cole didn't. He's innocent. Which means that everything over our holiday, everything that happened between us, was... real.

"I love you, big mouth," he whispers.

"Big mouth!?"

"Sorry. That sounded better in my head."

"Is your head filled with rocks?"

"Right now… it definitely feels that way. You never mentioned your dad was left-handed. I never saw it coming."

"Sorry."

I can't help myself. Cole grunts as I surprise him by throwing my arms around him and squeezing tightly. Cole wraps his arms around me and he squeezes tight.

"I love you, stupid," I whisper. "A lot."

"Stupid is a way worse insult than big mouth."

"Yeah. You're right."

I pull away and sigh.

"Why can't we just… love each other? Without the insults. I'm so bad at that."

"I love you, babe. Definitely. And I don't mind your insults. You keep me on my toes."

"That's just what a strong woman does," I tease, punching Cole's chest a little. He winces. Oops. I forgot that my dad kind of kicked his ass.

"I swore to you, I didn't do this, and I won't rest until I kick the ass of whoever did."

"You have a game. Right now. And you're hurt…"

"I know. I left right before the first period when Jayce let it slip they had you 'tied up somewhere special' for me."

"Your friends are total idiots," I remind him, in case he forgot for a moment.

"I know. Forgive me?"

"Maybe. We'll see."

"Kya…"

"Of course I forgive you. You did nothing. I'm the one who didn't trust you."

"Why should you trust me? I treated you like dirt for a long time. I was wrong about you. I thought you were… just another Laguna Grove rich chick."

"And I thought you were just another hockey player. We're still both those things, but… I care about you, Cole. A lot."

"I don't want you to be my girlfriend, Kya."

"Um… okay? Now I'm confused."

"I want you to be my fiancée. I want to prove I'm serious about you so that the next time I see your dad, he doesn't call me a punk ass white boy and lay my ass out in front of the Laguna Grove Regency."

"He did that?!"

"Yes. But until I make it… somehow… I can't ask you to marry me. But I can ask you to wait. To graduate college. And when you're done… I promise, I'll make you Mrs. Seabrook. Or you can keep your last name or whatever. But like… I'd rather make you Mrs. Seabrook."

For once, I'm the one who wants to shut Cole up. I wrap my arms around him again and kiss him. Hard. He kisses back, pressing me up against Dustin's truck as his hands travel to my waist. I could lose myself in that kiss forever, but then reality strikes me. I pull away.

"Cole. Get back on the ice. Right now. The game isn't over yet. I'm going to go inside and you are not going to give up."

"Kya. My friends kidnapped you. You're probably like… traumatized or whatever."

"Traumatized or not, you shouldn't even be skipping hockey to do this! We're playing the War Hogs!"

"Since when do you care?"

"Since I fell in love with the hat trick guy. Now let's GO!"

He takes my hand. "We'll take the back entrance in. Your friends are in your seats. They're worried sick."

"I'll handle my friends… you handle the War Hogs. Got it?"

"Got it, princess."

"Love you, babe," I tell him.

"Babe?"

"Get used to it, Seabrook. I'm a babe girl now."

"You're my girl," he whispers. "Forever."

Once we're in the building, Cole and I kiss one last time and he races over to the ice where I can see Tuck Murphy red in the face, tearing into him. Ouch. As long as he gets ice time, maybe this doesn't have to ruin everything. Maybe Cole still stands a chance…

❧ 29 ☙

THE WAR HOGS

COLE SEABROOK

I'm in my gear and ready to head onto the ice, but there's someone in my way. Tuck. I've never seen him this furious before. Then I look at the score. Fuck. 4-2. How the hell did we let them get four goals in when I was gone? Tuck looks like he wants to kick the shit out of me.

"I'm here. Put me in," I tell him, ignoring the fact that he looks like he wants to stab me.

My heart races. I've never seen him so pissed, but we both know we don't have time for that. He can kick my ass when the game is over. This isn't about the league anymore. It's about the boys. My friends. The idiots who would kidnap my ex-girlfriend if they thought it would help. Dumb thing to do, but their hearts were in the right place — and so is mine.

I have to win this game for them. For myself... and for Kya. I don't want to disappoint her. I want to keep chasing her impossible standards for the rest of my fucking life because Kya Ambrose… is worth it.

"Put me in. Kill me after."

"That sounds good," Tuck grunts.

Tuck whistles. I notice a few missing faces on our bench. What the hell happened to Jayce? Dustin? Hargreaves? No time… I skate out to replace Nick, who shouldn't even be playing offense. What the fuck happened out there? When I hurtle toward the puck, I finally get it. The War Hogs are some of the biggest fucking guys I've ever seen and they aren't afraid to hit dirty.

One of their forwards slams me into the boards, stealing the puck and flicking it hard to their center, who tears toward our end of the ice. Not so fucking fast… With a solid intercept by Marc Kane, the puck lands right against my stick. I weave around their taller defensemen and my body knows what to do before I do. I smack the puck into the net and with only thirty seconds on the ice… I score. The crowd goes crazy. I pump my fists and skate around to fist bump my teammates, but my eyes are only on one girl who is banging her fists like a crazy person against the clear boards cheering for me. Kya.

Tuck pulls me off the ice for the next face-off.

"Good job," he says. "But where the fuck have you been?"

"We have half of this period and the entire third period. We'll be fine."

"Answer my fucking question. Your agent and half the scouts in the league are here and believe me, they noticed your absence."

"I got back, and I scored. What more do you want from me?"

Tuck sighs. I'm right. He can kick the shit out of me once we win. If we win. No. I can't think like that. I'm Cole Seabrook. If I can take a punch from Dwayne Ambrose, I can take a few hits from a bunch of War Hogs.

"Listen," Tuck murmurs. "Jayce is in the penalty box for another 3 minutes and Rathbone's with the medics. I think he broke two of his ribs, possibly his nose. These guys play dirty, Seabrook."

"That explains the guys."

"We can't let them lose hope. And neither can you. At this point… with you gone… if we don't win this, Cole… That might be it."

"I get it."

"Play like it's your last," Tuck says, meaning every word.

"Thank you, coach."

"I hope that girl's worth it. I know mine would've been," he says to me, which is as close to approval as I can hope for from Tuck Murphy. I only need another minute breather before I head back onto the ice. Our second string does a good job of defending the net before I get back out there, but that doesn't mean we're any closer to scoring. One more goal. That's all we need to tie this game… one… more… goal.

Everything disappears except that one goal. Everything. I sail around the War Hog's center and watch the puck dance around our end of the ice for a second before Kane sends it up to me. I weave around their defenseman, but I'm not fast enough. He steals the puck. I spin around and lunge back for it. By some fucking miracle… I get it back.

The crowd goes wild. I pass the puck to our newbie forward, the Boston frosh Dale Miller. I nod, giving him encouragement to take the shot. I hope he fucking takes it. Dale might be a newbie, but he's no slouch. He weaves around the short stocky War Hog defenseman and flicks the puck into the net. The goalie lunges and everyone holds their breath until the buzzer.

WE MADE IT IN. WE TIED THE GAME.

The crowd goes absolutely insane. It's Miller's first goal in a few games and his excitement is visible. Nothing beats that feeling. But the game is still 4-4. Anything can happen and our two quick goals have definitely pissed off a couple of the War Hog dicks. If we can hold this score until the end of the second period, they'll be out for blood by the third.

The last few minutes of the period are a brutal fight to hold the score together. I can feel every muscle in my body aching and I know that I won't get to stop — I don't get to stop until the game is done. When we're off the ice, Tuck puts his fury with me aside temporarily to discuss our strategy for the third period.

"You all need to work together. You need to play to your strengths. You need to fucking score. Every game matters. But the one you're playing now matters most. Vipers on three…"

I don't feel like I've had enough time to breathe when we're ready to start the third. But I feel ready to win. Even down a few men, I know we can take the War Hogs. We may be a bunch of assholes, but we're a great fucking team. I start the period, but lose the face off to the seven footer they have playing forward. Then again, every guy feels like he's seven feet tall when you face him on the ice.

That shit doesn't scare me. What scares me is losing. What scares me is losing Kya. I chase the puck like my life depends on it, pulling crazy tricks that could make me lose my balance until I grab the puck.

The crowd goes wild. Then their screaming gets louder. I'm so lost in the moment that I don't even realize why until I hear the announcer cheering. I scored. From halfway across the ice, I landed a corner shot in the net. The craziest goal in Vipers history. One goal away from another hat trick. We're 5-4 now. One goal ahead and if we can keep it here… we'll win.

But my goal gets my blood hot. I don't just want to win anymore. I want to destroy them. It's just practice anyway, because I have someone else to destroy after this — the person who leaked Kya's filthy smut. I don't know who it is, but when I find out who it is… I'll destroy them.

Halfway through the third period, Dale Miller scores again, this time with Marc Kane on the assist. The crowd goes crazy. I want to make another hat trick and really wow everyone, but I don't get a chance before the end of the game. It doesn't matter. It's not always about being the star. We pulled ahead and won 6-4. The War Hog coach looks like he's boiling, but Tuck Murphy has the biggest fucking smile on his face I've ever seen.

The guys are happier than I've ever seen. Tuck reminds us that there's a big party organized by the moms in the green room and we're all welcome to celebrate the big game once we take showers. The guys grunt approvingly and mop sweat off their faces. Partying, showering, sitting down all sound good… but right now I want to see Kya. I take my skates off and lumber down the hallway in my pads until I hear her shriek.

"COLE! YOU WON!"

She takes a running leap into my arms, and I grunt as I catch her. She seems to get a hold of herself when her legs wrap around my hips and she feels how sweaty I am.

"Oh. Sorry."

"Hey. Stay right here." I pull her close against me and kiss her. Every winner needs a post-game kiss, right? The guys — and Kya's friends — all cheer. I can tell Kya definitely wants me to stop kissing her and making her the center of attention, but I don't care. I want to kiss her. I earned this kiss. I tug at some of her hair as I keep kissing her. Eventually, the cheering gets to her enough that she pushes against my arms and I set her down.

"Congrats," she mutters shyly.

"Yeah," I whisper. "Winning feels pretty good."

"You were great out there."

The crowd thins now that we're not kissing anymore. Makeba and Raven hover a few feet behind Kya, but eventually step forward.

"You were okay," Raven says. "For a guy with a black eye."

Kya sighs. "They told me everything. I guess you were pretty honorable."

"You gave me the motivation to break up with my dumb boyfriend," Makeba blurts out to me. "If you can take a punch from Dwayne Ambrose, I can do that… That shit was inspiring.”

“Thanks,” I mutter, unsure if this is how exactly I want to be an inspiration.

“You inspired me to give up on real love,” Raven says with a smile on her face.

“Raven!” Kya chides her. “That’s horrible.”

“No offense, but… I don’t want anyone to punch me in the face. I’ve seen y’all fall in love and it’s too complicated for me right now. I’m going back to my romance novels.”

“Sorry to disappoint,” I grumble.

“No!” Raven insists. “It’s not that. It’s just… let’s be real. Is there going to be another guy on this campus who could stand up to Kya’s dad? Congrats, Kya. You won the prize.”

“No,” I tell Raven, turning to Kya finally and pushing some of her hair out of her face so I can see her big smile properly. “I’m the one who won the prize.”

I put my arms around Kya’s hips and pull her close. “And I need the three of you to help me.”

“You do?” Kya asks me.

“We still don’t know who leaked your stories, babe. That’s not cool. I’m going to do something about it.”

Makeba blurts out, “You’re together now! Who cares!”

“She’s right,” Kya says. “I don’t want to think about that. I’m hungry.”

“There’s a little after party. Why don’t you ladies go ahead?”

I can see some of the new agents I was courting coming toward me and I don't know what the hell is going to happen next. I don't want Kya to hear me getting torn to shreds. I was late for the game. I didn't score my signature hat trick. We might have won, but my NHL future is far from guaranteed.

"Seabrook, you got a minute?"

It's Dylan. My palms sweat and I don't want anyone to see how nervous I am, but holy shit, I'm nervous. He wants to work with me and tonight was the big test to see if I was worth his time. I don't know if I screwed up too much by being late. I'm holding my breath because if this doesn't work out, I don't know what I'll tell Kya.

"I want to talk about your performance tonight…"

He puts his arm around my shoulder and pulls me away from the crowd. Kya turns back to her friends and they're gushing about something on Kya's phone.

Dylan gives me the bad news first. They want me to play another semester at Laguna Grove. For bad news, it's pretty good. I can finish my junior year and have more time with my new girlfriend. Then I get the good news. After that semester, I have four contract options. They want me to wait, but they want to offer me big money. Four teams. They want me in Buffalo, Boston, Seattle and Atlanta. I can't believe it.

There it is. My future laid out before me. All I have to do is play one more semester and I can have it all: my million dollar dreams and my million dollar girl, Kya… I can't wait to tell her. As I walk down the hallway to the green room, giddy with the news and eager to tell Kya, something nags at my mind.

When I brought up the emails of filthy smut, her friend Makeba acted pretty weird. I wonder if she knows more than she was letting on. I wonder if she has a secret.

"Cole!" Kya calls to me, distracting me from that thought. "What happened? What did Dylan say?"

"I have good news, babe," I tell her, taking her hand. "Good news for me and good news for us."

"Us?"

"Yeah. I'm thinking about us. Always."

"I love you," Kya blurts out.

"I love you too. Now come on. I've got a lot to tell you… Big things about our future."

"Our future?"

"Yeah, babe," I whisper. "Our future."

MAKEBA'S CHAPTER

MAKEBA WINSTON

My hands shake as I prepare myself to confront him. I don't know what I was thinking dating B.J. I guess I thought an easy-going laid-back guy like him would be easy to date and that once we started going out, he would put an effort in. I mean, we had a good time together, but we were always closer to friends than anything else. We kissed eventually, but never went further. I listened to him. I thought I understood him.

I should have listened to him when he said he had a dark side... but I didn't realize it was this dark. I know where I'll find him because it's where he spends 90% of his time while the rest of Laguna Grove watches hockey games or rages at frat parties. I knock on the door to his dorm room, the blue glow from his computer screen already spreading out into the hallway from beneath his door.

"Just a sec."

"It's Makeba. It's important."

I know we're broken up, but it was B.J.'s idea to stay friends, so I don't think he'll mind that I showed up here. He might mind when he finds out what I've actually come to talk to him about. I owe it to Kya to get to the bottom of things, but I don't want her crazy boyfriend to punch a hole through B.J. just in case I'm wrong.

I didn't want to tell Cole about my suspicions without talking to him first. After what feels like forever, B.J. throws the door open. He's wearing an oversized teal t-shirt and sweatpants, his copper hair a total mess.

"What do you want?"

"Can I come in?"

"Sure. Beer?"

I thought he would be a wonderful boyfriend because of things like that. B.J. was always so polite.

"No. I'm good."

"Tired of watching the jocks get rewarded for playing dumb sports?"

"No. I... I need to ask you something."

"Okay."

I can seriously never read B.J. Even now, he just keeps staring at me and I can't tell what he's thinking or if he's already guilty. I'm just trying to get to the truth.

"Did you hack Kya's computer?"

"What?"

"Did you hack Kya's computer?"

He heard what I said.

"Why would you ask something like that?"

"Because someone using the email address bojangles0606 at some weird website sent Kya's erotic stories to her dad. That's the username you have on your Japanese gaming site."

He's disarmingly calm.

"Yeah," B.J. explains. "But I don't use it on every website. You have your first name as your email address, but you don't use that name everywhere. Your Instagram has a different handle."

"I know, but… someone sent those stories to her dad."

"Wasn't it that idiot hockey player?"

"That's what I thought."

"Until?"

"I learned the truth."

"Let me guess, Kya bought his lie and now they're back together, so she's casting suspicions on someone else. Makeba, I'm an English major. I'm not some stupid misogynistic jock."

"I know that."

"Then you don't need to ask me any more dumb questions."

"It wasn't a dumb question. Someone hurt my best friend. I'm just looking for answers."

"You should be looking for better clothes," B.J. snaps.

"Ouch. What was that for?"

"Look. I don't know why you came here. We didn't work out. I'm cool hanging out, but you show up here accusing me of shit I didn't do. It sucks."

"I don't know that you didn't do it," I snap, suddenly getting really mad. B.J. always does this. For the brief moment I had my head in the clouds and actually wanted to date him, I thought it was just one of his quirky little traits or something. That all guys were like that. His gaze flickers to mine and I detect something beyond his usual disdain for all life forms. Anger.

"Why are you attacking me?" He asks. "Like, seriously? I don't have it out for Kya. I don't have a motive."

"I don't care about your motive. I want you to answer me directly. Look me in the eye and tell me you didn't hack my best friend's computer."

"I didn't."

He's lying. I know he's lying and once he looks into my eyes, he knows that I know that he's lying. B.J. slowly licks his lips and I watch his right hand curl into a fist.

"Makeba... I don't want you to do anything stupid. I swear. I had nothing to do with that."

"Your birthday is June 6th, B.J. It's your handle. I know it is."

"It's not me," he snarls.

"I'm going to talk to Kya."

"No," he whispers. "You're really not."

I lunge for the door, but he's too fast. He yanks his gaming keyboard off his desk and hits me hard in the head. Really hard. I scream and fall against the door. Before I can get my footing, he tosses the keyboard to the side and kicks me hard in the side. I scream again. There's no one in the dorms this time on a weekend. Literally everyone else is at various hockey game after parties across campus.

No one can hear me scream and B.J. knows it. That's okay. I can fight back. I think. I mean, I've never been in a fight and I've definitely never been in a fight with a guy. I scramble as fast as I can across the floor of his room, searching for a weapon. I find one of his L.L. Bean boots and fling it at him, hoping I can distract him enough to make a run for his bedroom door and get out of there.

I miss his head, and don't even give myself enough time to run. He grabs my arm and slams me against the wall. I scream again and try kicking him, but he wraps his hands around my neck and squeezes. Tightly. I try kicking him in the nuts. I think I hit him because his face suddenly turns cherry, but his hands only tighten around my neck.

"Say anything, and I will kill you," he snarls. I can't breathe. I reach for his hands to pull them away. My nails dig into his skin as tears erupt. I just need oxygen. I choke and claw at his hands again, but B.J. doesn't let go. He refuses. His hands grip my neck tighter. I can't breathe. I scratch harder, but it doesn't work.

"One word," he whispers. "And you're dead, Makeba. You're fucking dead."

Click here to order Makeba & Jayce's story

Click here to get updates when my next release comes out.

ABOUT JAMILA JASPER

The hotter and darker the romance, the better.

That's the Jamila Jasper promise.

If you enjoy sizzling multicultural romance stories that dare to *go there* you'll enjoy any Jamila Jasper title you pick up.

Open-minded readers who appreciate **shamelessly sexy romance novels** featuring black women of all shapes and sizes paired with smokin' hot white men are welcome.

Sign up for her e-mail list here to receive one of these FREE hot stories, exclusive offers and an update of Jamila's publication schedule:
bit.ly/jamilajasperromance

Get text message updates on new books:
https://slkt.io/gxzM

JAMILA JASPER

Diverse Romance For Black Women

MORE JAMILA JASPER ROMANCE

<u>Pick your poison…</u>

Delicious interracial romance novels for all tastes. Long novels, short stories, audiobooks and more.

Hit the link to experience my full catalog.

FULL CATALOG BY JAMILA JASPER:
https://linktr.ee/JamilaJasper

PATREON

For a small monthly fee, you get exclusive access to over 375 chapters of my first completed bwwm dark and spicy serial romance, as well as the spin-off serial...

DESPICABLE

The second serial, despicable has 300 chapters available for all Patreon subscribers to access instantly and... we officially have a **third completed spin-off bwwm romance series.**

And yes you get access to all of this at the $5/month tier with more benefits at more pricey tiers.

The third serial is about Clover + Thomas. Thomas has a shocking connection to a character in the second serial and Clover is an all-new African American female lead.

POWERLESS

This series has three *very long* "seasons" of chapters, the length of five full-length novels all-together.

You will probably have over three months of binge-reading before catching up to current content, making this one of the most 'bang for your buck' author Patreon subscriptions out there.

Don't take my word for it.
Check the post history:
www.patreon.com/jamilajasper

PATREON HAS MORE THAN THE ONGOING SERIAL...

INSTANT ACCESS

- NEW merchandise tiers with **t-shirts, totes, mugs,** stickers and MORE!
- **FREE paperback** with all new tiers
- **FREE short story audiobooks** and audiobook samples when they're ready

- #FirstDraftLeaks of Prologues and first chapters **weeks** before I hit publish
- Behind the scenes notes
- Polls and story contribution
- Comments & LIVELY community discussion with likeminded interracial romance readers.

LEARN MORE ABOUT SUPPORTING A DIVERSE ROMANCE AUTHOR

www.patreon.com/jamilajasper

THANK YOU KINDLY

Thank you to all my readers, new and old for your support with this new year.

I look forward to making 2023 an INCREDIBLE year for interracial romance novels. I want to thank you all for joining along on the journey.

www.patreon.com/jamilajasper

Thank you to my most supportive readers — my Patreon subscribers!:

Martha

Nikki Valentina

xjkpop

Valeria

BlkBae

SweetS

Msteeq

Rhonda

Darrah

Killa

Shavon

Misty

India

Kassandra

Imani

Nala

Chantell

Benvinda

Roger

Lexi B

Zapphire

Vbrooks

Tasha G

Kiera

Valencia

Stacy

YANITZA

Texansgurl76

Emma

Tinette

Jenny

Mariah

Nale

Tanisha

Trenita

Shelle

dulcemaria413

Shanice

Letarsha

Tania

Neeka

Julia

Linda

Lisa

Jiannie

Jillian

Tameka

Asia

Scarlette

Olwyn

R W

Fayefaefee

Brianna

Tiffany

Katie

Diamond

Kera

Tia

Love Reading

Dominique

Sheria

Jennifer

Georgette

Monique

Wendolyn

King Turtle22

Jessica

Nic M.

JustChill

DJC

Atira

TheeLastHokage

Yvonne

Chrissy

Janelle

Rian

LaRonda

LaRonda

Deanna

dlawson382

Jasmine

Haley

Belinda

Sercee

Yvonne

Jadelock

Farah

Tamiya

Quin

J.Payton

Geek Girl

Ashley

Rubi

Pilar

Sandra

Jurnee

Anni

Shannet

Joneesa

GlitzyHydra

Amanda

Barbara

Brianna

Jamica

Lyons

MARY ANN

Marketia

SarahD

LoverofHawaiiHearts

ceblue

Yolanda

MonaGirl Lewis

Dianna

Mary

amna

Nysha

fayola

Ty

Abria

Shyra

Andi-Mariee

Jamila

Naee's World

KEISHA

Jennett

Fredericka

Candece

Chante

Pholuv

Lydia A

Sabrina

JM

Jackie

Mo

Natrilly83

Ashaunte

Tolu

Margaret

Wendolyn

Lori

Dionne

ZLB

Kristina

Nicol

ELBERT

A. Harris

Jesi

Brenda

Desiree

Angela

Frances

LaShan

Only1ToniD

Debbie T.

Tiffanie

April L

shawnte

Kay

Lisema

Yvonne F

Natasha

Colleen

Julia

Amy

Jacklyn

Shyan R

Kiana B

Pearl

Javonda

Sheron

Maxine

Dash

Alicia

margaret

Love2Read

Juliette

Monica

Sandhya

MaryC

Trinity

Brittany

June

Ashleigh

Nene
Nene
Deborah
Nikki M
Dee
TyKira
Kimmey
Laytoya
Shel W
Arlene
Judith
Mary
Shanida
Rachel
Damzel
Ahnjala
Kenya
momo
BJ
Akeshia
Melissa
Tiffany
sherbear
Nini J
Curtresa
REGGIE A.
Ashley
Mia
Tink138110
Phia
Sharon
Charlotte
Assiatu C
Regina

Romanda
Catherine
Gaynor
BF
Perpetua
Tasha G
Henri Ann
sara
skkent
Rosalyn
Danielle
Deborah J
Kirsten
ANA
Taylor R.
Charlene
Louanna
Michelle
Tamika
Lauren
RoHyde
Natasha
Shekynah
Cassie
AnnaBooms
Keitheena
Nick R
Gennifer M
Rayna
Anton
Jaleda
Kimvodkna
JaTonn
Jazmine

Anoushka
Raynischa
Audrey
Valeria
Courtney
Donna
Patrisha
Jenetha
LaKisha J.
Ayana
Taylor
Christy
Monica
FreyaJo
GRACE
Kisha
Christine
Alexandra
Amber
Natasha
Stephanie
LaKisha
kristylove7
Cynthea
DENICE
Latoya
monifacd .
Doneishia
Mariah
Gerry
Yolanda T
Yolanda P
Susan D
Phyllis H

Alisa K
Daveena K
Desiree S
Kimberly B
Robin B
Gary S
Stephanie MG
Georgette A
Kathy
Marty
JanetDaniels
Megan
Shelle
Delores
Janet
Lydia
Phyllis
Freda
Charlott R

Join the Patreon Community.